COUNTRY COUSIN

A hard-up parson's daughter from Yorkshire, Eleanor might have felt out of her depth when she came South to stay with her mother's friends, the well-off Mansel family. But they couldn't have been nicer or kinder, and Eleanor liked them immensely. What a pity she couldn't feel the same way about the son of the family, the uncompromising Edward . . .

Books you will enjoy
by JACQUELINE GILBERT

SCORPIO SUMMER

Frances had done old Lady Ravenscar a very good turn, as a result of which the two had become friends—and the old lady was particularly anxious that Frances should meet her son Felix. Someone ought to have warned Frances that the gentleman in question was a Scorpio, the sign whose sting can sometimes be fatal. Or would she be able, once she had met him, to work that one out for herself?

EVERY WISE MAN

When Olivia Darcy went to work as secretary in the delightful Raynor household, she got on happily with everybody—with her boss, Charles Raynor, and two of his sons, Paul and Julian. Everybody except one, the third son, Matthew, who had seemed to take an instant dislike to her. But why? It wasn't as if he could possibly know her secret . . .

DEAR VILLAIN

Liz was looking forward immensely to her new job as deputy stage manager at the splendid new Queensbridge Civic Theatre—until she learned that the director was going to be Adam Carlyon. For Adam Carlyon was a man she had no wish whatsoever to meet again . . .

COUNTRY COUSIN

BY

JACQUELINE GILBERT

MILLS & BOON LIMITED
17–19 FOLEY STREET
LONDON W1A 1DR

First published 1978
Australian copyright 1979
Philippine copyright 1979
This edition 1979

ISBN 0 263 73215 0

Set in Linotype Plantin 10 pt

Made and printed in Great Britain by
Richard Clay (The Chaucer Press), Ltd., Bungay, Suffolk

For Rex

CHAPTER ONE

'Then fly betimes, for only they,
Conquer love that run away.'
Thomas Carew

As the driver lifted the cases from the taxi-cab, Eleanor Rose Ferrers stared wide-eyed at the house, feeling a quickening of interest, the first she had had since leaving home that morning. Nothing her mother had said had prepared her for the beauty of Priory Lodge. It was all very well being told that the old part of the house had been built in Elizabethan times, that there were four acres of ground situated in an exclusive part of Surrey, but when the real thing was in front of your eyes, it was time to take stock of this unlooked-for holiday of hers.

A small cough indicated that the driver was waiting for his money, and shifting the art folio to her other arm, Eleanor fumbled in her shoulder bag, paid him, and watched the cab drive slowly out into the lane.

She then turned her attention back to the house and grounds, delighting in the colourful display of flowers and shrubs, the immaculately kept lawns, the surrounding hedges and trees. Leaving the cases where they were, she walked over to the paddock and leaned on the fencing, grateful for the cool shade from the trees. It was September, but the day was as warm as midsummer. Eleanor took off her suit coat and pulled the cotton blouse stickily away from her body, thankful that it was fine and short-sleeved. Her long-abandoned hat she used as a fan, and she gazed contentedly at the two horses grazing on the other side of the paddock.

Perhaps things aren't going to be so bad, after all, she mused, resting chin on hands, and thinking of the situation she had left behind her. She would have to be a bridesmaid

... Kate was her sister, after all, but the wedding was seven months away and time and distance should do wonders. By then, she thought firmly, she should be used to the idea of Kate and Guy being married. Mr and Mrs Guy Slade. Eleanor remembered the first time she had met Guy and how she had been instantly attracted to him, and seemingly, he to her. Of the bemused and happy state she had been in—she went red-hot now whenever she thought of herself then. Poor Guy, how awful being brought home to the Rectory only to fall head over heels in love with her sister Kate! It's worthy of a comic song, she thought wryly, idly noticing that the horses had seen her on the fence and were cautiously making their way over. Thank goodness she had seen what was happening before she made a complete fool of herself, she reflected, hoping that no one but Guy had guessed how she felt about him, but she knew she was kidding herself. The parents must have had a suspicion, she acknowledged, hence the alacrity with which she was dispatched to Surrey. Remembering Guy's embarrassed last words on York station just before the train left of 'don't forget us', she didn't know whether to laugh or cry! Irony is a bitter pill to swallow. 'Forgetting' was what this trip was all about. Never again, she vowed fervently, would she allow herself to be so vulnerable.

The horses were approaching her warily and she lifted herself gently on to the first bar of the fence and held out her hand. They allowed her to stroke them, showing their disappointment when she had no titbit to offer by nudging her sharply.

'Never mind,' said Eleanor, giving them a final pat. 'The minute I can find something you shall have it.'

She walked slowly back to the impressive oak front door, swinging her jacket with one hand, the other shading her eyes from the contrast of shadow and sunshine. She stared thoughtfully at the bell.

'Well, here goes,' she murmured, and pressed her finger firmly on it. A dog barked somewhere ... there was the sound of a lawn mower in the distance, and a blackbird was singing his heart out high up in one of the sycamore trees.

She rang again, almost knowing that it wouldn't be answered.

'Darn it,' she muttered, 'they're probably out searching for me!' and she recalled once more the look of horror on Guy's face when he saw the flat tyre, knowing that he couldn't hope to change it in time for Eleanor to catch her train. She looked at her watch. With all the missed connections she was nearly three hours late. Uncertain what to do, she hesitated, nibbling her thumb, and then wandered round the side of the house towards the orchards at the rear, more out of curiosity than in the hope of finding someone.

Ivy covered this gable wall and she peered through a window, not surprised to find the inside equally elegant and satisfying, for it was to be expected; as one of the Mansels, she couldn't remember which one, ran an antique business. It seemed to be a study as she could see a handsome rosewood desk and a huge leather armchair, set before a wall entirely filled with bookshelves. Eleanor drew back from the window and the interior receded, leaving the image of herself reflected in the glass. She pulled a face and ran a hand half-heartedly through her straight brown hair. Two hundred miles of train travel had left its mark and she was dying for a cup of tea.

Losing interest, she carried on down the side of the house and was disappointed to find that the path led only to the kitchen garden and greenhouse beyond. Access to the back was barred by a six-foot-high laurel hedge.

'Well, that's that,' said Eleanor, preparing to return, when her wandering eye caught sight of some crisp, green apples, growing on a tree, the branches of which overhung the other side of the hedge. Her mouth began to water, but she resolutely turned her back, rejecting the idea that had immediately come to mind, even taking three steps away, before swinging round and eyeing the apples again. None were within reach from the ground.

'Eleanor Ferrers, don't do anything you'd regret,' she told herself firmly, seeking possible footholds with the eye of a professional. 'Why ever not? I'm sure if they knew how thirsty I am...' and without pausing for second thoughts, she began to climb. It was easy, but because the skirt she was wearing was new and she liked it, she took care and her time. The chosen branch was attained and the apple plucked. With satisfaction Eleanor polished it vigorously on the sleeve of her blouse and took a deep bite. Strong white teeth broke through the crisp green skin and juice trickled down her chin. After a couple of mouthfuls, she parted back the leaves and peered down below, to find that she was perched above a terrace on which white wrought-iron chairs and a table were placed.

An earwig dropped on to her bare arm and she flicked it off with a shudder. She could stand most insects but did draw the line at earwigs. Easing her limbs, prior to making a descent, she suddenly froze. A brindle bull-terrier came barking on to the terrace from the house and a man's voice called out sharply:

'Quiet, Sykes!'

Footsteps followed. Eleanor drew up her feet and sat as small and as quiet as she could, her heart hammering away against her knees, her eyes closed in anguish ... almost as if the fact that she couldn't see them meant that they couldn't see her.

What a fool you are, she groaned to herself, and nearly fell out of the tree when she heard her own name come floating up to meet her.

'Blast this Eleanor Ferrers! How have we missed her?' The voice was female and cross.

'Correction—how have *you* missed her? You're sure you checked on the times of the train in the first place?' The man's voice was a bored drawl.

'Of course I did!' was the indignant reply. 'I'm not a complete fool.'

'There's no of course about it, little sister.'

'Edward, I did, honestly! And she must be somewhere ... or how can those two cases have suddenly arrived out of the blue? I'm fed up with the girl already. Mother invites these waifs and strays and it's me that gets lumbered. She'll probably be as strait-laced as hell ... a ghastly goody-goody with an awful northern accent.' Her voice was now full of gloom.

'What a little snob you are, Van,' observed Edward carelessly. 'I seem to remember Mother saying that the Reverend Hilary Ferrers met his wife when they were both up at Oxford, so your fears of an accent appear groundless. And in any case, accents are extremely attractive on the right person.'

'I'm sure you've had first-hand experience,' grumbled Vanessa, 'and it's all right for you—you're adept at keeping out of the way of Mother's schemes—at least, you are usually,' and her voice took on gleeful interest. 'What brings you down here this weekend, anyway? Come to look Little Miss Muffet over?'

'You can hardly expect the visit of a parson's daughter to excite much interest in my breast, Van,' replied her brother, as bored as ever.

'Oh, I don't know,' drawled Vanessa, sitting herself beneath Eleanor, 'she might prove amusing for a while. Your women never last long anyway, you're so scared of getting hooked, and it might give the poor creature something to remember her visit by—that is, if she ever turns up. She'll make a change from your usual types ... you know—innocent girl from the backwoods and all that sort of thing.'

'No, I do not know,' said Edward repressively, 'and I always did think you had a particularly lurid imagination. I've told you before,' and his voice had a slight edge to it, 'keep your nose out of my affairs.'

'Darling, I would, only I'm not allowed to. You'd be surprised how popular I am with all the aspiring females that live in a fifty-mile radius—all eager for me to introduce them to my tall, dark, handsome brother! And don't you think you could use a word other than affairs?' she added sweetly.

'Don't push too far, little sister,' Edward said lazily, 'or I might turn the tables. For instance, Philip Nolan seems to be one of your more frequent escorts these days.'

Vanessa replied carelessly: 'What of it? He's useful and good fun.'

'Mmm ... older than your normal boy-friends, isn't he? I hope you know what you're doing?'

'Edward dear, are you giving me the concerned brother act?'

'No, but I doubt the parents would approve. Nolan's over ten years older than you are, and has a reputation for fast cars and fast women.'

Vanessa snorted. 'You're a fine one to talk! I wonder what . . .'

'We're talking about you, not me, and a word in Mother's ear could curtail your activities somewhat. We both know how involved she is in her charities and committees, but if she thought it necessary, she'd drop them like a shot.' He paused and his cynical tone softened. 'Don't burn your fingers, Van.'

'I wish you'd realise that I'm not a child any long . . . ouch!'

'What's the matter?'

'An apple dropped on me. Look here, Edward, I'll make a bargain—you keep out of my affairs and I'll keep out of yours.'

'Mmm . . .?'

'Aren't you listening? I said, I'll make a bargain with . . .'

'No bargains,' replied Edward firmly. 'Why isn't Duffy answering the telephone?'

'Sam's taken her to the dentist, poor darling, she was in agony with the toothache.'

There was a pause while a chair scraped the paving and Edward Mansel said dryly: 'It might be our lost parson's daughter waiting to be rescued.'

'I'll organise some tea,' said his sister languidly, and Eleanor heard them walk into the house. For a few seconds she sat rooted to the spot, thoughts whirling round in her head. It was one thing for her not to want to come on this visit, but quite another to find the feeling reciprocated! 'Straight-laced! Goody-goody! I may be a parson's daughter,' she fumed, 'but I'm no innocent from the backwoods, and if that's what they're expecting, then who am I to disappoint them?'

She thrust herself hastily down the tree, deeply thankful

that she had not been discovered ... that would have been dreadful! The half-eaten apple must have rolled uneaten side up, or else it would certainly have given her away. She brushed her skirt free of dust and leaves, picked up the abandoned folio and shoulder bag, and hurried to the front of the house—bending low beneath the windows as she went.

Things had altered since she was there last. The two suitcases had disappeared and on either side of the curved drive were parked a bright red Spitfire and a sleek, silver-grey Jensen. A fleeting vision of the mud-splattered family estate back home came to her, and unreasonably her indignation gathered strength.

Rummaging in her bag, Eleanor found sunglasses, large and horn-rimmed, and put them on. Next she stuffed her hair into the crown of her hat and pulled the brim ruthlessly down. There was nothing she could do about her clothes, but she scrubbed at her lipstick with a handkerchief, and fixing an inane smile upon her face, raised a finger once more to the bell. This time the door opened to reveal a young girl, attractively dressed in a cream trouser suit. Before she could say anything, Eleanor stretched out a hand, and in a broad Yorkshire accent, gushed:

'Happen we missed each other at t'station. I'm Eleanor Ferrers, and you must be Vanessa. How-do.'

The girl visibly winced. 'Oh ... yes ... hullo,' and gingerly held out her hand.

'Aye, I reckoned I was reet,' continued Eleanor cheerfully, shaking it vigorously. 'I'm that glad to meet you.'

'Won't you come in?' Vanessa asked, her face now a polite mask. 'We're on the terrace, it's still warm enough in a sheltered spot to sit out.'

Eleanor followed, well satisfied with results. Vanessa Mansel seemed stunned and, determined to give full measure, Eleanor continued non-stop chatter, about how she had missed the train, as they walked through the house and out into the garden, taking a mental picture of low ceilings, mellow wood, pictures, soft carpets, sparkling china, beautiful furniture, with her.

'I'm sorry you had to make your own way here . . .' began Vanessa, as her visitor was compelled to take breath.

'Nay, don't look so fatched, luv,' broke in Eleanor. 'I've been nobbut a nuisance to you, and I'm not a dafty. 'Twas reet easy to find a taxi.'

She heard a footfall behind her and saw Vanessa give an agonised look somewhere over her right shoulder—no doubt our bored Don Juan! she thought grimly.

'There you are, Edward!' Vanessa was saying thankfully. 'This is Miss Ferrers. My brother, Edward, Miss Ferrers.'

'Nay, then!' protested Eleanor, thoroughly enjoying herself. 'I shan't know who you mean if you call me that! Eleanor's the name—more homely, like.' She turned and held out her hand, keeping eyes coyly lowered. Hum . . . she thought, as a tall shape stepped from the shadows of the house—black leather shoes, very expensive, well creased grey flannels—and then her hand was held longer than was necessary, and he said:

'I'm so glad we've found you at last, Miss Ferrers. Did I hear you telling my sister that you'd had a puncture on the way? How annoying.' The drawl was instantly recognisable, although the boredom seemed to have disappeared. Good, thought Eleanor with satisfaction . . . evidently the sight and sound of her had demoralised him too! She was released, his hand transferred itself to beneath her elbow, and she was led firmly to one of the garden chairs.

'Aye, it was reet inconvenient,' she babbled on, inwardly blanching at how awful she sounded, but too launched into the act to stop. 'My sister Kate's fiancé was giving me the lift into York, and he was that mad when we picked up this puncture. Eh, lad, I said, not to worry—worse things happen at sea.'

'How true. Sit here, Miss Ferrers, and Vanessa will bring the tea. I'm sure you must be ready for a cup after your long journey. Off you go, Van,' the deep voice ordered, and his sister disappeared willingly.

Rather intrigued, despite herself, to see the owner of this attractive voice, Eleanor thought she could abandon coyness and take a peep from under the brim of her hat, but before she could do so, his next question startled her into stillness.

'And what have you done with your family, Miss Ferrers?' There was an infinitesimal edge to his voice that made her stiffen. Even the bull-terrier lifted his head uneasily.

'Eh, there's nobbut me come to stay.'

'Really? Dear me, how heartless you are. Have you disposed of the rosy-cheeked baby and small boy with a liking for steps? It seems you can dispose of an impeccable accent equally well.'

With deep foreboding, Eleanor slowly lowered the glasses to the end of her nose and peered over them. Standing before her, hooded blue eyes staring down at her, was the Good Samaritan from the railway station! Retribution! Of all people, it had to be Edward Mansel!

'You appear to have lost your Yorkshire tongue, Miss Ferrers,' he observed with soft sarcasm.

Eleanor's heart sank like a stone. She took a deep breath.

'You came to meet the train?' she asked, using her normal voice.

'Naturally,' was the dry reply. 'Each train has been met when you were not on the expected one. Since there didn't appear to be a girl travelling on her own, I assumed you were not on that train either. It seemed I was wrong.'

'I'm sorry,' said Eleanor miserably. 'You've been to a great deal of trouble. I . . . travelled down with a young family and while the mother collected the cases and pram from the guard's van, I looked after the children for her.'

She could see herself now, walking along the platform, the baby in her arms, the toddler by her side. She had had to drop the little boy's hand to rescue the baby's shoe and finding himself free, he had ran on ahead to unsteadily climb the steep iron steps alone. Eleanor had hurried after him as fast as she could, hampered by the baby and her handbag, and had caught him half-way up, only to slightly overbalance herself as she made a grab for him. A steadying hand from a fellow pedestrian forcefully resumed her equilibrium and for a few seconds she was held in a firm grip, and found herself looking into a pair of amused blue eyes. She heard a quiet 'allow me' and the boy was lifted effortlessly under the Good Samaritan's arm, much to his glee, and the ascent achieved with hardly a pause. When Eleanor breathlessly joined them at the top, she gasped:

'Thank you ... I think I need three pairs of hands for this pair!' and taking a firm hold of the chuckling truant, she smiled up at the owner of the blue eyes. The amusement was still there, and deepened as he very gently tweaked Eleanor's hat back into place. Beneath his scrutiny, for some completely inexplicable reason, she felt a blush sweep across her face, and feeling a fool, watched him give a brief smile to the children and then walk away.

The blue eyes were not amused now, merely coolly curious. She ground her teeth, remembering that blush, and wished she could get up, go out, and never come back.

'I wonder why you deemed it necessary for a spot of play-acting?' Edward Mansel was saying reflectively. 'Are you a frustrated actress?'

'Good heavens, no!' exclaimed Eleanor.

'Yet you did your best to create a wrong impression. Does it give you satisfaction to put others at a disadvantage?'

'Certainly not,' snapped Eleanor, her remorse rapidly disappearing. 'I would never have done it if you...' and she stopped short, biting her bottom lip.

He frowned. 'Now, how could I...?' and then his brow cleared, and the tip of his black shoe flicked the dropped apple on to its side, and his eyes moved upwards. 'I see... you were sitting in the apple tree listening to our conversation.'

'Not intentionally, I can assure you,' said Eleanor coldly, getting to her feet. 'Believe me, had I had any choice in the matter, I would rather not have heard your enlightening conversation.'

'It upset you, it would seem.'

She stared at him. Even at the station she had thought him worthy of a second look. It wasn't any one thing that set him apart, but rather the inseparability of the whole. He was tall, slim and moved with unhurried deliberation which had its own particular grace. Dressed with fastidious elegance, he had a deep, pleasing voice which lapsed into a drawl at times, sleepy blue eyes that evidently missed nothing, and an arrogantly assured, urbane manner that Eleanor immediately mistrusted.

She said frostily: 'I do not think you a fool, Mr Mansel, and would be obliged if you would not treat me as one. I can refresh your memory quite well. Strait-laced, waif and stray, goody-goody, innocent from the backwoods, is to quote but a brief outline.'

His eyes narrowed slightly. 'I wouldn't have thought you so touchy.'

Part of Eleanor agreed with him. All their lives the Ferrers children had come up against the fallacy that living in a Rectory automatically rendered them abnormal until proved otherwise. At any other time she would have shrugged philosophically and dismissed what she had overheard, but without realising the fact, she had come to view Priory Lodge as a safe bolt-hole, somewhere where she could relax from the knife-edge balance on which she had been living the past few weeks. To find that it was nothing of the kind was the final straw. All this flashed through her mind, but she had no intention of taking this man into her confidence.

He took unhurried steps towards her and before she could protest, had plucked the glasses gently from her nose, saying:

'I think we can dispense with these, and this,' removing her hat to allow her hair to fall free. 'It was unfortunate that you heard...' 'Unfortunate!' Eleanor could hardly believe her ears, so casually this was said. 'Unfortunate for you, perhaps, but...'

'Van says many things she doesn't mean. There ... that looks much better,' and his hand accidentally—or was it?—brushed her cheek as he released a strand of hair. He smiled. 'You have a good ear for accents. Had I not heard you speak at the station, you would have fooled me completely.'

Eleanor caught her breath. The treatment, when turned

on full power, was devastating ... and she felt a stab of pity for the girls in the fifty-mile radius.

'I can't imagine there are many women who can boast that,' she said stonily. 'I refuse to be charmed, Mr Mansel. Innocent and from the backwoods you may think me, but I have no wish to be a prototype, as your sister recently suggested.'

There was an ominous pause while Edward Mansel lifted a brow and allowed his eyes to travel slowly from her head to her feet and back again.

'Really?' he drawled. 'How kind of you to tell me.'

Eleanor felt the blood rush to her cheeks beneath his gaze. He continued:

'Whatever sympathy I may have felt has quickly died. Prejudging is not restricted to the South, after all. I'm rather relieved, I must confess. Having a saint as a guest could be trying.'

Eleanor bit her lip and stared down the garden. Insufferable man! but he had reminded her that she was a guest, whether she liked the idea or not, and she had said far too much already. The silence was broken by the arrival of Vanessa, and Eleanor turned thankfully and accepted a cup of tea.

'You will stay and have tea with us, Edward, won't you?' said Vanessa, her tone very pointed.

'I shall be delighted,' her brother replied smoothly, obediently seating himself, much to Vanessa's obvious surprise and Eleanor's chagrin.

'We've had a transformation scene in your absence, Van,' and Edward waved a hand in Eleanor's direction. 'Miss Ferrers had the bright idea of hoaxing us into believing her a country bumpkin, and if you're surprised at what was hidden beneath hat and glasses, I can assure you that her voice is like music.' His own was mocking. ' "Where there's music there can be no evil." '

'Don Quixote, I believe ... how appropriate,' said Eleanor, holding his stare above the rim of her cup, pleased to see the flicker of surprise at her knowledge. She turned to a perplexed Vanessa. 'It's your brother who's trying to hoax you now, Miss Mansel.'

Vanessa obviously thought the whole thing incomprehensible, but the relief afforded her by the change in their guest was plain to see, and she launched into small talk. As she drank her tea, Eleanor compared her surroundings with her own home and gave an inward smile. It was difficult to imagine her mother connected with anyone wealthy, so complete was her identification as the busy parson's wife, making a modest income stretch as far as she could. Constance Ferrers and Eve Mansel had faithfully kept in touch by letter over the years, sustaining an early friendship that outwardly seemed incongruous. Yet there was a deep affinity between the two women, despite their totally different environments. Eve had made frequent invitations for the three Ferrers girls to visit, but for some reason they never had. When her latest letter arrived, once more offering hospitality, Eleanor had seized upon it as a lifeline. It was a means of escape from an intolerable situation, and she was thrown into a whirlwind of preparations, the day of her departure arriving before she could catch her breath. And now here she was, drinking tea on the Mansel terrace, having earned two black marks against her—not an auspicious start to her visit!

'More tea, Eleanor?' Vanessa waited expectantly, teapot in hand.

Eleanor rose to her feet. 'No more, thank you, that was lovely.'

'Right ... just let me take the tray into the kitchen and I'll show you to your room,' responded Vanessa, stacking the cups and saucers. 'Mother sent her apologies for not being here to greet you, but she had a meeting she couldn't put off.' She paused at the french windows. 'Do call me Van, by the way. I like your name, it's pretty.'

Eleanor watched her go through to the house and when the silence became unbearable, said stiffly:

'I'm sorry for what I said.'

'You're not, you know,' Edward answered smoothly, 'a lifetime's indoctrination in good manners is hard to throw off.' He raised a brow. 'Does the thought occur to you that when you entered into your little charade you might have been compelled to play it out for the whole of your visit? Think how tiring it would have been—might even have proved fatal... the temptation to bump you off in the dead of night could well have become irresistible!'

Drat the man, thought Eleanor, squashing a bubble of laughter that his words provoked. How disconcerting to find herself warming to him, when she was determined to dislike him. Refusing to catch his eye, she said primly:

'What a lovely house you have, and a beautiful garden—quite a fantastic view.'

'Quite beautiful and quite, quite fantastic,' mimicked her companion in an equally prim voice, and the bubble threatened again. She took a quick breath and said with a rush:

'Look, whatever we may think of each other...'

'I'd be interested to hear your opinion on such a short acquaintance.'

Eleanor bit her lip. There were one or two highly descriptive words that immediately leapt to mind, but sense prevailed.

'You're not going to enlighten me?' There was exaggerated disappointment in his voice. 'Never mind—I have the feeling that you will... in time.'

'Oh, you're hopeless,' accused Eleanor, a quiver in her own.

'Yes, I am, aren't I?' he agreed with satisfaction. 'Come, no one with a sense of humour can be stiff-necked for long, and there's a smile just itching to be used, I saw it a few seconds ago and it gave me hope.' He rose indolently to his feet and stood staring at her. 'Shall we agree to forget our false start? I think, when you've had a good night's sleep and we're not so strange to you, that you'll see things in a much better light.'

'Do you always get your own way, Mr Mansel?'

He gave this his consideration. 'Nearly always. That is what's probably wrong with me. As for Van, she's a thoughtless creature, but there's no malice in her. If you can be bothered to try, you may find something worth your while. There she is, calling you now.' He opened the door and ushered her into the house. 'By the way, I think you'll have to make the effort and call me Edward . . . for the look of the thing.' He lifted a brow. 'It shouldn't be too difficult, after the first time.'

'Not difficult at all,' said Eleanor, with wide-eyed innocence. 'I once had a pet toad called Edward—I'm quite used to the name,' and giving him a bright smile, she swept past.

'I suppose I must be thankful it wasn't a snake in the grass,' murmured Edward Mansel, as he followed her in.

'Duffy', of toothache fame, turned out to be Amy Duffield, cook-housekeeper, who had been with the Mansels for longer than she cared to remember. Eleanor took to her immediately, recognising in the brusque, matter-of-fact manner that there was a warm-hearted confidante available if necessary. Duffy, on her part, sensed the girl's homesickness and encouraged visits to the large, comfortable kitchen, and with her warmth and interest in some measure filled the void of family contact in Eleanor's life. Sam, Duffy's implacable husband, a sturdy, weatherbeaten individual, was as indispensable to the well-being of the estate as Duffy was to the house.

Another safe haven, apart from the kitchen, was the study, with its well-stocked bookshelves, and she spent many hours curled up in one of the huge leather armchairs, her love of reading rescuing her from loneliness. There were ample opportunities while the weather lasted to go out with her sketch pad, and this she did, but the hoped-for intimacy with Vanessa did not materialise . . . how could it, when it had been made plain that Eleanor's visit was a bore? Not that Vanessa was openly rude, rather the reverse. She treated their visitor with a politeness that killed any overtures of a closer friendship stone dead, and Eleanor was too proud to beg for her company. It was a pity, because there was only six months between them in age and they ought to have found something in common.

James Mansel, founder of Mansel Airways, an air-freight business, reminded Eleanor of a picture of Edward Elgar that hung in the Rectory hall. He had thick white hair and moustache and an air of 'Pomp and Circumstance' too, being very upright with an old-fashioned courtesy. She thought him rather sweet. Her hostess, Eve, led a full life and was to be seen only fleetingly, at odd meal-times, or passing on the stairs. She was charming and anxious that Eleanor was having a good time and kept on saying how like her mother Eleanor was. Eleanor could see why the Mansel progeny were so self-sufficient; they had had to be with such busy parents.

Vanessa had great vivacity and Eleanor thought her pretty, with short, dark brown curls framing a heart-shaped face. She didn't lack escorts and dressed stunningly for each occasion, her slim, petite figure showing the clothes to advantage. Eleanor had the odd feeling, however, that beneath the gay exterior Vanessa was not as happy as she made out, and once or twice surprised a droop to the perfectly shaped mouth and a bleak look in the eyes that belied the fun and gaiety. Perhaps she had fallen for this Philip Nolan who was her most constant partner, and her feelings were not returned? Eleanor had first-hand knowledge of this situation and Guy's laughing face and their early meetings came, unbidden, to her mind. Stoically she told herself that even if their friendship had had the chance to survive Kate's introduction, it might have fizzled out, was bound to have done, for she and Kate were so unalike in temperament. Eleanor found these sort of arguments beneficial.

Edward was an irregular visitor, coming and going without warning, and she had not seen him since that first day. He had a flat in town and working hours were spent between the family business and the antique shop, in which his mother and sister also had an interest. What he did outside business hours was anyone's guess, and his private life was kept strictly private, although glossy photographs in society magazines showed him escorting some beautiful girl or another, indicating that he was no hermit. First impressions, although often not true ones, had a habit of sticking, and Eleanor's were not favourable. The fact that he made her feel extremely young and gauche did not help, and despite the lazy manner, she felt there was an underlying ruthlessness in him. She had every intention of keeping out of his way, for he brought out the worst in her, but some pricking of the thumbs told her that when Edward was around he would make his presence felt. She acknowledged that his looks were striking, but inscrutable faces always made her uneasy, she preferred a more open, friendlier disposition, and men whose eyebrows met—and his were extraordinarily dark and thick—she was mistrustful of. She guessed his was a popular name on the county guest lists—thirty and unmarried, presentable and wealthy, he was a challenge to every mother with a marriageable daughter, and Eleanor considered that many an eye would gleam with untold satisfaction when Edward Mansel put his foot across the threshold!

Contact with the Rectory was by a regular weekly letter. Constance Ferrers was a natural writer, her words came alive on the paper, bringing with them a mixture of emotions. Family and village gossip was read avidly, but among it, inevitably, were plans for Kate's and Guy's wedding.

Late on Friday evening, three weeks after her arrival, Eleanor slipped out of the house, to post her own letter home. The air had a seasonal nip to it, and she was glad of her coat, hugging it round her as she walked briskly to the post-box at the far end of the country lane. On the way back she paused to lean on the parapet of a small bridge, straining ears and eyes to see if she could locate any night-life along the river bank in the moonlight available.

She had a sudden rush of longing for her own river and felt the familiar wave of homesickness sweep over her. She fished in the pocket for a handkerchief and crossly blew her nose, telling herself that it was futile to indulge in self-pity. She knew why she was feeling like this now, at this moment, for her mother had made a surprise telephone call, her voice coming over warm and near. And then Kate had taken over, full of excitement about the wedding and giving details of the bridesmaid's dress Eleanor was to wear.

So busy was she with her thoughts that Eleanor gave no heed to the sound of an approaching car, and was only aware of it when a beam of light rounded the corner, blinding her momentarily. Startled, she flattened herself back against the brickwork as the car bore down on her, breathing a sigh of relief as it roared safely by, screeching to a halt a few yards ahead.

She realised that it had been foolish to linger on the narrow bridge in the dark, and as a door slammed and a tall shape loomed up out of the night, she felt a touch of fear until she saw who it was. She had an apology framed on her lips, but he gave her no time to get in first.

'That's a damned stupid place to be dreaming, isn't it?' his irascible voice demanded.

She felt a cold nose touch her ankle and saw unwinking, almond eyes staring up at her.

'Yes, it is, I'm sorry,' she answered readily, bending down to stroke the bull-terrier at her feet. 'There was no real danger, was there?'

Edward Mansel drew in audible breath. 'Only because I know the road. That bridge is a blind one, and too narrow for comfort.' He paused and searched her face. 'What were you doing?'

'Communing with nature,' she replied airily, standng up but keeping her face turned away.

'In future, do it where it's safer,' came the dry retort, Edward taking her arm in a firm grip and walking her back down the road.

'I didn't know you were coming this weekend,' Eleanor remarked. She hoped there'd been no trace of tears on her face.

'I don't advertise my movements,' was the repressive reply; and she bit her lip in annoyance. Drat the man, she thought crossly, surely he doesn't think I'm interested in whether he comes or not? Moving in front of her, Edward opened the passenger door of the Jensen.

'The back seat's rather cluttered, I'm afraid, but I think we can squeeze you in.'

'Oh, no, really,' protested Eleanor, 'I came out for a walk.'

'Then Hugh will walk with you,' he replied, 'it's too late for you to be out alone . . . next time, take one of the dogs with you. Hugh, this is Eleanor Ferrers who is staying with us for a while. She likes to commune with nature.'

'And a pleasant occupation it is, too,' agreed his friend, emerging from the car.

'There's really no need, I assure you...' Eleanor began feebly, and as her hand was warmly taken, she was cut off by an amused voice.

'When Edward commands, we obey, Miss Ferrers. How do you do? I'm Hugh Latimer. If I may whisper the truth in your ear, I'm very glad to be able to walk the rest of the way with you, as that brute of a dog resents anyone sitting on his seat. Look, he's established his right of tenure before the upholstery is even cold!'

Eleanor laughed with him, quickly liking his easy manner, and her eyes were drawn to the car window, where the brindle face of Sykes was staring, silent and immobile, through the glass.

'In that case, thank you,' she capitulated with a smile, and took his offered arm. 'Are you down for the weekend?' she asked, when the tail-lights of the Jensen had disappeared from sight down the road.

'For the whole week, and the thought gives me comfort. I can forget the office desk and relax in these beautiful surroundings. I'm lucky to have such an hospitable friend as Edward.'

'You've known each other long, Mr Latimer?'

'From prep-school days ... and if we're to be fellow guests, perhaps you will allow me to call you Eleanor?' He paused. 'But only if you feel you can reciprocate.'

Eleanor responded with a smile and said shyly: 'I think I can manage to do that.'

'Good.'

She studied her companion as well as she could in the light available. He was not tall, little taller than herself, and looked the bookish type. Hair fine and slightly receding, he wore rimless glasses and had a thin, clever face and a gentle manner.

'What conclusions have you come to?' Hugh asked, his voice teasing.

'Oh, dear, was I that obvious?' exclaimed Eleanor, giving him an apologetic grimace. 'To be truthful, I was thinking what an unlikely pair you made, you and Edward—not that I know either of you, of course.'

Hugh grinned. 'The suave, sartorial Edward and the comfortable, creased Hugh, do you mean? Ah, well, attraction of the opposites, I suppose.' He looked at her consideringly. 'What were you thinking of when you were communing with nature?'

Somehow Eleanor didn't mind Hugh Latimer knowing. 'I was homesick,' she confessed ruefully. 'Silly, isn't it? I was wishing I was standing on a similar bridge on my own Yorkshire soil. I don't transplant very easily, I'm afraid.'

'And where is your own soil? I know parts of Yorkshire very well.'

'Do you?' replied Eleanor. 'Do you know Rye Dale, where I live?' she asked eagerly, and for a few minutes they found common ground to discuss, and from there it was natural for Eleanor to go on to her family. 'My father is the rector of a rural parish, four villages as well as our own.'

'A happy family home is difficult to leave behind, but necessary if one is to find one's own identity, especially in a family of—three girls, did you say?'

'Yes. Poor father is sadly outnumbered, I'm afraid. I'm the eldest, then comes Katharine, she's eighteen, and then Dorothea who's fourteen.' They had reached the gates of the house by now and Eleanor turned to him in dismay. 'You shouldn't have let me go on so! I've monopolised the conversation!' She passed through the gate which he was holding open. 'I've given you no chance to speak of your own family,' she added, smiling her thanks.

'There's little to tell,' Hugh admitted, closing the gate behind them. 'The Latimers are rather thin on the ground, only a frail grandmother in Devon and me, so I latch on to Priory Lodge like grim death.'

'It's inevitable, I know,' Eleanor reflected, only wondering later how easy he was to talk to, 'but things are changing. Kate will soon be married and I shall have to be looking around for a job, and then we'll be split up.'

'But the fundamental unity will remain,' Hugh said firmly. 'What job will you do?'

Eleanor shrugged. 'I'm not trained for anything, that's the trouble. I went to art college for a year and then my mother became seriously ill and I came home. It wasn't a sacrifice on my part ... I wanted to be part of the family during that time. My sisters, being younger, were still at school and it would have been dreadful anyway at college, I wouldn't have been able to work.'

'And your mother?'

'She's made a remarkable recovery, thank goodness, and now they've insisted I have a breathing space before deciding what to do.'

'Can you resume your art studies? Are you good?' Hugh's brown eyes were turned on her consideringly.

'There are one or two whose judgment I respect, who think I may perhaps have something,' she admitted shyly. 'I've never given up studying and one of my professors insisted on seeing my work regularly which has been an added incentive to keep going.' She made the same little shrugging movement, trying for whimsical nonchalance. 'So I have a small talent, but is that enough in such a competitive field? I find I've acquired cold feet over going back to college. I'm not the same person I was two years ago.'

'There's plenty of time, don't rush things,' advised Hugh, bringing their slow pace to a halt. 'Ah, we will pause and allow Sykes to inspect us. I trust he satisfies himself that we are his friends. I'm a cat-man myself, and I rather think Sykes knows.'

Eleanor grinned at the pained expression on Hugh's face. 'He's beautiful, isn't he? but so aloof. There's an aristocratic look in his eye that I find daunting,' she confided.

'Hum ... there are some people who affect me the same way,' observed her companion dryly.

'We have a cross labrador back home who loves to be cuddled. How could you possibly cuddle Sykes?' Eleanor demanded.

Hugh smiled and pushed open the door. 'I'm all for mongrels in any set of circumstances. Too fine a strain can only be strengthened by an additive ... and talking of additives—we will proceed in the hope that Edward, as the true host he usually is, has liquid refreshment awaiting us,' and they entered the room, laughing together.

'Hugh! My dear boy, there you are!' Eve Mansel moved gracefully towards them and embraced Hugh warmly. After giving him a critical inspection, she said briskly: 'You're looking pale. You should have come to see us in the summer, you've neglected us dreadfully.'

Hugh kissed her on both cheeks. 'And you, my dear Eve, are looking as beautiful as ever.' He smiled. 'I've just been reminiscing with Eleanor and suddenly it all came back to me, that first day I came to stay ... what a thin, timid boy I was, and what a vision you appeared to my youthful eye.' He turned to Eleanor. 'She hasn't altered.'

'I adore Hugh,' Eve said with satisfaction. 'He's such a comfort to me in my old age.' She put an arm round Eleanor's shoulder. 'You've met each other, I see. Come over to the fire, both of you.'

The door burst open behind them and Vanessa erupted into the room.

'Hugh! I thought it was your voice! Edward didn't tell me you were coming down ... do come and see what I've found for you.'

'Give the poor man time for a drink, Van,' interrupted Edward mildly, following her in.

'You haven't told him, Mother, have you?' Vanessa demanded imperiously.

'I've hardly had time, darling. Do sit down, Hugh dear, and shake that ridiculous child off your arm. Vanessa, if you're determined to have no patience then you may go and bring it in—but be careful, it's very fragile.'

'I know that,' replied Vanessa, with impatient emphasis. 'It will ruin everything if I have to bring it in, Mother! I've set it to its best advantage on the Louis Quinze.'

'By all means, let us see it to its best advantage,' said Hugh, adding teasingly: 'You don't think it would ruin everything if my glass came with me?'

Vanessa grinned, moving quickly to the drinks table and

pouring him a generous measure. 'All the better. You'll be mellowed sufficiently to want to buy it!' and handing him the glass, she tucked an arm firmly through his.

'Hussy!' was the affectionate rejoinder as they left the room together.

Eve sighed. 'Really, Vanessa is so demanding at times, what must Hugh think of her?'

Eleanor supposed the question to be purely rhetorical, as she herself was in no position to answer, and Edward, immersed in the paper, made no attempt to do so.

'Oh, well, he's known her long enough to understand,' Eve continued, answering herself quite adequately. 'I'd better organise his room. Let me take your coat, my dear. Edward, Eleanor hasn't a drink,' and with a smile at her guest, Eve left the room.

The newspaper was lowered and a brow raised enquiringly. 'I'm sorry, what would you like?' He rose and strolled to the drinks table. 'There's all the usual stuff, or would you prefer a fruit juice?'

'In general a clergyman's daughter is expected to be abstemious regarding alcohol,' Eleanor reflected gravely. 'I always take a delight in correcting that view.'

'I can imagine,' Edward said dryly. 'And so?'

'Sherry, please, not sweet.' She watched him pour and added: 'In fact, my father is quite a connoisseur in his own small way.' She accepted the glass, murmured, 'Thank you' and picked up her book to indicate that she did not need entertaining. Her point was not taken, however, for Edward crossed to his chair and ignoring the paper, asked:

'What are you reading?'

'*Middlemarch*.' She hesitated and hurried on to say: 'It's your own copy . . . I'm sorry, I ought to have asked if I could borrow it.'

'My dear girl, take what you wish. I'm quite sure my books will be treated with the utmost respect,' Edward said carelessly, pausing to take a drink and adding: 'Have you settled here, Eleanor?'

She looked at him warily. 'Yes, thank you, Edward.'

'Happy?'

'Yes, thank you.'

'It was an odd time to be out walking, and alone.'

'I'd gone to post a letter home,' she replied, feeling slightly defensive.

'You seemed to be getting on well with Hugh.'

'Yes, but then he's easy to talk to, isn't he?' and as the following silence implied the unspoken—and you aren't—she added quickly: 'Am I allowed to ask what it is that Vanessa's anxious to show him?'

Edward frowned. 'I thought you were with her when she found it? Didn't you go to the Haxted sale with her last Tuesday?'

'Er—no ... I must have had something else planned.' Eleanor had no intention of saying that she hadn't been invited.

Edward regarded her thoughtfully. 'I see.' He crossed to the table and replenished his glass. 'Hugh collects snuff-boxes, and Van came across this one unexpectedly and snapped it up—hence her proprietorial manner. She's not often so lucky and is rather proud of herself.'

Eleanor smiled. 'I can imagine your friend surrounded by his snuffboxes,' and as Edward rested an elegant arm along the mantel and contemplated the liquid in his glass, she thought: And you I can see as the Beau, the eligible bachelor, leader of fashion, looking down your aristocratic nose at all the simpering, giggling girls making eyes behind their fluttering fans. Her thoughts evoked such a vivid picture that it was some time before she became aware that Edward was regarding her quizzically, the Technicolor splendour of the eighteenth century rapidly giving way to the twentieth, and the superbly cut, dark grey suit that he was wearing.

'Er—sorry ... did you say something?' she began in some confusion.

'I merely asked if you were interested in history?'

'Average interest, I think.' She wrinkled her nose thoughtfully. 'The romantic image is grossly overrated, don't you think? I'm more than grateful to be living in this century.'

He half smiled. 'Somehow I hadn't expected such a practical view to come from you. There's a seamy side to every age, and dealing, as I do, with material things from the past, it's a constant reminder that beautiful and intricate workmanship is often the result of sweat, blood and tears. But that's life, and only a fool expects life to be fair.'

'Is the snuffbox rare?'

'Comparatively so.' Edward bent forward, offering her a cigarette, which she refused, and lighting one for himself, he sat down, relaxing back and stretching out his long legs. 'It depends on how they're made as to value and rarity,' he continued. 'The ones of gold and silver, especially those decorated with precious stones, are obviously valuable, although horn, tortoiseshell and porcelain are all good collectors' pieces. Pewter and wood aren't so rare, being durable. The one Van's picked up is enamel with gold mounting, very fragile, hence its rarity.' He drew deeply on the cigarette and watched the exhaled smoke spiral and then dissipate. 'So . . . you're happy here,' he stated, after a few moments of silence. 'Why, then, were you crying tonight?' and he stared across at her with eyes more than usually hooded, the subdued lighting allowing the flickering flames of the fire to highlight the severe planes of his face, making it look more than usually austere.

Eleanor stared back, shocked surprise on her face, her mind a jumble of excuses.

'No man's worth crying over, you know,' he asserted calmly.

She flushed vividly and rose, putting her glass down with exceptional care. 'Why do you say that?'

He gave a cynical smile. 'My dear girl, it usually is the case when a young woman is found having a good cry all by herself in the moonlight. No man's worth it.' He downed his drink in one swift movement and added brusquely: 'Or woman, for that matter.'

'I'm sure you have a wealth of experience to draw upon,' Eleanor answered with tolerable composure, 'and I thank you for your advice. If ever I need to, I'll try and remember it,' and she walked to the door.

'Running away, Eleanor?'

'I don't care for the conversation.'

'Then we'll change it.' He rose and crossed to the desk. With a stab of dismay Eleanor saw that he was holding her art folio.

'That's my . . .'

'Drawings and paintings—yes, I know. I hope you don't mind, but I started to look through them just before you came in this evening.' Edward flipped open the cover and began to sift through the sheets which he examined carefully, one by one. 'These are good. Do you only do wild flowers?'

'No, but they give me pleasure,' she answered abruptly, and forced herself to go over and rescue her precious folio. His hands were still searching the pages and she caught her breath as he came to the charcoal section. 'I'm no good at portraits,' she said quickly.

'Oh, I wouldn't say that,' he replied, holding up a sketch of Duffy. 'Admittedly it's more of a caricature, but you've caught her expression. And this . . .' his voice trailed. Eleanor gave an inward groan. Why, oh, why hadn't she destroyed that wretched drawing! She nearly had done so, but it had pleased her, and now Edward was studying it with keen interest.

'Well, well . . . talk of the devil!' he said softly. 'So that's how you see me, Eleanor!'

'Edward, I . . .'

'Are my eyebrows really like that?'

'Of course not! You said yourself that I'm a caricaturist, and everything has to be exaggerated!' she replied, cheeks bright red.

'How reassuring,' was the sardonic answer. 'And the horns?'

'Oh, give it to me,' began Eleanor desperately, snatching at the drawing, only succeeding in making Edward spill the rest out of the folio. Dropping to her knees, she began to collect them together. Conscious of his sudden stillness, she looked up, and her heart sank even further.

'Now this one is interesting . . .'

She rose unsteadily to her feet. 'Please, Edward, may I have . . .'

'Now I wonder who this is—so lovingly drawn. No caricature, this.'

'. . . my drawings back?'

She waited, hand outstretched, and after a long moment Edward flipped the cover over and gave it to her.

'I'm sorry about the one of you . . . it was extremely rude of me,' she said stiffly, meeting his mocking eyes.

'Don't apologise, my dear. I now know in what light you see me . . . a dark one, obviously. And the other?' He watched her walk swiftly to the door. 'Is he the one you're crying over, Eleanor?'

Eleanor didn't reply, and left the room, taking with her a brief glimpse of eyes no longer sleepy, but surprisingly clear and calculating. When she gained her room, she took out the drawing of Guy and ripped it into tiny pieces.

CHAPTER TWO

'There is a certain relief in change.'
Washington Irving

HUGH was passing the foot of the stairs when Eleanor came down to breakfast the next morning, and he stopped, smiling up at her.

'Good morning, Eleanor. You disappeared last night before I could show you my new treasure. Do come now and see it.'

'Hullo, Hugh . . . thank you, I should love to,' she replied, running down the last few steps to join him. As they walked along the hall to the study, she added: 'You've decided to buy it?'

Hugh smiled ruefully: 'To tell you the truth, there was little doubt.'

'What else do you like doing, besides collecting snuff-boxes, I mean?' she asked, as he opened the door and ushered her through.

'Nothing very energetic—walking is my main form of exercise.' He pursed his lips thoughtfully. 'I go to concerts and the theatre, read, enjoy a good meal with people I like, follow the Test Match and...'

'Buy snuffboxes,' finished Eleanor. 'Oh, yes,' she breathed, 'it is lovely, isn't it?' and she knelt down by the small Louis XV table on which was displayed a charming box, smaller than Eleanor had anticipated, inset with intricately painted pictures of plump ladies reclining on frothy clouds. 'Quite lovely,' she repeated, and they smiled at each other, and into this companionable scene strolled Edward.

'So there you both are. Good morning, Eleanor, sleep well?'

Eleanor rose to her feet murmuring an appropriate answer and Edward turned to Hugh.

'I have to go to Wells today to look over a horse. I've suggested to Van that we all go and make a day of it.'

'Good idea,' agreed Hugh. 'You and Van can discuss the horse ... I'm sure that Eleanor and I can find something to do.'

'I'm sure you can,' said Edward. 'Come and breakfast, and we'll make a start.'

The next few days passed quickly, the four of them spending most of the time together. By Wednesday Eleanor had grown used to being included in the general plans and was surprised at how disappointed she was to find that the day was to be her own. Edward stated that he had business to attend to, and later, she heard Vanessa discussing with Hugh the prospect of visiting friends in Esher. As the only vehicle left was her Spitfire, which could accommodate two, Eleanor took the hint.

The weather looked promising, a thin gleam of sunshine was struggling through the cloud, and if she could find a sheltered spot, then she would do some work. Transport was the main difficulty, but she had spied a bicycle in the depths of one of the outbuildings and went in search of Sam. After listening to her, Sam was not enthusiastic.

'You won't want to ride this old thing, Miss Eleanor,' he protested, struggling to free the machine. 'It's hardly safe.'

'I think it is,' persisted Eleanor, giving it a closer inspection as he propped it against the wall. 'It looks worse because of all the cobwebs.'

'Used to be Miss Van's, but she's not used it for many a year. Let me test those brakes before you ride it. I don't think Mr Edward will like the idea,' he muttered under his breath.

'Mr Edward needn't know,' she replied firmly, rubbing the dirt off with a finger.

Sam produced a rag from out of nowhere and gave it to her. He shook his head, still not completely easy. 'The brakes seem good enough ... I'll have to lift the saddle, though, you've a fair stretch of leg.' He looked up at her. 'Why don't you give the horses their apple while I'm doing it? Else they might think you've forgotten them this morning,' he added slyly.

Eleanor took the two halves of apple from her pocket and grinned.

'There's not much misses you, Sam, is there?' and she walked over to the paddock fence and sat on the top bar. They came towards her expectantly and she held out her hand to each in turn. They blew gently and nuzzled, and she laughed and stroked each soft velvet nose. 'Don't be greedy,' she admonished fondly, and giving them a last pat, returned to Sam who was now filling his pipe, watching her.

'You're used to horses?' he asked, puffing briskly, shielding the flame of the match from the breeze.

'Not really. A farmer friend has let me ride occasionally, but not on anything compared to them. They're beauties, aren't they? I've watched Edward exercise them first thing in the mornings from my bedroom window. Now he's what I would call used to horses!' She nodded at the cycle. 'Is it okay?'

'Wouldn't say that,' returned Sam laconically, wheeling it over to her. 'This is as ready as I can make it at such short notice. I've given her a drop of oil and a bit of air, but there's no bell.'

'Not to worry, I'll just yell if anything gets in my way!' She slipped the straps of her art folio over her arms and wriggled it comfortably on to her back.

Sam thumbed the tyres doubtfully. 'Better not go too far, Miss Eleanor.'

'I won't,' she promised, balancing on one toe as she sat astride the saddle. 'I say, Sam, I wish you'd stop this Miss prefix, it's not my style at all.' Giving him a grin, she pushed off. 'There's no need to worry about me ... I've been brought up on a bike,' and wobbling as she negotiated the curve, she pedalled down the drive and out on to the road.

The day was a grand one for cycling, the breeze gentle enough to be cooling but not enough to have to battle against. Eleanor, lulled into an optimism that was misguided, forgot her promise and went further than she intended. Eventually she found a sheltered spinney and settled to work. A packed lunch, provided by Duffy, satisfied hunger pains at midday, and if she hadn't found a wild honeysuckle growing in a hawthorn hedge, which she couldn't resist, she would have started back much earlier. As it was, by the time she had packed up all her gear and dragged the bicycle through the undergrowth to the road, the sun had disappeared and clouds had begun to build up.

Eleanor zipped up her anorak and started for home. She would, she thought, be warm after a few minutes' hard work on the pedals. Not a quarter of an hour passed, however, before there was an ominous bump-bump from the back wheel and examination showed a two-inch split in the tyre.

'Drat the thing!' exclaimed Eleanor, frowning down at the wheel. 'Oh, well, heaven knows how far from Priory Lodge I am, but there's nothing else to do but push!' and this she proceeded to do. After a while the heel of her right foot began to shout for attention and realising that her minor road joined the main one a few yards ahead she made that her goal, and on reaching the junction propped the cycle against the road sign and sat on the grass verge, gingerly removing sock and shoe.

This revealed a king-sized blister, and winding a clean handkerchief round as best she could, Eleanor eased her sock and shoe back on. Intent on the job, she was unaware of passing traffic, and of one particular car which suddenly pulled up and then backed to where she was sitting. Then she did look up, surprise changing to wariness when she saw Edward alight, slam his door and walk over to her.

'What the devil are you doing here, Eleanor? I thought you were with Van and Hugh?'

'Oh, did you?' she said guardedly. 'No, I'm not.'

'I can see you're not,' he exclaimed impatiently. 'Surely Van told you the arrangements for today?'

'Er—something was said, but I fancied a jaunt more leisurely for a change.'

'You're extremely leisurely at the moment, it seems,' he said dryly, glancing down to her foot, taking in the tyre, flushed face and tousled hair. 'Where did that contraption come from?' and he nodded at the cycle.

'I found it in the shed and Sam helped me to . . .'

'Sam had no business to allow you out on . . .'

'It had nothing to do with him,' exclaimed Eleanor indignantly. 'Don't you dare go on at Sam, because it wasn't his fault. He wanted to tell you, but I wouldn't let him. He said not to go far because of the tyres, but . . .'

'You thought best. Don't get excited. Far from blaming Sam, I sympathise with the poor fellow. That dewy-eyed look of yours is all humbug!' He looked at his watch. 'I haven't time to take you back, you'll have to come with me.'

'You don't have to concern yourself with me, Edward. If you'd come two minutes earlier you would have missed me altogether. I can quite easily . . .'

'But I didn't miss you.' He picked up the cycle and heaved it over the hedge into the adjacent field, where it vanished into the undergrowth with hardly a sound.

'What are you doing?' protested Eleanor. 'That's a perfectly good bike, you know, and I've grown very fond of it...' Edward pulled her to her feet and steered her firmly to the Jensen. 'Suppose someone steals it?' she added worriedly.

'My dear girl, no one in their right mind would steal that thing, but if you insist, I'll arrange for its collection.' He opened the door. 'In you get.'

She did so, struggling with her folio which Edward took from her without a word and placed on the back seat. Soon the Jensen was bowling along the road, very fast.

'I'm sorry to be such a nuisance,' Eleanor said at last, seeing him glance briefly at his watch for a second time. 'I was going to wait for a lorry to come by and hitch a lift.'

'I see. Why didn't you dump the cycle, somewhere safe, of course,' he added caustically, 'and get on a bus?'

'Because I hadn't any ...' Eleanor checked the words abruptly.

'Money,' finished Edward. 'You ridiculous girl!'

'I never bother at home, there's always someone who knows me to help out.'

'You're not home now.'

'Oh, well, you came along,' she observed airily.

He shot her a side glance. 'So Van didn't ask you to go with them?'

His face told her nothing. 'Oh, it wasn't like that, and anyway, there was a shortage of car space.'

'Nonsense ... Mother's was in the garage.'

'She knew I had plans of my own today,' Eleanor said firmly, putting an end to the interrogation. She wasn't going to be accused of complaining and she launched into an account of her day.

'You don't bring anything back with you to draw at home?' Edward asked.

'It depends. You can't uproot wild plants these days without permission from the landowner. Some species are now protected by law because they're dying out completely.'

'I didn't realise things were so bad as that,' said Edward,

slowing the Jensen almost to a halt to turn right.

'I suppose something will be done when it's too late,' replied Eleanor rather forlornly. 'Where are we going?' she asked, as the car passed through an open barrier. 'It looks like a private aerodrome!'

'It is,' agreed Edward, winding down his window as a white-overalled man ran alongside, and saying briefly: 'Sorry I'm late.'

'Thought it was off, Mansel. Is this it?' The man indicated a large packet at the back of the Jensen.

'Yes. I'll park and you can take it.' Edward manoeuvred into a line of parked cars. He turned to Eleanor before alighting. 'I won't be a moment, someone's waiting for this,' and he heaved out the packet and strode off. He returned almost immediately and opened her door.

'Aren't we going home now?' she asked in surprise.

'I've arranged to meet someone here, so we might as well go into the clubhouse and make ourselves comfortable.'

'I'm not dressed for socialising,' Eleanor said doubtfully. 'I could wait in the car.'

He scanned her briefly. 'Don't be ridiculous. No one's going to notice what we wear,' and Eleanor allowed herself to be led meekly into the clubhouse, thinking that Edward's grey and white dog-tooth check pants and Aran sweater would stand scrutiny better than her own patched jeans and anorak.

'I suppose you fly,' she said, looking round her curiously.

'Yes.' Edward glanced at her briefly. 'I'll take you up one day.'

'Er—well, maybe . . .'

'Let me tell you, Eleanor Ferrers, that I have been piloting aircraft since I was seventeen, and I can assure you that you'd be far safer in my Piper Cherokee than riding that damned cycle!'

'Very well, I accept your offer. Never let it be said that parsons' daughters are chicken-hearted,' she replied demurely.

'There are times when I suspect parsons' daughters are

not spanked enough in their early, formative years,' he retorted jocosely.

Edward ordered a drink and sat her at one of the small tables at the side of the room, excusing himself to speak to someone at the bar.

I bet he's a good pilot, too, she thought, as she sipped her drink. She loved watching him ride the horses, and speed in the Jensen had no fears for her. Altogether, Edward was a comforting person to have around in that respect. In fact, she was enjoying herself ... rather to her surprise. After a while her eye was caught by a woman who had just come in and was weaving her way between the tables. Her route may have appeared haphazard, but she knew her goal, and when Edward turned and moved towards her, Eleanor was not surprised, just stupidly disappointed. Naturally, she told herself crossly, it's only to be expected that the most beautiful and exciting woman in the room should be claimed by Edward Mansel, but he might have warned me, and then I should definitely have waited in the car.

To her dismay she saw that after five minutes of deep conversation he was bringing the woman over. It was no use remembering her father's maxim that fine feathers do not necessarily make a fine bird—that philosophy is only acceptable when you feel that you have at least a few feathers existing of your own! She watched their approach with a sinking heart.

'Eleanor, this is Felicity Maddox—Felicity, this is Eleanor Ferrers, who is on a visit from Yorkshire.' He pulled out a chair and Felicity sank gracefully in to it. She was even more breathtaking close to, with ash-blonde hair, eyes a startling green and a voice attractively husky.

'Yorkshire?' she echoed, as though it were a county on Mars, and Eleanor nodded, reading the message loud and clear that emanated from the hard, green eyes.

Her glass was refilled—Eleanor knew she ought not to have had another on such an empty stomach, but it gave her something to do, for it was soon apparent that she might not have existed so far as Miss Maddox was concerned. Her feelings were not improved when Felicity turned to her, smiling sweetly, and purred:

'Do persuade Edward to stay on this evening, Miss Ferrers.' She tilted a shapely head to Edward and added reproachfully: 'Darling, you did promise!'

Edward smiled slightly and shook his head. 'I said perhaps.'

'There you are!' exclaimed Felicity, teasingly, 'I'm sure Miss Ferrers would enjoy herself.'

Oh, you do, do you? thought Eleanor grimly, a deep resolve forming that she would rather walk home than remain. And anyway, who did she think she was kidding? If Felicity could not induce him to stay, then an insignificant Yorkshire nonentity couldn't!

'We won't stay,' Edward was saying, 'but I'll do penance one evening next week, Felicity.' The drawl was very pronounced.

'Darling, that's a promise?' Felicity raised her brows provocatively. 'And I may choose your punishment?' she added softly, a smile gathering on her lips.

'You may,' replied Edward easily, then turning to Eleanor he said: 'Are you ready?'

More than ready, asserted Eleanor to herself, rising and shrugging herself into her anorak before he could help.

'So you think the horse will do?' Felicity asked.

'He'll suit you admirably.' Edward included Eleanor into the conversation by adding: 'That horse we vetted at Wells this week was for Felicity.'

'Do you ride, Miss Ferrers?' asked Felicity with charming interest.

'Yes,' answered Eleanor, thinking it wasn't altogether a lie.

Two minutes later she raised her flushed face thankfully to the cool air as Edward closed the clubhouse doors behind them. She saw him give her a keen look as he opened the car door, but there was silence between them until the Jensen was speeding along the road. As it had to be said and the longer she waited the more difficult it would become, Eleanor took a deep breath.

'I'm sorry I messed up the evening for you.' To her

disgust it came out prim and proper.

'You didn't,' replied Edward laconically.

She flicked him a glance beneath lowered lashes to see if she could read his face. He looked composed enough, but then he rarely displayed his real feelings. Those objectionable eyebrows were a thick line above eyes fixed steadily ahead.

'I'd feel better if you said what a nuisance I'd been,' she carried on irritably.

'That's a pity, as I have no intention of saying anything of the kind,' Edward drawled. 'What bee in your bonnet have you now, Eleanor?'

'If I'd realised that you'd arranged to meet Miss Maddox then I'd never have come with you. You could easily have put me on the bus and . . .'

'Thank you,' he returned dryly, 'but since I had no plans for staying this evening you need not concern yourself with outraged feelings.'

There was a car coming up fast from behind. As it zoomed past, the headlights flicked on and off and a hand waved. Edward responded with a similar reply and when the rearlights disappeared into the distance, Eleanor said flatly:

'Miss Maddox didn't stay on herself.'

'Evidently not.'

She slipped further into her seat and stared out of the window. After a few miles of silence, Edward said:

'Why didn't you tell me you could ride a horse?'

'You didn't ask me,' she prevaricated.

'I didn't ask if you could ride a bicycle, but that didn't stop you from doing so,' countered Edward uncompromisingly.

'That's quite different!' said Eleanor, indignantly.

'Why didn't you ask?'

'Because I can't ride well . . . it was stupid of me to say I could . . . I mean, I have, but I'm not much good and would certainly be outclassed by Miss Maddox.'

'I should imagine so. Felicity is a superb horsewoman,' Edward announced, sweeping into the driveway and pulling up in front of the garage doors.

She would be, muttered Eleanor under her breath as she climbed out of the Jensen, adding louder, as Edward joined her: 'I suppose she can fly a plane too.' There were no lights on at the front of the house and he took her arm to guide her along the path.

'She can indeed.'

'Anything she can't do?' replied Eleanor tartly.

'I suspect—ride a bike.'

There! He'd done it again. Completely taken the wind out of her sails with his totally unexpected humour. Remorseful, she stammered:

'I am grateful to you, Edward, for rescuing me from a long walk. I . . . I don't think I thanked you properly.'

There was amusement in his voice. 'I'll accept your thanks as said, Eleanor, if you'll only tell me what this is?' and he lifted her hand to inspect it in the light from the pale, watery moon.

Eleanor stared in puzzlement at her fingers. She had used pencil and pastel crayons for her drawings . . . so why were they stained? Her frown broke and she smiled up into his face.

'Oh! It's blackberry juice!' she exclaimed with a laugh.

Edward touched her chin with a finger and tilted her face to the light.

'You really are a child of nature, aren't you?'

For a crazy split second, Eleanor thought he was going to kiss her, and held her breath, her eyes mesmerised by his. Then he said brusquely:

'Run along and find something to eat. You'll not get very far on blackberries!'

Feeling like a twelve-year-old, Eleanor ran into the house, branding herself with scornful comments, and escaped to bed as soon as she could.

She had an early visitor the next morning, a chastened Vanessa.

'Thanks for not giving me away to Edward.' Vanessa moved from the bed to stare pensively out of the window at the steadily falling rain. She hunched her shoulders. 'I wouldn't have blamed you if you'd had a good moan. I know I've not been behaving very well since you came, and I'm sorry.'

'Well, I was wished on you in the first place,' comforted Eleanor, sipping the cup of tea Vanessa had brought in with her.

'Yes, but I could have been a little more gracious. Dear brother calls me a selfish brat, and I'm afraid he's right. You being decent about it makes things worse.' Vanessa turned and leant on the window ledge. 'I wouldn't say I was the easiest of companions at the moment, but if you can put up with me...' She eyed Eleanor thoughtfully. 'Edward reckons you'll be good for me.'

'I object to being spoken of as if I were a patent medicine! Was Edward beastly to you?' Eleanor pulled up her knees and clasped them with pyjama-clad arms. 'I don't think I fancy the idea of Edward being angry.'

'He can be rather blistering,' admitted Vanessa, 'but he is fair. And I can't complain—he's a decent brother, really, protective in a detached sort of way. He taught me to drive, and that should have reduced him to a raving lunatic, but it didn't,' she added with a grin.

'It's a pity he came across me yesterday.'

'Oh, he knew what was going on, but hoped I'd show sense without him having to lay down the law.' Vanessa pulled a face and Eleanor smiled at the other girl's matter-of-fact way in which she offered self-criticism ... it was heart-warming.

'He was probably more annoyed because I cramped his style, somewhat, last night,' said Eleanor.

'Oh?' Vanessa raised her brows. 'How?'

'There was this gorgeous blonde he'd arranged to meet,' explained Eleanor. 'A Felicity Maddox. She seemed to think I was expendable.'

'She would,' said Vanessa laughing. 'She's one of Edward's more persistent admirers. He taught her to fly, hence the proprietorial manner. You've heard of Maddox Enterprises? Well, she's the granddaughter. Mother's hopeful of an alliance—but I don't know, Edward's a dark horse, and she's one of many. Poor Mother is constantly frustrated. Goodness, I nearly forgot!' Vanessa felt in her pocket. 'Here's a letter for you.' She tossed it on to the bed and then walked to the door. 'Hugh and Edward are playing golf all day. I thought we'd buzz off somewhere. Duffy will pack a hamper if we ask her nicely.'

Eleanor looked out of the window, doubtfully. 'It's pouring with rain.'

'It won't last, Sam says so and he's always right,' declared Vanessa airily. 'See you in half an hour.'

Eleanor finished her tea thoughtfully and then opened her letter from home.

'Sam was right, as you see,' said Vanessa, peering up into the watery blue sky an hour later, as they walked towards the Spitfire.

'Look, Van, are you sure you want to go . . .' began Eleanor, and was silenced by Vanessa's vigorous shaking of her head.

'I don't often do anything that isn't basically geared to self. You can laugh, but it's true, although I don't think I'm wholly to blame. You must have gathered the sort of upbringing we've had . . . I'm not complaining, but it has resulted in my being encouraged to use my initiative and be self-sufficient. I've been told that both Edward and myself have our fair share of arrogance . . . it may be so.' She shrugged and eased the Spitfire out of a line of traffic, overtaking with confidence and expertise. 'Anyway, a few weeks ago something happened to shake both my initiative and self-sufficiency, and my arrogance is slightly dented. It doesn't excuse my behaviour to you, but it may help to show me in a more kindly light . . . yours is the nicer nature and I'm trading on that, you see.' Vanessa smiled wryly. 'The Mansels aren't used to being thwarted and I'm having to adjust to the idea that I can't have everything I want at the click of a finger. I'm not explaining too well . . .'

'You don't need to explain,' murmured Eleanor.

Vanessa carried on gruffly: 'Edward was right. He said that if ever you offered your hand in friendship it would be no mean gesture. I can't see you getting much out of it.'

'Oh, I don't know. I'll have a chauffeur for a start,' Eleanor said lightly, and began to ask questions about the route they were taking. It was no good trying to guess at what had knocked Vanessa off balance, and it didn't really matter. What did matter was how much of that conversation was revealing. For one thing, Vanessa wasn't so hard-boiled as she liked to make out, and for another, she was basically a truthful person, even if the truth was against herself.

'By the way, that letter was from my sister,' said Eleanor, 'the one who's being married in April, next year.' She fished the letter from her pocket and smoothed the creases. 'She says she has the chance of coming to London this week for a couple of days ... Guy is coming on business. It seems a pity not to take advantage of seeing her, as she'll be so near. According to this, which she wrote at the weekend, they should have arrived yesterday, and as Guy has a meeting tomorrow afternoon, Kate suggests I meet her then.'

Vanessa replied promptly: 'Good idea, and no problem. I have to do my stint at the shop for the next two days. Why not come with me, and we could perhaps arrange an evening out for them—a meal and a show. That would be fun. We'll rope Edward and Hugh in too.'

'It might not be convenient for them,' said Eleanor doubtfully, her motives confused. On the one hand she had hoped not to have to see Guy until the wedding, but perhaps it would do her good, be a testing? She would leave it to fate.

'You can ask,' Vanessa was saying decisively. 'We'll do it anyway, even if they can't. It will be a fitting end to Hugh's holiday.' She swung the wheel over sharply and took a right fork in the road. 'I'm making for Beachy Head, we'll have lunch there and watch the Newhaven-Dieppe ferries crossing the Channel.'

They spent an enjoyable day together, making tentative explorations towards friendship, each satisfied with the small inroads made. When they arrived back at Dunsmead, the silver-grey Jensen was parked in the drive and Vanessa brought the subject up of the proposed plans during the evening meal.

'Slade? You say that Kate's fiancé is Guy Slade?' Eve Mansel asked, hand poised with the coffee pot. 'Constance hasn't written me about Kate's engagement. She's very young, of course, at eighteen.'

'It only happened just before I came away,' offered Eleanor, aware of the interest round the table.

'We know some Slades, don't we, Edward? I wonder if they're the same?'

As usual with many of his mother's unanswerable questions, Edward ignored it, and turned to Eleanor.

'If you'll let me know where I can get hold of your prospective brother-in-law, I'll make arrangements for the evening.'

'We should have enough contacts between us to get into something decent,' Hugh acknowledged thoughtfully.

'Oh, anything will do,' said Eleanor eagerly.

'How refreshing to have such enthusiasm,' replied Hugh with a smile.

'If I remember rightly,' Eve continued, 'Guy is the good-looking one, a blond boy with a good deal of charm. Am I right?' and she looked expectantly at Eleanor, who was conscious of Edward's regard from across the table.

'Yes, he is fair,' she admitted, knowing her colour was rising.

'Not a boy now, though,' mused Eve, passing the cups round. 'He must be about twenty-five. What a coincidence that we know him! And how lovely to have a wedding in the family,' and she gave an exaggerated sigh and glared at her son and daughter.

'Don't despair, mater, old thing,' said Vanessa cheekily, rousing from an unusually quiet spell, 'we both might surprise you one of these years,' and her father said dryly:

'Do let us have notice in good time, my dear, for I'll need to take out a bank loan, knowing your mother,' and there was general laughter.

After a moment, Eleanor's eyes were drawn inexorably towards Edward. He was staring at her thoughtfully and she was pleased with the way she held his gaze and calmly refilled his coffee cup.

The next day the two girls set out early.

'It's a nuisance the shop being on the north side, but I suspect it was intentional on Edward's part.' Vanessa grinned and added: 'He's never liked being too close to the family, and knowing Mama's beady eyes, I'm not surprised.' She negotiated a set of traffic lights and hooted at a taxi that was cutting in. 'When I'm at the Crescent I don't use the car, I go by tube, much easier,' she added in exasperation.

'The Crescent?' Eleanor asked.

'The town house, just off Sloane Square. Quite a handy base. Mr and Mrs Hickman live in the basement quarters and look after the place for us. We have a couple of part-time helpers in the shop.' Vanessa pulled in at the kerb. 'Here we are—Camden Mews. This is the back. The front is a pedestrian walk, which gives problems for parking but is nice for the customers. Edward lives above, it's rather super—I'll show you round, he won't mind.'

Eleanor considered this a somewhat sweeping statement, but there was no holding Vanessa, and anyway, she was curious. Edward's home reflected his image, at least, the one he offered publicly, Eleanor thought, looking round the large main room. It was masculine to the point of austerity, furnished with excellent taste, and was immaculate. Very much a bachelor flat, she mused, returning down the stairs, hardly looking lived-in.

The shop was not like a normal one, in Eleanor's opinion, more like a huge sitting room displayed with treasures, and while Vanessa was reading the list of instructions that Edward had left for her, she made coffee and they set to work, dusting and polishing. Most of the customers were tourists and Eleanor enjoyed talking to them, and when things slackened off slightly she wandered round the other shops in the precinct, taking her time, noting that they were mostly antique and bookshops, the atmosphere exclusive and expensive. She returned to share a light lunch with Vanessa which they prepared in a tiny kitchen at the rear, and afterwards Eleanor asked advice as to where she should meet Kate.

Vanessa's finger moved expertly along Eleanor's new street guide.

'Bayswater Road ... Queensborough Terrace, yes, here it is. Why not meet here?' she suggested, stabbing her finger. 'Your sister won't know London, will she? It's better if only one of you charges about getting lost.'

'You say such encouraging things,' murmured Eleanor, peering over her shoulder. 'Yes, that's a good idea, Van. May I telephone Kate now?' It was convenient, so Eleanor dialled the number Kate had given her and waited.

'Eleanor?' Kate's voice came over with peculiar intensity. 'You *can* meet me, can't you?'

'Of course I can, you don't think I'd let you come all this way without doing so, do you?' exclaimed Eleanor, laughing. 'How about meeting at the entrance to the Queensway underground? That's the nearest to your hotel. Two o'clock ... and wait if I'm late.'

'I'll wait,' promised Kate. 'It ... it's lovely to hear you, Nell, I have missed you. 'Bye. See you at two.'

Vanessa returned as Eleanor was replacing the telephone.

'Anything the matter?' she asked, seeing Eleanor's face.

'Kate sounded rather strange,' said Eleanor, puzzled.

'The telephone is a terrible instrument, so impersonal, it distorts the most normal of conversations! I've been looking at the map again, Eleanor, and you might just as well go on to the Crescent when you've seen your sister and I'll meet you there. It's hardly any distance.' She ignored the sceptical look given her and folded the map, pushing it into Eleanor's bag. 'Are you and Kate alike?'

'Heavens, no!' exclaimed Eleanor with a laugh. 'Kate's beautiful ... lovely hair, the colour of ripe corn, blue eyes, a super figure.' She paused and said reflectively, 'I'm not surprised that Guy fell for her the minute he saw her.'

'I only hope it was more than looks he fell for,' said Vanessa slowly. 'Looks aren't really important, are they?'

'Oh, I know,' Eleanor put in quickly, 'and I'm sure there is something more. Kate's a bit silly sometimes, but she's still very young, isn't she, at eighteen? I'm sure she'll make Guy a good wife.'

'What a great champion you are, Nell. Okay, so sister Kate is a smasher, but don't do yourself down by comparison.' Vanessa looked her over. 'Hazel eyes, clear magnolia complexion, thick, glossy hair have their own attraction ... and you have lovely teeth.'

Eleanor burst out laughing. 'You sound like a television advertisement!'

'You wait. One of these days I'll go to work on you, and you'll be surprised at the results,' warned Vanessa, shooing her out of the door.

Eleanor followed the directions to the nearest tube station, thinking of the evening ahead. Kate had been thrilled with the idea of a theatre outing and so arrangements had been made through Edward and Guy for them all to meet at eight o'clock. They would see the show together and then go on afterwards for a meal somewhere. During this piece of news Kate had sounded perfectly all right; the rest of the conversation, however, had sounded odd, as if she was labouring under a certain amount of tension.

Eleanor sighed and boarded the crowded train. She would know soon enough if anything was the matter with Kate, and as for tension, she was labouring under some herself. She had to meet Guy some time and she supposed tonight was as good a time as any, but she wished it could have been less public. The others would be there, and Edward ... Edward, who knew how she felt about Guy, and whose sleepy blue eyes missed nothing.

No, tonight was not going to be easy to live through.

CHAPTER THREE

'It is impossible to be in love and be wise.'
Francis Bacon

As Eleanor emerged from the underground station she looked anxiously around until she caught sight of Kate, and seeing her face, she was sure something was wrong. The October day, although sunny, had a nip to the air, and she turned up the collar of her camel coat and tightened the belt as she hurried towards her.

Eleanor was surprised at the fierceness of her sister's hug when they met. They crossed the busy Bayswater Road and made for Kensington Gardens, arm in arm, matching their steps. When they reached the Gardens they made for the direction of the Round Pond and when all normal questions regarding the family had been asked and answered, Eleanor said quietly: 'Is anything wrong, Katie?' and was not surprised when her sister suddenly burst into tears. She immediately put her arms round her, asking quickly:

'Kate, whatever is the matter? Is it Guy? Have you fallen out with Guy?' Kate shook her head, unable to speak, and fumbled for her handkerchief. Eleanor continued firmly: 'What is it? Come and sit down on this seat and tell me.' She waited until Kate had gained some degree of control and asked again: 'What is it?'

After a few moments Kate began to talk in a low voice, stumbling now and again and interrupting the flow with shuddering sobs.

'I've been an awful fool, Nell, you'll not believe how silly I've been, and I can't go to Father for help and I just don't know what to do! It's my own fault ... I was stupid and I can't believe now that I let it happen. I can't tell Guy, I just can't! I love him so, and he thinks I'm p—perfect. I shall just die if his mother finds out, I can imagine what she'll say because she doesn't r—really approve of me, you know, and if she finds out ...'

'Kate, stop!' begged Eleanor, thoroughly alarmed at the

rising hysteria in her sister's voice. 'Calm down and don't worry. I'm here and I can help. Finds out what? You're not really telling me anything.'

Kate swallowed hard and began to twist her handkerchief nervously between her fingers.

'When I had the chance to come with Guy I was so pleased, Nell, you c—can imagine. Mrs Slade sent for me and told me I could b—buy some clothes and charge them to her account, as part of my wedding gift from her. Guy's cousin, Margot, lives in London and it was arranged for her to take me round. Mother wasn't too keen about that, b—but I persuaded her it would be all right, I wanted to go with Margot, although I'd never met her. She's older than us, Nell, about twenty-six, and awfully attractive and dresses out of this world! I liked her from the first, although she kept on teasing me about coming to London for the first time, she couldn't get over that. Anyway, it was all tremendously exciting and I was enjoying myself enormously, and then...' She stopped and stared miserably at the ground.

'Go on, Katie,' prompted Eleanor gently.

'I... I told you how good her clothes were, Nell—well, she took me to Harrods and sort of took over completely, and I lost my head and...' Kate paused and turned stricken eyes to Eleanor. 'It wasn't that I was ashamed of us, Nell, you must believe that, but being with Margot and having the assistants treating me like Royalty, I found myself pretending I was used to it, you know, keeping up appearances. Oh, it all started off in fun, but then I was carried away by the lovely clothes and everyone saying "You must have that" and Margot saying "Guy will love you in that" and it was as though the person in the mirror wasn't me at all! And then, as the parcels began to mount up, I began to be frightened. It dawned on me how expensive everything was, but when I tried to tell Margot that I thought I was over-spending she just laughed and said "Doesn't everyone, darling, and isn't Guy a good cause?" I felt sick then, and couldn't wait to get back to the hotel, and when I added up what I'd overspent...'

'How much?' asked Eleanor quietly, feeling sick herself.

Kate bit her lip and in deep misery mumbled: 'Over eighty pounds!' She turned and clutched Eleanor's arm. 'Oh, Nell, what am I to do? Eighty pounds! I can't ask Father for any more money—the wedding is going to cost an awful amount, and besides, he'd be so disappointed in me. He'd not say so, but I know he would be. He didn't want me to be engaged, he doesn't think I'm old enough to be married, and he's always trying to make me understand that vanity is such a paltry thing, that outward appearance is worthless! And look how I always go on at Dodie about not caring enough with her clothes ... what a smug fool I am!'

Eleanor listened aghast. Eighty pounds! Her thoughts in a tumult, she carefully controlled her facial expression and said as calmly as she could: 'Would it be possible to return any of the items?'

Kate shook her head miserably. 'I've already thought of that. It would look so odd, and Margot knows what I bought and it's all been put down to Mrs Slade's account.'

'Are you sure you can't tell Father? He isn't an ogre, you know. He'd understand.'

'I know he would, but he had all that worry over Mother and I know it's a struggle bringing us all up, and Dodie will have to go on to university, she's so clever ...' Tears trickled silently down Kate's cheeks.

'What about Guy?' pursued Eleanor gently. 'He loves you, Katie.'

'How can I go and ask him for money before we're even married, Nell? That would only confirm his family's doubts about me. Oh, I'm introduced as a "sweet girl", but I'm not their choice of a bride for Guy. I've not bothered about it before because I know I can be anything Guy wants me to be—I'll work hard and help him, but I want to start off with a clean sheet. You do understand, don't you, Nell?' Kate besought her anxiously.

'Yes, I understand.'

'Do you ... have you any ideas, Nell?'

'One or two, but they need thinking over carefully. Dry

your eyes, Kate, I can't deliver you back to Guy looking like this.'

Kate obediently mopped up and the sisters began to walk back the way they had come. Kate took a deep breath.

'I do feel better, now I've told you, Nell.' She gave Eleanor a hug. 'What a comfort you are! You're the best sister anyone could wish for. I've told Margot all about you and she's longing to meet you tonight.' She smiled at Eleanor's surprised look. 'Yes, tonight! When Edward Mansel telephoned Guy they found out they know each other, isn't it funny? At least, Edward knows Margot, their families mix.'

'When I mentioned Guy's name, Mrs Mansel said she knew the Slades,' reflected Eleanor. 'Well, if we're going to be looked over, we shall wear our prettiest dresses tonight and show London what Yorkshire can provide in the way of beauty!'

Kate squeezed her arm and grinned. 'Margot went on quite a bit about the Mansels, especially Edward . . . I think she likes him.' She flashed Eleanor a quick glance before saying airily: 'I told her you know them well. Very well, in fact.'

'What have you been saying, Kate?' asked Eleanor warily.

'I was jolly annoyed with Margot going on and on about us living in the wilds, making out we were country cousins, you know the sort of thing?'

'Yes, I know. And?'

'There's no need to sound like that, Nell. All I said was that you'd known them for years—and that's partly true, Mother's known Mrs Mansel for donkey's years, and surely you've been with them long enough to be called friends?' Kate demanded crossly.

'I expect I have.'

'I mean, you'd call Edward Mansel a friend, wouldn't you?'

'We aren't enemies,' conceded Eleanor with a short laugh.

'There you are, then!' Kate picked up a ball that had

rolled towards them and threw it back to its owner. 'Tell me about Vanessa and Edward.'

Eleanor, glad to see the colour back in her sister's cheeks, was quite willing to keep her mind off the awful eighty pounds.

'Vanessa's small, pretty and has short curly hair. She's full of life, and can give the impression sometimes of being superficial, but she's not. I like her.'

'Oh, dear,' groaned Kate, 'she scares me already.' She tilted her head. 'And Edward?'

'Rather remote and too sure of himself. I prefer to feel that a man is vulnerable somewhere, purely for fellow feeling.'

'That doesn't sound like the Edward Margot knows,' protested Kate. 'She says he's good-looking, dresses superbly, knows what he wants and is able to get it.'

Eleanor laughed. 'Oh, we know the same Edward, I think.'

Kate wrinkled her brow. 'He's thirty and not married?'

'Marriage doesn't form an important factor in everyone's life, you know, and Edward doesn't have to beg for female company.'

'Yes, that's what Margot said. Quite a cool customer, I gather.'

'Very cool. I wouldn't like to fall into Edward's bad books,' declared Eleanor fervently. 'But he can be amusing and charming, and when he makes the effort, he's good company.'

'Let's hope he makes the effort tonight. Who else will be there?' asked Kate eagerly.

'Hugh Latimer, a friend of Edward's. He's not tall or good-looking, but he's a very nice man, easy to talk to and kind.'

'Aren't the Mansels kind?'

Eleanor hesitated. 'It's not a word that instantly springs to mind in connection with them. They don't suffer fools gladly.'

Kate pulled a face. 'I wish I hadn't asked about them. I feel terrified now!'

Eleanor laughed and gave a shiver. 'I'm feeling cold—come on, let's run!' and catching each other's hands, they reached their point of separation, breathless and laughing.

The Mansel town house was a tall, elegant, three-storied gabled property. The man who opened the door to Eleanor's ring introduced himself as Hickman and said he had been expecting her. Following him up the stairs, Eleanor was told that Vanessa had rung, and he showed her into a pleasant bedroom where her small overnight case stood by the window.

'Mr Edward dropped it in,' explained Hickman, seeing her surprise. 'I understand that Mr Latimer will be calling for you at seven-thirty as Miss Vanessa is going to the theatre from the shop.' He turned at the door, saying deferentially: 'May I suggest, Miss Ferrers, that you have a tea-tray, here in your room, as it will be some time before you eat this evening.'

'Thank you, that sounds a lovely idea,' lied Eleanor, and he left her, promising to return with the tray.

The thought of food appalled her, but when it came, she forced herself to eat something and thankfully drank two cups of scalding hot tea. The problem of where to find eighty pounds had been going round and round in her head since leaving Kate, and as she took a look at herself in the mirror her white face compelled her to shut her mind and try to rest, or else the evening would be in ruins.

But to shut her mind was easier said than done. The more she thought about it, the more convinced she was that Kate should tell Guy, and it worried her that this was evidently beyond her sister's capabilities. If I found myself in trouble, she reflected, would I feel the same way? She sighed. Oh, I don't know, of course, but I hope that I'd be able to open my heart to the man I loved. What was the point of spending the rest of your life with someone from whom you had to hide things? she argued, as she tossed and turned on the bed.

She had still found no solution by the time she was ready to leave. Looking critically in the mirror, Eleanor gave thanks for the discovery of cosmetics. A subtle application of warpaint had disguised her extreme pallor and if she smiled and made an effort, she thought she could pass without comment. Her dress was of fine pleated chiffon, with flattering cape sleeves, in three layers. The colour, a deep bronze, brought out the copper tones in her hair, which she had brushed and now framed a face which could confront the world with reasonable composure.

When Eleanor and Hugh arrived at the theatre, they found they were the last, and the dreaded meeting with Guy was smooth and easy among so many introductions. Margot Slade was attractive, in a hard, glittery way, and Eleanor was glad she could dislike her on sight. Margot's partner was a good deal older and apart from their introduction, Eleanor had no occasion to speak further to him all evening.

Kate, following her sister up the stairs, murmured excitedly:

'Isn't it a marvellous theatre, Nell? I've heard of Drury Lane, of course, but never imagined it to be like this. Guy says he doesn't know how they managed to get tickets because the show is supposed to be a sell-out, but I know how—one look at Edward is sufficient!' She cast a quick look at him walking a few yards ahead of them, and rolled her eyes comically. 'I think you need glasses, sister dear. He's a dish!'

'You haven't told Guy about...?' Eleanor asked hopefully, and Kate shot her an agonised look.

'No! Nell, I told you I can't!'

'Kate, I'm sure it would be better if you did,' began Eleanor, and seeing her sister's distress, added soothingly: 'No, all right. Forget it.'

'Come along, you two, stop whispering,' and Guy came between them, smiling. 'No secrets are allowed.'

'Nonsense!' exclaimed his cousin Margot. 'Wedding plans are full of secrets, Guy darling! We've lots of lovely secrets, haven't we, Kate? Lovely trousseau secrets! What a pretty wife you've chosen, Guy.'

'Yes, I have, haven't I?' answered Guy, with a proud smile, putting his arm round Kate, who smiled radiantly back.

'Your programme, Eleanor.'

She turned and found Edward by her side, face inscrutable as his dark head bent to her, guiding her to their seats.

Eleanor supposed the play to be good. She applauded loudly at the end and said the appropriate words in praise. Two days later it could have been in a foreign language for all she could remember it. That evening she was only completely aware of three people. Edward—polite and watchful, Margot Slade—curious and probing, and Guy—talkative and merry. Guy. Self-revelations take their toll under any circumstances. Eleanor's emotions, already taut and brittle over the thought of meeting him, and further shocked by the knowledge of Kate's dilemma, became even more confused and mixed as the minutes slowly ticked by, leaving her more and more desolate and numb. The meal was a trial of superhuman effort to appear normal . . . delicious food had to be forced down and conversations maintained. The evening was interminable, yet it had to be suffered.

At last, when Eleanor thought she could stand no more, the lateness of the hour was remarked and the party broke up. She found herself, in the bustle of last-minute travelling arrangements, left with Edward as the only passenger in the Jensen, and was jolted out of her apathy to ask tiredly:

'Where's Vanessa?'

Edward stared ahead, concentrating on driving, and after a pause so long that Eleanor thought he hadn't heard, said:

'We're expecting an early delivery tomorrow, so she's sleeping at the flat—I thought she'd told you. You'll not mind staying in the house without her? The Hickmans are downstairs.'

'No, I won't mind,' Eleanor replied. She glanced at him, wondering at his tone. Something had upset him. His voice was clipped and out of keeping with the usual indolence that Edward affected and there was a rigidity of jawline that boded ill for someone, and she was thankful it was not her. She closed her eyes. Edward's silence suited her.

If only her head would stop aching and her thoughts quieten! But she knew they wouldn't. She shrank from self-analysis, but it was inevitable. Seeing Guy and talking to him throughout the evening had rapidly revealed that he was nothing to her other than a prospective brother-in-law. The revelation, instead of lightening her spirits, plunged them to the depths. How, she demanded of herself, how could she fall in and out of love so easily? Was she so shallow? Had she been catapulted into love by his good looks and attractive personality? Flattered because he had noticed her in the first place? Could the grand passion, the heartbreak, be healed by the absence of a few weeks?

The questions hurtled round and round in her head until she could scream, and behind them all lay the enormous burden of eighty pounds.

The house was in darkness as Edward opened the front door. Eleanor followed him slowly into the study, slipping off her coat and stifling a yawn. He switched on a small table lamp, which cast a warm glow round the room. There was something odd about the continuing silence between them, and although she was really too tired to cope, Eleanor felt that she ought to make an effort.

'Thank you for this evening, Edward. It was kind of you to take so much trouble to give Kate a good time. She enjoyed herself thoroughly.' Her voice trailed. 'And ... so did I.' She couldn't think of anything more to say and was slightly unnerved by Edward's stillness. He brooded for a moment longer by the lamp, its light casting a weird shadow on to his face, and then he turned to the highly technical piece of stereo equipment, twiddled a few knobs and after satisfying himself with the soft, dreamy music that came forth, walked towards her.

'You didn't dance with me this evening.'

Eleanor couldn't see his expression, his face was in the shadow and his voice gave nothing away, and yet the feeling persisted that something was wrong. She gave a tentative smile and said awkwardly:

'You didn't ask me.'

'No, I didn't, did I?' he replied quite brusquely, and drew her into his arms and they began to move slowly round the small confines of the room.

The incongruity of the situation, plus its unexpectedness, was enough to make Eleanor stiff and awkward in his arms, and she wasn't surprised when their steps slowed to a standstill, and she broke away with relief.

Edward walked impatiently and switched off the music. 'There's some talking to be done between us, I think.' He crossed and poured a drink. Eleanor stood where he had left her in the middle of the room, blinking uncertainly.

'There is?'

He looked over his shoulder and said caustically: 'I've already had experience of your acting abilities, Eleanor. Please don't over-strain the wide-eyed innocence.'

She was suddenly, acutely aware that he was angry, and that the anger was barely controlled. She rubbed her forehead in confusion as he returned to stand before her, offering her one of the glasses in his hand. She shook her head.

'No, thank you, I...'

'You'll drink it and do as you're told,' he told her crisply. 'It's brandy and will do you good. I don't know what's been the matter with you tonight, but I don't want you fainting at my feet and expecting sympathy.'

Eleanor took a deep breath, drastically wide awake.

'That's the last thing I shall expect from you, Edward,' she was stung to reply, taking the glass roughly, her eyes bright with a rush of stupid unshed tears. 'And nothing's the matter with *me*!'

'Good. I'll put your wan face and lack of appetite down to the excitement of the evening, and leave other possible reasons for the moment. Drink up.'

'I *wish* you'd stop treating me like your little sister!' she retorted crossly, nevertheless taking a sip, and Edward, doing the same, his eyes never leaving her face, said evenly:

'Maybe that's where I've gone wrong.'

Eleanor stood still, a flicker of shock running through her at the look on his face. He was still very angry, and it seemed, amazingly, that the anger was projected against herself.

'W ... what do you mean?'

'I mean, my dear Eleanor, that it has been brought to my notice tonight that you are not in any shape, way or form, my little sister.' There was a pause and then he took her glass and placed it with deliberation on the mantel with his own.

'I can see you're angry . . .' she began, her voice trembling despite the effort to keep it steady.

'I was, but I've now realised that there are compensations.' Edward reached out and gently caressed her cheek, travelling lightly, persuasively down her pale, slender neck, along the line of her shoulder and down her arm to take her inert hand in his. He lifted it to his lips, kissing the throbbing vein at her wrist, and all the time his blue eyes were holding her own.

Her hand felt on fire.

'Why are you doing this, Edward?' she asked in a low voice.

A dark brow lifted quizzically. 'Why? Come, you do yourself an injustice, my dear. You shouldn't compare yourself to the chocolate-box prettiness of your sister. Good bones, a melodious voice, and expressive eyes appeal to me much more.'

Eleanor shook her head in silent protest as Edward drew her slowly and effortlessly into his arms, holding her against the long length of his body. A few moments ago, when they were dancing, she had been rigid in his clasp, now the strength had left her, drained mysteriously away, and she would have fallen had she not been given his support. She went to speak again, the words dying as his mouth came down on hers.

After a long moment she breathed: 'Let me go, Edward . . . please.'

His drawling voice came to her from a distance.

'I'm sorry, isn't that what you wanted? Have you suddenly changed your mind? The idea was a good one, but perhaps now that it's beginning to bear fruit you're getting cold feet.' The questions were thrust at her with intense ridicule. 'Too used to milksop boys, maybe I've frightened you? Yes, that's it . . . I should have asked Margot how far our relationship had gone.' He laughed derisively. 'If you believe that we're still at the holding hands stage, I shall have to disappoint you. Not with a man of my reputation, dear girl.' He pulled her roughly to him. 'No, definitely not,' he said harshly, lips touching eyes, cheek, hollow of neck and finally, with bruising intensity, her mouth.

When she could speak, Eleanor said painfully:

'Edward, I know you're angry . . .'

'My God, I am angry! My only satisfaction is that you didn't realise who you were taking on! If we're lovers, my sweet little innocent, then I shall demand my dues!' He studied her bright red cheeks with grim pleasure. 'Margot Slade is the biggest gossip in town and no doubt couldn't contain herself once the opportunity was so readily available. She was dying to congratulate me, but even Margot daren't go that far without a formal announcement!' This was said with such a knife edge that Eleanor flinched, and he abruptly let her go.

It was all becoming too clear. Kate . . . silly, romantic Kate! She was having total recall of Kate saying to her that afternoon—I've said you know the Mansels very well. What else she had said was only too apparent.

For a split second she was consumed by a blinding anger equal to Edward's. How dared he think that she was capable of such intrigue! Well, it didn't matter what he thought, she told herself bitterly, and giving a brittle laugh, said lightly:

'My goodness, I can't see why you're so angry, Edward, it was only done for a bit of fun! Surely you're used to this sort of thing?' She turned away from the light with a shrug.

'I am, but somehow I didn't expect it from you . . .' His eyes narrowed. 'So you admit it?'

'It would be silly not to, wouldn't it? You can't blame me for trying with such an eligible bachelor on the premises. And I only dropped the teeniest of hints to Margot . . . she must have exaggerated dreadfully.'

Disturbingly, he was right there, behind her. 'No, I can't blame you,' came the soft drawl. 'And don't be disappointed. I don't like disappointing a lady. I can't promise marriage . . . but perhaps you can help me change my mind,' and he began to expertly unzip her dress.

Eleanor froze, his fingertips scorching her bare back, and she flew round, eyes wide, a protest on her lips—silenced by the watchful, intense look on his face. A slow, painful flush crept over her face.

'You're hateful!' she whispered vehemently, voice trembling.

'And you're a foolish, silly girl!' Edward let out an explosive breath. 'It's not games we're playing now!' he lashed out. 'My God! If I wasn't so furious with you, I'd laugh!'

'*You're* furious? Well, let me tell you, Edward Mansel, you're not the only one!' and Eleanor began frantically to wrench up the zip.

'Here, let me.'

'Don't you dare touch me!'

'Don't be ridiculous!' Edward's voice was curt and he thrust her hands away, zipping her up coolly and efficiently. 'You do ask for trouble, don't you? Do you realise what you were letting yourself in for?'

'Obviously not!' she flashed round on him, 'and I don't think I was the only one playing games!'

'It seemed the easiest way of getting at the truth.' He lifted a brow. 'If you had meant what you said then you would have allowed me to continue.'

'I see,' said Eleanor icily, shaken to the core by the conflicting emotions whirling inside her, and finding refuge in outraged anger. 'Perhaps you would be good enough to tell me what Margot Slade said to you tonight?'

Edward broke away and went to the mantel, leaning an elbow and looking back at her thoughtfully.

'No, I don't think I shall.' He saw her look of surprise and added evenly: 'Margot isn't particularly a nice character, you know. She's the ultimate in predatory females and has never forgiven me for not falling for her fatal charms. This, I'm afraid, coloured our conversation slightly, and I won't bore you with details. Suffice it to say that she made enough insinuations to leave me in no doubt as to what she meant.'

'I see,' said Eleanor doubtfully.

'You don't see at all,' Edward replied roughly. 'By getting at you she thought she was getting at me, you little innocent. And my hands were tied until I could speak to you.'

'What a high opinion you do have of yourself, Edward,' Eleanor choked out furiously. She lifted her chin and continued cuttingly: 'Inconceivable though it may be, I have no wish to be coupled with your name.' There was silence and Edward, eyes hooded, face enigmatic, looked at her consideringly, and she added in no uncertain tone: 'Unlike the majority of females that come into contact with you, I do not care for arrogant, conceited egotists!'

'So I see.'

'I'm very glad that you do. How could you think that I...?' and she pressed her lips together, remembering all that he had said.

'I apologise for being so obtuse.'

'I should think so!' Again she waited, and then demanded: 'Is that all you're going to say?'

He raised his brows and shrugged slightly. 'What would you like?'

She gazed back, nonplussed. 'How can you be so *blisteringly* angry one minute, making horrible, sarcastic remarks and taking advantage of the situation by...' Here she stopped short, realising just where this was leading her, and amended it hurriedly to: 'How you can change and be so casual and calm about it, I just don't know!'

'My advanced years are an asset, no doubt. Your anger will pass when you consider that I had good reason.'

'And I suppose I hadn't? You thought I could trick you ... set up a situation so that you'd have to act the gentleman ...' Words failed her and after an exasperated breath she tried again. '*You* be blackmailed by good manners?' she asked incredulously.

'I can see how wrong I was,' offered Edward, outrageously shamefaced. 'You obviously know me far better than I'd at first realised.'

'As if you would...' She stopped suddenly, unsure, and looked at him suspiciously, his words sinking in. She bit her lip. 'And now you're making fun of me. You have a perverse sense of humour, Edward Mansel, and are completely without scruples . . . and I'm still—very—angry!'

He said soothingly: 'Come, Eleanor, sit down and stop pacing like a caged animal.' He touched her arm gently and she shot away from his contact, regretting the involuntary reaction the minute it was made. She retreated to the settee and Edward sat in the armchair opposite, remarking casually:

'So it was all little sister's doing?'

Eleanor looked at him, indecision all over her face. There was no way out. What a mess it all was! If only she could tell Edward everything . . . and with a blinding flash she knew that if she was in Kate's shoes now, she would be able to tell Edward, knew it with a clarity that astounded her. But she couldn't tell him. He was nothing to her, merely a stand-in host. Someone who had thought her capable of trying to ensnare him into marriage. She nodded reluctantly.

'I'm afraid so,' she said in a constricted voice. 'She wouldn't realise how it could escalate. I think Margot rubbed her up the wrong way by being condescending about our background and Katie began to boast that . . . She probably sensed that Margot was interested in you.' She lifted a hand helplessly. 'I have no idea what she said.'

'It need not have been much. Margot would have done the rest,' Edward said dryly, 'and lost no time in going into action.'

'What did you say to her?'

'Mmm . . .? Oh, I parried her inquisitive jabs with the usual enigmatic replies I save for these occasions!'

'It's happened to you before?'

He smiled thinly. 'Don't accuse me of boasting, Eleanor.'

'So you didn't confirm or deny anything?' she persisted.

'No.'

They sat quietly for a while and then Eleanor asked hesitantly: 'What shall we do, Edward?'

Receiving no reply, she looked at him fully. He was sitting in the shadows, the flickering light from the fire playing on his face which was in deep repose.

Those eyebrows are unbelievable, she thought idly, and had a strong impulse, which she resisted, to smooth the fall of hair from his forehead. It didn't seem right, somehow, for the immaculate and sartorial Edward Mansel to be untidy ... didn't seem fair, for it made him more human. Over his collar lay a fringe of tiny, dark tendrils and the hand resting on the arm of the chair had fine, dark hairs smoothing back to a deceptively slender wrist. His legs were outstretched, his coat thrown open, the white ruffled shirt was a startling contrast to the black cloth of the evening suit. Eleanor wondered for a wild moment if he had fallen asleep, so relaxed was his attitude, and then as her gaze wandered back to his face, she was aware that the thick, black lashes were no longer fanned across the high cheekbones, but were raised. Speculative blue eyes were watching her. She repeated her question hurriedly and Edward lazily sat up and ran a hand through his hair, rubbing the back of his head thoughtfully. He stretched his arms wide and rising indolently, stood broodingly over her, lips pursed.

'What shall we do? Why, nothing. It will all die a death.' He shrugged. 'Your sister leaves for home tomorrow and we'll give Margot a wide berth from now on. Forget it.' He held out a hand. 'It's late ... you'd better go to bed.'

Eleanor hesitated and then gave him her hand, allowing him to draw her to her feet, removing it from his grasp as quickly as decently possible. She moved directly away, making for the door. Edward switched off the lamp and followed her into the hall.

'Goodnight, Edward,' she began awkwardly. 'I'm sorry the evening was spoilt.'

'Oh, it wasn't all disastrous.' An odd tone in his voice made her look at him sharply, but his face was bland as he felt in the pockets of his jacket for the Jensen keys. Finding them, he said abruptly: 'You were looking like death when you arrived at the theatre tonight. Was meeting Slade so traumatic that it made you physically ill?'

He had caught her unprepared, a wave of colour suffused her face.

'I wouldn't have thought him your type,' he went on. 'Do for your empty-headed sister, but not for you.'

'You really are the most objectionable . . .'

'Do you still love him?'

She held his look, grinding her teeth, and then said furiously: 'I'm flattered you take such an interest. No, I'm not . . . in love with him.'

'Keep telling yourself often enough and you might even come to believe it.' His voice was cynical. 'The longer I live, the more wary I become of this thing called love. It's not to be trusted, I fear.' He made to go, hesitated and walked back to her. Eleanor stood on the first step of the stair, almost on a level with him, holding her breath as his eyes flickered over her face.

'I was angry with you tonight, Eleanor. I'm not always so brutal,' and he leaned forward and gently kissed her lips. 'I was angry with myself, which didn't help. Goodnight,' and turning, he walked briskly along the hallway, opened the front door and disappeared into the night.

Eleanor remained staring blankly at the closed door, finger tips raised to her lips. It was all too much, she thought helplessly. How could she start out the evening believing herself in love with one man, and end up completely the opposite—and bedevilled with some very disturbing thoughts of another? She shook her head wearily. No, it was too much to comprehend at this moment. About to turn and make her way to bed, she froze as she heard the key in the lock.

'Forgot something,' Edward announced calmly, showing no surprise that she was as he had left her. He walked to the study, returning some seconds later with papers in his hand. He paused and looked over his shoulder. 'By the way, Eleanor, I meant to ask you before. Whatever happened to Edward?'

'Edward?'

'Mmm . . . you know, your pet toad.'

Eleanor stared at him, hardly able to believe her ears. When she found her voice, she said with relish: 'He came to a bad end. He was squashed to a pulp by the school bus.'

His lips gave a sudden quirk. 'Ah! I thought he was heading that way. Poor old Edward. Goodnight,' and he closed the door quietly behind him. A few seconds later she heard the Jensen start up and move away.

How could anyone begin to describe a man like that? Eleanor asked herself despairingly, as she made for her bed. Impossible, utterly infuriating, unpredictable man! She was too tired to think of a wider vocabulary. That would do very well for a start.

CHAPTER FOUR

'Be good, sweet maid, and let who will be clever'
Charles Kingsley

'Two egg and chips, one spaghetti bolognese, one beef curry, Ken, please.'

Eleanor received confirmation of her order and looked at her watch. It was nearly two o'clock. Within half an hour they would be able to take a breather before getting ready for the afternoon tea brigade. Maisie, the other waitress on this shift, passed her, carrying a tray of steaming hot lunches.

'Whew! We're busy today, Nell, aren't we? I say, look out for number seven. He's the bloke I was telling you about—the fault-finder. It's a wonder he's bothered to come back ... perhaps he fancies one of us!' and raising her eyes to the ceiling expressively, Maisie grinned and wound her way expertly between the tables to the one occupied by a group of smiling Italians, lured in by the name over the door, and with whom she had already progressed to a teasing backchat.

Eleanor smiled her thanks for the useful information. She

had learnt a great deal from Maisie, who had taken it upon herself to mother the newcomer to Luigi's.

Eleanor's job had come about within three days of talking to Kate, an accumulation of events making this possible. The first, and probably the most important, was a nine-year-old boy's passion for roller skates. The boy was the grandson of Edward's part-time assistant. The widow, visiting her daughter, stepped on a skate left in a dark passageway, took a short ride and broke her leg. Someone once said that calamities are of two kinds: misfortune to ourselves and good fortune to others. Eleanor was sorry for the widow, but it meant that Vanessa was now needed to take her place for much longer hours at the shop, and thus suitably out of the way, Eleanor's time was her own.

The next step, following on naturally, was Vanessa's move from the country to the town house, and Eleanor jumped at the chance to accompany her, thinking that a London base would make it easier to find a job, and sightseeing a good reason for her absence from the house when she found one.

Before looking for a job, however, she decided to have her grandmother's ring valued and consequently set off to find a suitable place to have this done. She found a small, respectable-looking jewellers off Shaftesbury Avenue. To her disappointment she found it was not their custom to give an assessment instantly, and before she could think whether to go elsewhere, her name and particulars had been duly taken.

She left the shop feeling slightly frustrated. It began to rain, a fine drizzle, and finding herself lost in a labyrinth of small, narrow streets, she spied a café. Deciding that a morning coffee would be a good idea, for she could study her street map in comfort, Eleanor opened the door and went in.

That was how she found Luigi's. Afterwards, she learnt that the proprietor hailed from no further than the Midlands, and far from having a romantic Italian name and birthplace, he was Ken Wilson from Birmingham and his accent proclaimed the fact.

While partaking of the excellent coffee, Eleanor found that they needed a waitress. She applied there and then, the hours being from ten until three with two evenings, and she began the next day.

It was hard work, but she was doing something constructive towards Kate's problem, and as she had no specific training, this job was as good as anything she could hope for with the limited hours at her disposal.

Maisie, her co-partner, was a cheerful girl and very popular with customers. She had a boy of four and was bringing him up on her own, her husband having walked out on them both when the baby was a few weeks old. Her opinion of men in general was low and graphic.

'Two egg and chips, one spaghetti bolognese, one beef curry—coming up!'

Eleanor was jolted out of her reverie by Ken shouting her order. She flexed her back gingerly and wriggled her toes. In the future, she would view waitresses in a completely different light! At this moment all she wanted to do was sit down and take off her shoes, but looking at the clock, that was just wishful thinking.

'You on again tonight, Nell?' Maisie asked, as they met at the kitchen doors, and Eleanor nodded. 'I'm supposed to be,' carried on Maisie worriedly, 'but I've got baby-sitting problems.' She pulled a face. 'I don't want to lose this job if I can help it, the hours suit me, but young Joe's a problem.'

Eleanor could understand her new friend's difficulties and admired her for adapting to being a one-parent family.

'Try and change with one of the other girls and I'll sit another night for you,' she offered, and Maisie's face brightened.

'Will you? Oh, Nell, thanks. I'll see if I can manage to.'

As the days passed and her luck held, Eleanor began to relax. Her life continued in some semblance of routine and if she felt physically weary most evenings, she collapsed into bed and consoled herself that each day knocked some more off the eighty pounds.

She went out with Vanessa odd evenings and pretended

she was having interesting and educational sorties during the day. She was, but not in the way Vanessa thought. It was not history she was seeing but life, and it was all very illuminating.

Edward could have been a problem, but he made things easy by going to Ireland on business. Mr Mansel frequented the town house on occasions and she received a smile and a courteous question as to her health when he did. Eve Mansel divided her time between town and country, leaving a heady trail of perfume, asking questions but not really listening to the answers.

Two weeks after first walking into Luigi's, Eleanor felt as though she had been doing the job all her life. As she travelled home one Wednesday afternoon she gave a grin of amusement as she negotiated the journey. It hardly seemed possible that a short time ago she had never been on her own in London before. The day had been a particularly busy one and she was due in again that evening. She staggered into the house and flopped on one of the armchairs, accepting a cup of tea from Hickman with a grateful smile.

The next thing she knew was that she had a crick in her neck and the stabbing pain brought her reluctantly out of an exhausted sleep. Sitting up with a groan, she rubbed her neck, stretching cramped legs, and a few seconds later became aware of a still form in the chair opposite, watching her thoughtfully. She sat equally still, all movement suspended.

She had not seen Edward since that traumatic night of Kate's visit.

'Oh! Hullo, Edward . . . so you're back. I didn't hear you come in,' she said brightly, settling herself upright. 'Have you been here long?'

'About ten minutes. You were so far gone that you didn't even wake when Hickman brought in the trolley. You'd better have another cup of tea . . . this seems to be cold,' and he indicated the cup by her side. 'You must have been tired. Having some late nights?' He raised a brow as he passed another cup.

'One or two,' agreed Eleanor, smoothing her skirt. 'I

hope I didn't disgrace myself? You know—snore or anything?'

'No, you didn't disgrace yourself.' Edward lighted a cigarette and leaned back comfortably in the armchair, eyes flicking over her lazily.

Eleanor, to her annoyance, felt the colour rise in her cheeks as the blue eyes surveyed her, remembering vividly their last meeting. She made a great business of stirring her tea. So, she thought, Edward is back ... to complicate things, and in more ways than one. She could still feel his kisses and the hardness of his body against hers. He had made her aware of herself as no other man had before, and that was difficult to come to terms with—she didn't even like him. Raising her eyes above the rim of her cup, she caught a fleeting expression on his face that surprised her—an almost brooding resentment, as if his thoughts reiterated her own, a fancy which she discredited as quickly as it came as being ridiculous.

'You look very fit and well, Edward,' she said lightly. Tanned and brimming over with good health and vitality, he was dressed with misleading casualness in a cool blue cashmere sweater and navy cords.

'I wish I could return the compliment,' Edward replied evenly. 'Admittedly you were not on top form when I left for Ireland, but I hoped you'd recover the roses in your cheeks when your sister and Slade went back.'

'Perhaps black doesn't suit me?' began Eleanor lamely, beginning to feel uncomfortable beneath his scrutiny, knowing that the black jumper and skirt, dark stockings and comfortable flat shoes which constituted her uniform were not flattering.

'It matches the smudges under your eyes—and you've lost weight.'

'It must be all the walking round London that I'm doing,' she joked quickly. 'How was Ireland?'

'Green and beautiful.' Edward reached for an ashtray. 'You must have been neglected shamefully these past two weeks, Eleanor. Where are you off to tomorrow?' He crossed an elegant trousered leg and eyed the polished tan calf of his shoe as though he suspected a speck of mud had had the temerity to land there.

Luigi's with any luck, thought Eleanor grimly. 'The Tate and National, throwing in the Royal Academy, if there's time,' she said aloud, congratulating herself on her improvisation. Satisfaction was shortlived.

'Would you like me to come with you?'

'Oh! Er ... how nice of you, Edward, but you must be terribly busy, just getting back. There's no need for you to worry about me, I'm quite used to going around on my own. Perhaps another day, when it may be easier for you?' She waited anxiously for his reply, hoping her smile was not as uncertain as it felt.

'Very well.' If he was relieved, he didn't show it, merely opened up his briefcase and began to study some papers, and Eleanor breathed easily again.

'May I pour you out another cup of tea, Edward?' she asked. He looked up and nodded absently, returning to his papers.

Eleanor collected his cup and took it to the trolley. She glanced down at her watch—she would have to be on her way in half an hour. On her return, Edward murmured:

'Will you come out with me this evening?'

So much for relaxing and dropping her guard.

'Oh, lord!' she exclaimed in dismay as her hand jumped with the shock and the tea slopped, the spoon dropping to the carpet.

'Was that maidenly delight, or horror, at my suggestion?' came the dry response.

'Neither,' said Eleanor, going to her knees and mopping up a spot of moisture from the carpet. 'The cup wasn't on straight.'

'Well ... do I get an answer?'

'Er ... tonight? Sorry, Edward, but I'm already going out.'

His hand grasped her by the wrist gently, staying the rather fevered mopping up process. 'Not scared of me, Eleanor, are you?'

'No . . . of course not,' she said breathlessly. 'I . . . I have a date, truly.'

'I see. Who's the lucky fellow? One of Van's friends?'

'No. His name's Joe,' replied Eleanor, collecting her scattered wits, her tone conveying an end to the catechism. Removing herself from his grasp, she rose to her feet. 'Let me wipe the saucer for you, Edward, or else you'll drip tea over yourself.' She returned to the trolley, purposefully keeping her back to him. The silence behind her seemed to be shrieking.

'Some other evening, perhaps? If . . . Joe doesn't mind?' said Edward equably.

'Mmm . . . that would be lovely. Here you are, I've managed better this time,' and smiling, but not meeting his eyes, Eleanor said briskly: 'Goodbye, Edward, thanks for the tea,' and walking as casually as she could to the door, she made her escape.

Edward and the traffic delayed her and she was a few minutes late. Eleanor rushed into the staff cloakroom and threw off her coat, quickly donning cap and apron. Behind her the door opened and Maisie's head popped round.

'Oh, you've arrived,' she exclaimed thankfully. 'Thought you weren't coming,' and Maisie came in, shutting the door behind her.

'I got held up,' explained Eleanor, fixing her hair with another grip to make it more secure.

'You all right?' Maisie asked anxiously, and receiving a nod shot her new friend a sharp glance. 'You don't say much about yourself and I don't want to pry, but you're not in any trouble, are you? Man-trouble, I mean,' she added darkly.

Eleanor smiled, touched by her concern. 'No, Maisie.'

'That's all right, then,' carried on Maisie. 'I mean, it's obvious you're only filling in with this job, but if you're in a mess, and I can help, then I'd like to. Most messes we women get into are man-made.'

Eleanor said thoughtfully: 'One of these days I might come to you for advice on somewhere to stay. I'm with friends of my family at the moment and they haven't said anything regarding the length of my visit, but I can't impose on them for very much longer—although I think it's going to be difficult to make them see that. So I might need digs later on.' She dived into her basket and brought out a paper bag. 'Here ... I saw these and couldn't resist them. They're for Joe ... oranges.'

'Nell, you shouldn't! You're always buying him something.'

'He's my favourite boy-friend.'

'Go on! I can't believe that!' responded Maisie with a grin, and following Eleanor out, reflected sagely that whatever her friend said, there was a man lurking somewhere about!

The next day Hugh's Porsche was parked outside the house on Eleanor's return and she found him in the study, writing a letter. He looked up on her entrance and smiled a greeting. Eleanor, glad to see him, said cheerfully:

'Hullo, Hugh, can you stay to tea? I've put in the order.' She threw herself into a chair and kicked off her shoes. 'You don't mind, do you?' she appealed, indicating her stockinged feet. 'They're killing me!'

'Sightseeing is hard on the feet, but worth the agony,' Hugh observed. 'I'm writing a note for Edward, will you see he gets it? Van can deliver it to the shop when she goes in tomorrow if he doesn't drop in here tonight. I tried to reach him by phone this afternoon, but had no success.'

Eleanor wriggled her toes in ecstasy and murmured: 'He's in Holland, I think, chasing some missing freight. Anyway, leave it with me, Hugh, I'll make sure he gets it, one way or another. And talking of letters, this was waiting for me, do you mind if I read it?' and she pulled an envelope from her pocket. Hugh shook his head, continuing his writing, and Eleanor opened up her letter from home.

'Still homesick for Yorkshire?' he asked after a moment.

Eleanor gave the question due consideration. 'Now and again. It's done me good to get away—I know that now.' She leaned forward, warming to her theme. 'I've done things I wouldn't have dreamed I'd be doing a few months ago, and I'm meeting people and seeing different ways of life—and how can you choose your own unless you do that?'

'How indeed?' agreed Hugh, folding his letter and placing it in an envelope. 'It seems that you transplant easier than you at first thought. I'm glad, for your sake. The hot-house plant leads a rather narrow life.'

Hickman entered with the tea trolley and Eleanor sprang to her feet and took over, saying fervently:

'Thank you, Hickman, this looks lovely.' When he left the room Eleanor began to pour out, saying with amusement: 'Just look at all this food—sandwiches, scones and cakes!'

Hugh crossed to the mantel and placed the letter in a prominent position.

'My dear Eleanor, why do you think I planned my arrival so opportunely?'

Half an hour later, Vanessa burst into the room to find them sitting chatting companionably—Hugh in the armchair, Eleanor on the rug by the fire.

'Well! What a cosy scene! I hope there's some left for the workers of the world?' She ran a hand through her curls and threw herself into the other armchair. 'What a menace the traffic is. How are you, Hugh? We haven't seen you lately.' She picked up a sandwich and began to nibble it. 'Awfully busy, are you?'

'Fairly.' Hugh smiled and added mildly: 'The way you burst into a room, Vanessa, makes me shudder for the safety of Edward's precious treasures.'

Vanessa swung a slender leg. 'Oh, I can be ladylike when required. Thanks, Eleanor,' she said, as a cup of tea came her way. 'Have you had a good day?'

'Mmm . . . rather. Do have the left-over eats,' offered Eleanor, before she was made to provide some necessary lies.

'I haven't been too busy to remember my promise to take you to the Festival Hall, Vanessa,' broke in Hugh, answering Vanessa's earlier question more thoroughly. 'There's an interesting programme offered next week. Can you make the Friday?'

'Friday?' Vanessa stirred her tea, frowning thoughtfully. 'Yes, I'm free.'

'Eleanor?' Hugh turned to her.

'Sorry—I'm already booked for that night.' To her relief, neither questioned her further.

'I'll ring you later to make arrangements, Vanessa.' Hugh took off his glasses and began to polish them, adding casually: 'Don't you want to know what they're playing?'

For once Vanessa appeared disconcerted. 'Oh . . . well, you know I leave my musical education to you.'

'Dvorak's *New World* is being offered, plus some Prokofiev and Berlioz.' Hugh replaced his glasses and flicked the handkerchief into his top pocket. Vanessa watched him and grinned at Eleanor.

'Have you noticed,' she said, 'how defenceless Hugh looks without those specs of his? I don't think he really needs them, you know, Eleanor. He uses them as a camouflage. He hides behind them and considers they give him dignity and authority as he deals with the country's weighty problems!'

He walked slowly to the door, tweaking a curl as he passed behind her chair. 'There are those who never show due respect to their elders,' he said, voice full of resignation.

Vanessa said darkly: 'I shall be twenty-one next month, and come into my independence—then I'll show you how respectful I can be, I'll astound you! By the way, what did you think of Archie Lord's exhibition the other day? I caught a glimpse of you there. You didn't stay long.'

'No, I didn't, did I?' Hugh replied dryly. 'I saw one or two worthwhile things, but for the most part it was way above my head.'

Vanessa grinned. 'Yes, it was weird, wasn't it? How come you were there?'

'I know his elder brother and felt obliged to give my support.'

'Poor old Hugh,' teased Vanessa, taking another sandwich.

'And you?'

'Oh, I went with Phil Nolan. He knows the family quite well.'

'I see.' Hugh regarded her thoughtfully for a moment, and she met his gaze wide-eyed.

While their conversation had been going on, Eleanor had been re-reading her letter, but now she glanced up at them both, having caught the tail end. For a few seconds it seemed as though Hugh was going to answer the unspoken challenge but he merely made his goodbyes and left. They heard the front door bang. Vanessa stared into the fire, leg still swinging, humming a fragment of a tune.

'Do you like Hugh, Nell?' she asked suddenly, and Eleanor looked up.

'Why, yes, of course,' she replied, somewhat surprised.

'You might not have done,' argued Vanessa indifferently, 'although thinking about it, you're the sort I could imagine him marrying, if ever he gets around to it.'

Eleanor found herself colouring, but ignored the remark and asked a question of her own. 'What exactly does Hugh do?'

'Mmm ...? Oh, sits behind some dreary desk, in a dreary Ministry somewhere.'

'You're quite awful to him, you know,' commented Eleanor, returning to her letter.

'Yes,' agreed Vanessa, unrepentant. 'He thrives on it, actually. We're the nearest to family he has and it gives him a sense of security to come and be teased. Of course, both he and Edward still see me as a grubby schoolgirl with a pony-tail.' She grinned. 'I was awful to Hugh then, too, I used to plague the life out of him, he was a safer bet than Edward.' She rose restlessly to her feet and walked to the window. 'It's my lifelong ambition to make Hugh lose his temper, but I'm beginning to think it's not possible.' She turned and added carelessly: 'I say, Eleanor, are you really not available on that Friday?'

'Why?'

'Well, I could easily get a foursome together.'

'Thank you, but I won't be free—and if one of the foursome is to be Philip Nolan, then I don't think Hugh would be very pleased, do you? I don't believe Hugh cares for your Mr Nolan.'

'Do you know, I get that impression too.'

'Why is that, do you think?'

Vanessa strolled leisurely to the door. 'Oh, Phil's been a bit wild in his youth, but he's steady enough now. I suspect Hugh considers him rather old for me . . . I know Edward thinks so.' She paused, head on one side. 'Phil's thirty—and he's not too old. What do you think, Nell?'

Eleanor said reflectively: 'I don't think it matters—if the man is right.'

'Exactly,' said Vanessa coolly. 'It's the man that counts, not the years.'

November was trying to become the wettest on record, and succeeding. On the Friday that Hugh was taking Vanessa to the Festival Hall, Eleanor was working her evening shift. It was a particularly blustery and wet evening and customers were coming in with raincoats glistening with water, shaking themselves like wet dogs and steaming gently in the warm atmosphere.

Maisie was also on duty and as there were only half a dozen people in, the two girls had the chance to chat in the occasional lull.

'I don't think you ought to be in tonight, Nell. You haven't really recovered from the 'flu,' said Maisie, looking at her friend critically.

Eleanor grimaced. 'I'm all right. I shall have the weekend to rest up and . . .' Her voice trailed as she gazed blankly at some new arrivals.

'You'd think folk would eat at home on a night like this,' Maisie grumbled goodnaturedly as they watched the customers settling themselves at the tables. 'You take number four, Nell, and I'll do number ten,' she added, as she moved away.

Eleanor didn't argue. As she gave a glance in the mirror her heart sank at the wan face that looked back at her. She pulled half-heartedly at her cap, picked up her pencil and pad, and looked across at number four, who was waiting with studied patience. Stiffening her back, she made her way over, standing quietly at his side as he studied the menu.

Maisie swept past, giving her a wink and raising her eyebrows appreciatively at number four. Eleanor eased her weight fractionally from one foot to the other, and then back again.

'What do you recommend?' he asked at last.

'I'd try the Spanish omelette, sir. It's very good,' suggested Eleanor, noticing that the dark grey suit and crisp blue shirt were spotted with rain, and a small puddle was forming on the floor from the large black umbrella which was hooked on to the back of the chair.

'Very well, the omelette,' agreed Edward, lifting his eyes from the menu for the first time, his gaze steady.

Eleanor pressed her lips together to stop them trembling and escaped to the kitchen where Maisie, eyes sparkling, was eyeing him from the door.

'Hey, Nell, he's a smasher, isn't he? Just take a look at the cut of that suit! What's he doing here—slumming?'

Eleanor managed a smile. 'Maisie, we get all sorts in here, you know that. The food is good, quick and reasonable...'

'The waitresses kind and beautiful!'

'And word spreads around.'

'Dearie, if word spread around to good-lookers like that more often—my faith in manhood would be drastically restored!' Maisie said dramatically. 'Imagine sitting opposite that every morning at the breakfast table! What a pity I didn't take a better look when he came in, I'd have grabbed him like a shot and left you with the five Geordies.'

They both knew that she had chosen the five Geordies to help Eleanor.

'I say, Nell, are you sure you're okay? You look dreadful. Don't you think you ought to go home? I'll ask Ken, he'll let you go, we're not busy.'

Eleanor shook her head. 'No, Maisie, there's not much longer to do, and I'm all right, honestly.'

The omelette was ready far too soon, and taking a deep breath she made her way back to table four—and Edward. He was reading the evening paper, folded into an oblong, which he put down on her arrival. She wiped the table before placing the dish before him.

'Will you require a sweet, sir?' she murmured politely.

'If you sir me once more, Eleanor, I'll give you something else to think about,' Edward said softly. 'No, I'll have just coffee. I don't suppose you can join me?' He lifted a brow. 'No . . . very well.'

Colour high, Eleanor returned to the kitchens and Maisie gave her an odd look.

'You look as though he's made you an improper suggestion!' she joked.

Eleanor hesitated and then said awkwardly: 'Actually, Maisie, I know him.'

'You do, do you? You're a sly one.' She looked thoughtfully at her and nodded. 'I suppose I ought to have guessed. He's your type.' She peered round the door again. 'He doesn't look too hungry to me.'

'I think he has other things on his mind at the moment,' offered Eleanor rather bleakly.

'Meaning you?' and when Eleanor nodded, Maisie added casually: 'Is he sweet on you?'

Eleanor gave a short laugh. 'Quite the reverse,' she answered dryly. 'I'm a complete nuisance to him. He didn't know I'd got this job and he's rather angry.'

'I see. Has he walked in here, on the off-chance, and it's come as a shock to him?'

'It's come as a shock to him, but he knew I was here—I could tell the minute he walked in. How he knew, I don't know, but he'll tell me, later.'

'So that's why you went as white as a sheet when he came in.' Maisie frowned. 'Let me take his coffee,' she offered, and Eleanor nodded her agreement, and watched her go over to the table.

'He has a lovely smile,' said Maisie, on her return.

'I don't think I'll see much of it tonight.' Eleanor pushed a stray wisp of hair behind an ear.

'What I can't understand,' said Maisie softly, 'is why, if he's not sweet on you, he's bothered about what you do? It doesn't make sense to me.'

Eleanor shrugged, and tried to explain.

'He feels responsible for me. I've told you, I'm a nuisance he can do without, but family ties make it impossible for him to ignore me.'

She looked up at the clock. 'Nearly closing time.'

He walked by her side in silence. It had stopped raining and the roads and pavements were bright with the distorted reflections of light. Passing traffic hissed as their tyres hit the wetness. Holding her arm easily, but with an underlying forcefulness, Edward led Eleanor to a side street, where she saw the sleek, silver-grey Jensen parked in waiting. A flicker of wry amusement came to her as she thought how impressed Maisie would be with the car, and with the way she was now being handed into it. It didn't mean a thing. Edward Mansel's urbanity was as natural as breathing, but would good manners be enough to shield her from his so obvious anger? Once before she had felt the whiplash of his tongue when his emotions were barely controlled. The quick look she had given him as they left Luigi's had not been reassuring.

Edward drove quickly with his usual efficiency through the streets, finally pulling up on a quiet section of the embankment. He wound down his window and they could hear the muted sounds of the city, and nearer, a street cleaning lorry moved along on the opposite side, brushes whirling in the gutter, lights flashing. When it had passed, Edward said in a level voice:

'Are you ready to tell me what this latest escapade is about?' The question was not addressed directly to her. He lighted a cigarette, the flame illuminating his dark, lean face. Eleanor bit her lip. She had learned not to trust the outward langour of this man. Stalling for time, she leaned foward, concentrating on a rivulet of rainwater making its way down the windscreen, and asked hesitantly:

'How did you find out?'

'I had you followed.'

She made an instinctive recoil from him, a shiver running down her back.

'You ... had me ... followed?' she stammered, shooting him a horrified look. Edward drew deeply on his cigarette and shrugged.

'It's quite simple if you know the right people.'

She stared at him incredulously. In her mind's eye she saw herself walking blithely to work, and looming in the background, a faceless person. How offensive the thought was! But not so amazing, for hadn't she always been aware that coupled with his astuteness was a ruthlessness alien to her? It had been extremely silly of her to underestimate Edward Mansel.

'The knowledge is distasteful to you?' Edward's voice cut through her thoughts. 'It seemed the easiest way of gaining information. Would you have told me?'

Eleanor flushed at his tone. 'What made you ... have me followed?' she asked, her voice low, fixing her eyes on the lights on the far side of the Thames.

'A call came through from Hanley's, the jewellers. I took it. They stated how sorry they were to have been so long in valuing your ring, but your address had been mislaid.' He turned and looked at her for the first time since stopping the car.

'I see.'

'I'm glad one of us does,' he answered sarcastically. 'Perhaps you will tell me why you find it necessary to sell your jewellery, Eleanor, and work in a café as a waitress?'

'You needn't use that tone of voice, Edward! Luigi's may not be up to your high and mighty standards, but to ordinary, decent people it's perfectly acceptable,' flashed Eleanor angrily.

'I quite realise that I do not constitute being ordinary or decent, I'm well aware of your opinion of me, Eleanor, but do not try and evade the issue. You haven't answered my question.' His voice was hard.

'Because I need the money! That's why people work, isn't it? Even you, Edward! And now, will you please take me home, I'm rather tired.'

'No, I will not take you home. We're getting to the bottom of this, here and now. Why do you need the money?'

'I don't think it's any of your business.'

He smiled thinly. 'I've already gathered that, Eleanor, but I'm making it my business. Apart from anything else, don't you realise that it puts my parents in an impossible situation?'

Eleanor lifted a shoulder disdainfully. 'Oh, I see—you're bothered about the look of the thing!'

'Continue in that way, my girl, and I'll put you over my knee!' promised Edward dangerously. 'Whatever your personal opinion of us—and you've been quite happy to take our hospitality and use us to the best of your advantage—you *are* our responsibility! When you entertain a young girl as a guest, no matter how little time you spare her, it must come as rather a surprise to learn that she is not, as you had supposed, seeing something of the city and having an enjoyable holiday, but is, in fact, working all hours God sends serving people meals! Even *you* must realise that!' he added scathingly.

There was silence. Eleanor was numb with humiliation. She could see how it must appear to him, could understand his anger. She swallowed the tears threatening to overwhelm her, hoping that the darkness inside the Jensen was sufficient to hide her distress. Every word said so contemptuously was true. The fact that they had been thrown at her in such an unpalatable way made no difference. When she was able, she said in a low voice:

'I'm sorry ... I didn't mean to insult your parents' hospitality. They're very kind. I thought they need never know. I couldn't think of anything else to do.' She broke off miserably. 'You wouldn't understand.'

'Try me.'

Eleanor hesitated, seeking the right words.

'Don't wrap it up,' Edward carried on remorselessly. 'Fancy words don't obliterate the facts.'

'Oh, by all means, let's keep to the facts,' Eleanor answered bitterly, 'but sometimes the facts aren't the whole story!'

'No, but they're the backbone. I'll use my imagination for the rest.'

She lifted a hand and rubbed her forehead, saying more calmly:

'When Kate came to London she over-spent her allowance by eighty pounds. This was on her future mother-in-law's account at Harrods and she was dreadfully upset, nearly hysterical. I promised to help her get the money.' There was a long silence and Eleanor continued defensively: 'She's not usually like this. It's a difficult time in a girl's life. She's vulnerable. It's hard for you to understand, you're strong and don't care what people think of you, but for Kate, young and wanting to make a good impression, this one silly mistake could do untold damage.'

'Why couldn't she tell Slade?'

Eleanor swallowed. 'I ... don't really know. I wanted her to, but ... she couldn't.'

'If the man's in love with her, surely it was the most sensible thing to do?'

'Probably it was ...'

'Probably? Don't you think so?'

'Yes! Yes, of course it was.'

'We are agreed on something, then.' He paused. 'So little sister hands over all her troubles to big sister.'

'What else could she do?' answered Eleanor defensively. 'I won't have you sneering at Kate! How can you understand? Money can never have been a problem to you!'

'Money, in one way or another, is always a problem,' said Edward evenly. 'Why didn't you go to Eve?'

Eleanor put her hands wearily to her eyes. 'As you've pointed out, I was already indebted to your parents. I'm nothing to them, I couldn't go to them.'

'I disagree. You are far more to my mother than I think you realise. She's not a demonstrative woman, but she's very fond of you. I believe she sees your mother in you and it brings back happy memories.'

'My mother?' Eleanor's voice wobbled dangerously.

'You disagree?'

She choked on a laugh. 'If you saw photographs of her

when she was young, so would you! She had a lovely face . . . and still has.'

His thumb tapped gently on the steering wheel. A couple passed, arms entwined, oblivious to everyone and everything but themselves. They stopped a few yards ahead and kissed, and then moved dreamily away until the darkness swallowed them.

'Love's young dream,' murmured Edward cynically, reaching for the keys.

'What are you going to do? Will you tell . . . your parents? Can I carry on at Luigi's?' Eleanor asked hesitantly.

His hand paused. 'No, you cannot. I'll give you the money tomorrow. You can go back to being a quiet little parson's daughter seeing the sights of the big city—and try and keep out of any further trouble, if you can. And we'll keep this just between ourselves.'

Eleanor stared at him in amazement. 'You'll give me eighty pounds, just like that?' Her voice rose incredulously. 'Why?'

'Because I have it,' said Edward repressively, starting the engine.

'But how can I repay you?' she asked helplessly.

'Certainly not by serving meals.' He shot her a sharp look. 'You don't feel like accepting the money from me?' His eyes gleamed sardonically. 'No, you don't! Why not?'

'Why not? Because . . . well, you . . . I . . .' floundered Eleanor.

'You don't seem to know why not,' he said silkily, 'or maybe good manners make it impossible for you to enlighten me?'

Eleanor, cheeks flushed, replied in a quivering voice:

'It's you that's impossible! I don't want to be beholden to you in any way whatsoever!'

'That's a pity,' he drawled, engaging gear and driving smoothly away, 'because Kate will—quite easily.'

Eleanor was silenced, as he'd known she would be. With certainty, she knew that Kate would have no qualms about where the money came from, so long as it was paid.

As the Jensen turned in the Crescent and halted outside the house, Edward said laconically:

'Well?' He studied the rebellious jut of her chin and amusement crept into his voice. 'At least you couldn't be accused of being a money-grabber, Eleanor.'

'I should hope not!' Eleanor turned on him indignantly. 'Not to have to worry about money must be comforting, but I'd sooner be hard-up and happy than rich and miserable!'

'I applaud your sentiments. Do you think you could be rich and happy?' He paused. 'I believe it has been proved possible.'

'We're getting away from the point,' she told him coldly. 'If I do take the money from you ... and I've no choice really, have I? ... then I only take it on the understanding that I pay you back.'

'How do you propose doing that?'

'I don't know exactly. I'll ... find digs and then I won't be your parents' responsibility. I was going to have to find a job eventually, anyway ...'

Edward gave an exasperated sigh. 'Don't be ridiculous, Eleanor. I thought the whole idea was to keep it from your parents? Leaving the Crescent would cause comment, it was agreed you'd stay indefinitely, until you decided what you were going to do. Can you really see my mother allowing you to live in some poky bed-sit? She's very clever at getting her own way and would shoot down any arguments in flames.'

'How shall I pay you back?' repeated Eleanor stubbornly.

'There is a way,' Edward said slowly, looking at her, brows lowered. 'You'll have to come and work at the shop.'

'But I know nothing about antiques!'

'You can learn.'

'You don't need anyone else there, surely?'

'It so happens that we do. We've been looking round for suitable premises for Van to start up on her own. These have now been found. It would be quite feasible to offer you to Mother, as her replacement.'

'I see. I didn't know that. Is Van pleased?'

'My sister is rather a puzzle to me these days . . . I think she is.' He paused, thinking hard. 'Yes, that's the best idea.'

'You don't seem very enthusiastic,' Eleanor was goaded into saying, stung by his tone.

'I'm not. I don't want you there—it only adds to complications.'

'I don't see why,' she argued, voice small, absurdly hurt. 'I'm a good worker.'

'I'm sure you are, my dear Eleanor, and you wouldn't see the complications even if they were stuck under your nose,' Edward said dryly. 'But it's the obvious solution. I can't trust you not to go looking for another job and my mother will accept you helping us out.'

Eleanor suddenly realised how naïve she was. Of course he didn't want her working there! He lived over the shop and liked his privacy.

'Just don't forget that I'm the boss.' His voice broke her thoughts.

'I don't think you'll allow me to do that, Edward!' She sighed and continued hesitantly: 'Look, I *am* grateful, truly. I know I haven't sounded it, but . . .'

'I don't want your thanks, Eleanor,' Edward cut in evenly, 'we'll take them as given.' He gave her deep scrutiny and his voice, though not unkind, was unyielding. 'Now, is there anything more? Let's have everything cleared up. You haven't been doing anything else I ought to know about?'

Eleanor stared doggedly through the windscreen. He had every right to demand his pound of flesh. It had started to rain again, she noticed absently, and the street lamps cast small pyramids of shimmering light, making a regular pattern along the pavement ahead.

'Well?' demanded Edward. 'I don't want you coming to me another day saying, I think I ought to have told you, Edward! If there *is* something more, tell me now. If not, if there's no more Ferrers family skeletons in the cupboard, we can go in.'

Eleanor sighed deeply. 'I expect you're fed up with us, one way or another,' she said awkwardly. 'Kate and me.'

There was a pause and then Edward said smoothly: 'I think I'll be able to survive.'

Eleanor sighed again. 'And now I'm afraid there's Dodie.'

He stirred in his seat. 'Dodie?'

She nodded, still gazing out in front. 'My youngest sister, Dorothea.'

'What has she to do with it?'

'Well, you see, Edward, I'm awfully sorry, but she's walking towards us now,' Eleanor informed him, fatalistically calm.

Edward turned his eyes slowly from her face to the direction of her gaze, and watched the small figure coming along the Crescent towards them, looming in and out of the ring of light, her velour hat hanging limply with the wet, her plaits sticking out at a comic angle. Her step was sturdy and strong, the lateness of the hour seeming not to bother her. Every now and again she would pause, search for a number, and carry on. In one hand she held her school satchel, and in the other, her violin case.

'This is your sister Dorothea,' stated Edward, just as calm.

'Dodie for short.'

'Who you thought fast asleep in her little bed in Yorkshire?'

'Uhuh.'

His lips twitched imperceptibly. He slowly wound down his window and waited as the approaching figure came abreast of them.

'Good evening, Dorothea. If you're looking for Eleanor, she's here.'

Dodie stopped instantly at his voice and peered uncertainly into the Jensen. Seeing her sister there, her face at once broke out into a wide smile, the freckles standing out sharply in the eerie light.

'What luck! Hullo, Nell. I bet you're surprised to see me!'

'She's not surprised at all,' remarked Edward, with his usual drawl. 'Why should you think that?'

'Oh, Dodie,' breathed Eleanor despairingly, 'what are you doing here?'

'I have the feeling it's going to be a long story.' Edward's voice was resigned. He opened the car door and got out. 'We shall be more comfortable inside,' and taking Dodie firmly by the hand, walked her up the front steps, his key poised ready for the lock.

Eleanor followed, not knowing whether to laugh or cry.

CHAPTER FIVE

'I do desire we may be better strangers.'
William Shakespeare

EVE MANSEL passed some hot buttered toast to her unexpected guest and frowned worriedly.

'So you decided to come to London and take the music examination without telling anyone,' she stated, trying to be phlegmatic about the whole affair and failing abysmally.

'Thanks!' Dodie accepted the plate with unconcealed pleasure. 'I'm absolutely famished—this is great!' she exclaimed fervently, tucking in with relish, and then realising that some sort of an answer was expected, nodded and added serenely: 'Yes, that's right. I knew Nell would help me this end.'

Eleanor was torn between a mixture of amusement and exasperation. What an evening this was turning out to be! She looked broodingly at Dodie. Her young sister was wearing a pair of pyjamas and an enveloping red dressing-gown, both belonging to Vanessa. The red, combined with Dodie's carrot shade of hair, made a bright splash of colour among the subdued greens and beiges of the Mansels' lounge where they had finally congregated.

The first half an hour after Dodie's abrupt arrival had been filled with explanations, through which Edward had organised things quietly and efficiently, treating Dodie, whom he called Dorothea, with a dry kindness. Then Vanessa and Hugh had arrived on the scene and finally Eve.

Edward then allowed his mother to take over, retiring to the background, not saying much, but, Eleanor thought bleakly, he must have been thinking plenty! She reflected that this latest Ferrers episode couldn't have come at a worse time, on top of everything else that had happened that evening. She still cringed when she remembered the icy contempt in Edward's voice as he proclaimed in no uncertain terms his opinion of her behaviour, especially relating it to his parents' hospitality. And now this hospitality was being offered unreservedly and with great kindness to another member of her family, sinking her deeper into remorse.

There was absolutely no doubt that since unburdening herself to Edward of Kate's troubles, distressing as it had been, the weight of those troubles had been considerably lightened. Dictatorial and arrogant he might be, but he was also a strength to lean on. There were so many inconsistencies in Edward's make-up that it was difficult to form an opinion that lasted for any length of time. Her eyes turned in his direction. Seated on her far right, he caught the movement and held her glance . . . and smiled.

Eleanor drew in breath. Maisie was right! he did indeed have a lovely smile, when it was a genuine one, like this, and not as so often the case, a mockery of one. It transformed his face completely, and with the smile, right out of the blue, came the dimple. Not a fat, rounded dimple usually associated with roly-poly babies, rather a lean, sleek one—but a dimple, nevertheless, changing a face usually austere and remote into one almost sweet and little-boyish! It was a revelation, and each time she was privileged to see it she was aware of a lightening of her spirits and a desire to grin idiotically back.

With a start Eleanor found that the dimple had gone and the lift of a quizzical brow made her realise that she had been staring. She turned with relief as Eve Mansel addressed her.

'Eleanor, my dear, do you think it too late to ring your parents?' and her good hostess looked anxiously at the clock and then back again to Dodie, who was sitting with complete unconcern, drinking a glass of milk.

'There's no need,' asserted that young madam calmly, 'everything's arranged. I'm thought to be visiting my best friend. They won't be worried. I'm at Jane's,' she added ingenuously to Eleanor.

'Dodie darling,' Eleanor said helplessly, 'what a harebrained scheme! Anything might have happened to you and it would have been Monday before anyone would have realised.'

'Well, thank goodness nothing has happened,' soothed Vanessa philosophically, 'and Dodie's arrived here, safe and sound, though rather wet.'

'I don't see why we have to telephone at all,' put in Dodie, a ring of milk round her mouth. 'If I'm supposed to be at Jane's . . .'

'But you're not at Jane's,' replied Eleanor firmly, 'and we'll ring tonight, I think, Mrs Mansel, if you don't mind. Just in case they've accidentally found out.'

'Very well, my dear, I'll go and do so now,' and Eve went purposefully from the room.

Dodie, her face full of resignation, muttered: 'Blow!'

'If you do mad things then you must accept the consequences,' Edward said repressively, but Dodie obviously saw something not apparent in face or tone because she gave him a quick grin and finished off her milk.

'Have a biscuit, Dodie,' offered Vanessa sympathetically. 'Take two, they're chocolate.' Dodie, after a quelling look from Eleanor, took one.

'You say your music teacher felt you should enter for this exam?' asked Hugh with kindly interest. 'If you pass, I gather this enables you for a scholarship to the college?'

'Yes, if I pass,' agreed Dodie heavily. 'That's why I kept it a secret. I can't possibly go unless I get a scholarship and there's no point in fussing now if I don't get through.' She shrugged. 'Even if I pass I don't know whether I'll stick with music as a career. Anyway, I had enough money saved up for the train fare, and I knew Nell would sort things out for me.'

'Good old reliable Nell,' murmured Edward.

'What time is this exam tomorrow?' asked Eleanor, ignoring Edward and moving the plate of biscuits out of reach.

'Half past one,' answered Dodie reproachfully, turning a cautious face to Eve Mansel as she came back into the room.

'Did you get through?' asked Eleanor and Eve nodded, looking relieved.

'Yes, I spoke to your father, who happily knew nothing. We kept explanations short and to the point. I've said we'll send her home on Sunday, and your father will meet you in.' This last was addressed to Dodie, who asked with exaggerated unconcern:

'Did Daddy . . . well, did he seem cross?'

'Not in the least,' answered Eve dryly. 'He appeared well used to dealing with errant daughters.'

Vanessa crossed to sit by Hugh who had picked up the violin and was studying it. 'How about giving us a tune?' she suggested, plucking the strings with a slender finger.

'Really, Vanessa, the child must be tired,' protested her mother.

'I'm not a bit tired,' declared the incomparable Dodie, wiping her hands expressively down the front of the dressing-gown. 'What would you like?'

Eleanor was acutely aware that her sister was playing to the gallery, but after taking a swift look round the room and seeing that they were all enjoying her immensely, decided to let her carry on.

'Make it something short,' she said warningly, 'and then you really must go to bed, Dodie.'

'Play something you're doing tomorrow, Dorothea,' encouraged Edward, leaning back and resting chin on hands, and as Vanessa curled up beside Hugh on the settee and Eve seated herself on a high-backed chair by the door, a resigned Eleanor sat rather reluctantly on a small stool by the fire.

Dodie looked at her in surprise. 'It's no good sitting there, Nell. I need you to play for me,' and she set the music on the piano, received the violin from Hugh and waited expectantly. Eleanor gave a laugh and crossed to the piano where Dodie proceeded to tune the violin from its pitch. Eleanor quickly studied the piece before her and, fairly satisfied, turned to look at Dodie, who gave a confident nod in return, and they began. At the end Dodie received a round of applause and, to Eleanor's relief, Eve rose briskly to her feet, saying:

'That was lovely, Dodie. We'll cross our fingers for you tomorrow. And now it's bed. Come along, child, even if you aren't tired, you should be. Mrs Hickman has made up the bed in Eleanor's room for you.'

At the door, Dodie gave composed goodnights all round, and a lingering look in Eleanor's direction, which prompted her to say hastily:

'Yes, I'll be up.' As Eleanor folded away the music and replaced the violin in its case, she heard Edward say to Hugh:

'What's the child like? She seemed good to me, but then I'm no judge.'

'Neither am I,' parried Hugh. He looked at Eleanor consideringly. 'I think she has talent, certainly has a feel for the instrument, and it's not the easiest of things to play.'

'It's difficult to make decisions at fourteen, and to be successful one has to be so dedicated,' she replied soberly.

'Dorothea seems capable of being single-minded if the desire takes her,' observed Edward dryly, and Eleanor reluctantly laughed.

'I'd better go upstairs or she'll not sleep,' she said, and left them, meeting her hostess on her way down.

'What an extraordinary child—all that energy!' Eve exclaimed. 'She's waiting for you, Eleanor, but I wouldn't stay too long talking, she really is tired. You'll be able to have a long chat together tomorrow.'

'How kind you've been, taking it like this,' said Eleanor

gratefully. 'I can't thank you enough.'

'Nonsense, my dear, I love having Dodie here.' Eve placed a hand on Eleanor's shoulder and smiled her pleasure, eyes pensive. 'Just as I love having you. I'm so glad ...' She broke off and patted her gently, saying again with more emphasis: 'I *love* having you with us,' and giving her a brief, surprising kiss on the cheek, continued on her way down.

Dodie was sitting up in bed, waiting. 'I say, Nell, what a super place this is! All these heavenly carpets! And what a fantastic car you were in—I couldn't believe my eyes when I saw you. I timed my arrival spot-on, didn't I?' She eyed her sister warily.

'Oh, Dodie, what a menace you are!' exclaimed Eleanor, breaking into a laugh, and Dodie grinned her relief and threw her arms round Eleanor's neck.

'I know I am, Nell, and I'm sorry. I knew it was a daft thing to do the minute I was on the train and had time to think about it, but it was too late by then. Oh, well, it's done and they don't seem to mind me being here.' She released Eleanor and carried on nonchalantly: 'I could see how you felt about the whole thing, so I did my best to be ... entertaining. I thought I brought it off rather well, didn't you?'

'Yes, you horror, you were quite a hit,' laughed Eleanor, pushing her down beneath the covers and tucking her in. 'Now get some sleep or else you won't play well tomorrow and the whole escapade will have been wasted.'

'Nell, who is Hugh?'

'A friend of Edward's.'

'He's nice,' affirmed Dodie sleepily, 'but I like Edward best.'

Eleanor waited a moment, but as nothing more seemed to be forthcoming, she closed the door quietly behind her.

Hugh met her with a drink as she re-entered the lounge. He nodded in the direction of the threesome by the fire.

'There appears to be a family consultation, so we'll sit here and amuse ourselves.'

Eleanor smiled and sank into the deep cushions, realising

how tired she was. 'Did you enjoy the concert?' she asked.

'Yes, it was good. A pity that you and Edward couldn't have joined us, I'm sure you'd have enjoyed it.'

She shot him a quick look, feeling her cheeks redden at the implication that she had been with Edward all evening, but before she could say anything Eve bore down on them, her face wreathed in smiles.

'My dear Eleanor, I'm so pleased!'

Eleanor's eyes flew to Edward who was leaning against the mantelpiece, a drink in his hand and no help in his face.

'Er . . . you are?' she managed.

'Yes, my dear. Edward has just been telling us. How kind of you to offer to help out at the shop. Normally it wouldn't matter, but we are short-staffed at the moment.' Eve turned to Hugh. 'Has Edward told you he's found premises that will do admirably for Vanessa?'

Hugh shook his head and looked across to Vanessa, who was standing next to her brother, her usually animated face rather devoid of expression, but on Hugh's 'You didn't tell me,' she answered airily:

'Oh, I can keep secrets too, you know, and anyway, big brother's only just confirmed it with me. It's near the old Covent Garden Market and as I'll not be far from your stuffy hideout, Hugh, I'll expect you to drop in on me frequently, so I won't feel lonely,' and as Hugh murmured: 'You? Lonely?' she tilted her head at Eleanor and added wickedly: 'What an asset you'll be to us, Nell. You'll deal with the customers beautifully. They won't be able to resist buying after you've got them talking about their grand-children and showing you their photographs. That's what happened when she helped before. I'm not so sure about big brother, though. You'll have to make sure he doesn't bully you.'

'Really, Vanessa,' her mother said crossly, 'I'm sure Edward wouldn't dream of bullying Eleanor, what a thing to say!' and Eleanor was uncomfortably aware of both brother and sister eyeing her with amusement—the one mockingly, the other teasingly. Before it became necessary to make some noncommittal reply, Eve turned to the mocker.

'Edward, it would be a good idea if you were to take Eleanor and Dodie to the Academy tomorrow.'

There was the smallest of pauses as Edward regarded the liquid in his glass, and when he spoke, his voice was amiable but smooth.

'I'm sorry, Mother, but that isn't possible.'

His mother frowned, fingering the pearls at her neck, a habit when thwarted. 'Can't you drop what you're doing...?'

'Please,' began Eleanor desperately, acutely embarrassed, 'I...'

'I don't think Felicity would care to be dropped,' observed Edward gently, looking calmly at his mother and ignoring Eleanor's interjections. Vanessa began to laugh quietly.

'Oh, I see ... Felicity!' exclaimed Eve, indecision all over her face.

'There's really no need...' Eleanor tried again.

'I shall be happy to go with Eleanor tomorrow,' intervened Hugh mildly, and Eve turned to him gratefully.

'How kind of you, Hugh. I'll leave you to make the necessary arrangements with Eleanor.' She walked to the door, saying crossly: 'Really, Vanessa, I fail to see what's so funny!' and after a general goodnight, Eve left the room.

'Honestly! Mother's the limit!' gasped Vanessa as the door closed. 'Your face, Eleanor, was a picture!'

'I still say there's no need for anyone to come with us,' Eleanor said, turning awkwardly to Hugh. 'It would be grand, of course, but...'

'I wouldn't miss a day out with Dodie for anything,' he answered with his warm smile. 'We'll do something afterwards, Dodie might as well get the most out of her trip.' He glanced at his watch and declared his intention of leaving.

'And I'm off to bed,' announced Vanessa, following him out. About to say goodnight, Edward stopped Eleanor from doing so by saying quietly:

'I'd like a word with you, Eleanor, if you're not too tired?'

She hesitated and came back into the room, waiting for him to speak. He took his time, eyeing her for so long that she felt herself colouring.

'You'll just have to get used to her,' he said at last in his mocking drawl. 'I mean my dear mother's managing ways. You'll have to get used to them and learn not to be inveigled into doing something you don't want to do.'

Nothing could be plainer than that. 'Your mother's very kind,' she said, and he replied dryly:

'Be wary of the Mansels when they're kind, Eleanor—there's usually a very good reason,' and he moved to the far end of the room to switch off the standard lamp.

'Do you always have to be cynical about everything?' she demanded.

'You call it cynicism, I call it realism. Your rose-coloured view of life scares me to death.'

'And you'd hate to be thought kind, wouldn't you, Edward?' she said gently.

'It's very easy to be kind when you've nothing to lose. What did you think I'd do, turn Dodie from the door? I know exactly what you're thinking, Eleanor, but I'm no Knight in Shining Armour, and I'll have no labels pinned on me. I'll pay off this eighty-pound debt because it's easy for me to do and because I don't want my mother to be upset.' He drew level with her. 'And what the hell you think to achieve by screwing your hair up in this ridiculous bun I don't know,' and he deliberately tugged at the back of her hair, which had been steadily falling all evening, bringing it tumbling down round her shoulders. 'You look like little orphan Annie!' he added sardonically.

'I had to tie it back to work at Luigi's. I quite realise how I look, thank you.' Eleanor took a deep breath. 'I think you want me to dislike you, Edward. I just don't understand you.'

'Good. There's no necessity for you to do so.' He moved abruptly to the cigarette box on the table, taking his time to select one, snapping the lid before saying crisply: 'You'll go to the jewellers tomorrow and collect your ring. I've paid for the valuation, but they wouldn't hand it over without a receipt. I'll go into Harrods and place eighty pounds against Mrs Slade's account there. You may write to your sister and tell her the money is now available—I leave it to you whether you tell her where it's come from. If you do tell her, I don't want her thanks.' He lighted the cigarette and turned his back, looking into the fire.

'Very well. Goodnight, Edward.'

'Goodnight, Eleanor.' He waited until she reached the door and then added: 'One thing more. So far as my mother is concerned, you're a friend of the family, and your help in the shop is a justifiable blessing. We both know that the only basis on which it could possibly work is on a business one.' A moment's pause, and then: 'You agree?'

'I agree ... and understand perfectly. Goodnight,' and Eleanor left the room and went wearily to bed.

There was an envelope marked 'Dorothea' written in bold, black writing, left on the piano, which they found the next morning.

'I think it's from Edward, he's the only one who calls me Dorothea,' exclaimed Dodie eagerly, ripping open the envelope and hurriedly scanning the contents. 'He sends his best wishes and good luck for the exam; he's sorry he can't take me himself, but has an appointment he can't break, and I'm to buy myself a present to remind me of this visit.' She peered at the inside of the envelope and her eyes widened. 'A fiver! Golly!' and she took it out reverently. 'I say, Nell, he must be awfully rich!'

'Hush, Dodie. He's very generous, certainly. Come along and let's get ready,' urged Eleanor, giving her a little push in the direction of their shared bedroom.

'Mrs Hickman's washed the rain splashes out of my white socks, they look quite decent now. She's a super cook, isn't she?' Dodie hardly waited for Eleanor's reply before rattling on. 'The house is terribly tidy, Nell, isn't it? I think I'd find it an awful strain,' and Eleanor, a sudden vision of the Rectory flashing through her, laughed and said:

'Yes, I should think you would!' She ran a comb through her hair and looked at her sister in the mirror. Her own face, above Dodie's, looked like a ghost, but it was hardly surprising, for she had not slept well. 'What do you think of the Mansels, now you've met them? Are they as you imagined from my letters?'

'Mostly,' admitted Dodie, experimenting with Eleanor's perfume spray. 'Mrs Mansel smells nice, doesn't she? and I suppose she's jolly decent really, though she does fuss. Vanessa's pretty. Do you think I should have my hair cut short, like hers, Nell? Ouch!' She pulled a face as Eleanor brushed out her own long, corrugated locks. 'I don't mind Edward calling me Dorothea. I think he's great, and not just because of the fiver,' she added ingenuously.

'He was certainly very kind to you last night,' agreed Eleanor. 'There, you look quite reasonable. Have you a clean hankie? Here's one of mine and don't lose it. Come on, it's time to meet Hugh.'

They deposited Dodie at the Academy and wandered leisurely around, Hugh pointing out various places of interest. They went into a small art gallery and Hugh mentioned that this was where he had seen Vanessa that time a few weeks ago, but thank goodness, he observed with a smile, the pictures today were not so weird as then.

Eleanor remembered that Vanessa had been with Philip Nolan that day and as they made their way out into the street once more, she was prompted to say:

'Hugh, how old are you?' She saw his startled face and added hastily: 'You needn't tell me if you don't want to, of course.'

'I don't mind telling you in the least,' he assured her mildly. 'It was the reason, rather than the nature of the question that surprised me.' He paused slightly. 'I'm thirty-one.'

'I see.' Eleanor looked at him consideringly. 'I don't feel that the ten years' difference between us is a barrier to our friendship, do you?'

'Good heavens, no!' exclaimed Hugh.

'Then why should it make a difference between Vanessa and Philip Nolan?' she asked casually. 'Vanessa is, in fact, six months older than I am and Philip a year younger than you are. What have you against him?'

Hugh was silent for a moment. 'How do you know I have anything against him?' he answered guardedly.

'My dear Hugh, you bristle every time his name is mentioned!'

He laughed and shook his head. 'I can't believe that.' He frowned slightly. 'I don't consider him to be a particularly steady person. He wouldn't do for Vanessa.'

'But she's old enough to decide for herself,' persisted Eleanor. 'Van's awfully level-headed, you know. I don't think she'd rush into anything really important. You and Edward are so used to her you don't see her properly. I'm a newcomer, so it's easier for me. I think that once Vanessa makes up her mind about something, very little will shake her off course. Take a good look at her, Hugh, when you see her next. She's not a little girl any longer.' She let her words sink in and then asked interestedly: 'Where are we?'

'Mmm...?' Hugh looked about him. 'Oh, just leaving Wimpole Street.'

'Ah, the tyrannical father, Mr Barrett,' stated Eleanor with relish.

'Eleanor, do you think Vanessa is serious about Nolan?'

She replied promptly. 'I don't know. Why don't you ask her?'

'Heaven forbid! I'm not that brave,' Hugh exclaimed with a laugh, adding with a vague gesture of the hand: 'I just wondered if she'd told you.'

Dodie was already waiting for them when they went to collect her. She seemed outwardly composed, but Eleanor wondered whether this insouciance was real or merely assumed. Apart from saying that the theory paper was 'a stinker', she'd played 'all right' and the interview 'seemed okay' Dodie gave no further details.

As Eleanor might have supposed, Hugh rose to the occasion and they were borne off to the Planetarium and then on to Madame Tussauds, where Dodie's impassivity died a death, volubility taking over from then on. They had an impressive tea at Fortnum and Mason's and to round the day off, Hugh produced tickets for the National's production of *Blithe Spirit*. At this, Dodie was once more rendered speechless.

It was a tired but very happy Dodie who snuggled down to sleep in the twin bed that night, and when Eleanor returned from tucking her up, she tried to thank Hugh.

'She'll never forget today, even if she doesn't pass the exam. You've made it memorable, Hugh, and I'm truly grateful. On my own behalf too.' She held out her hands impulsively and he took them in his own, drawing her to him. She raised her lashes shyly. 'May I thank you in the time-honoured way?' she asked, eyes laughing.

'You may,' assured Hugh, making it so much easier by lifting her hands and placing them securely on his shoulders. He folded his own with just the right amount of firmness around her and they stood for a moment, smiling at each other, and then their lips met.

'A perfect ending to a perfect day,' he murmured, and kissed her again. Lifting his head, he regarded her whimsically. 'Any doubts that may have been still lingering as to how old you are have irrevocably gone.'

Eleanor gazed demurely back. 'Good.'

And then the door opened and Edward walked in.

Eleanor's first reaction was to leap at least five yards away from Hugh, but she wasn't allowed to. Hugh's arms remained firmly round her as he said mildly:

'Edward. You're back early.'

'Too early, it seems,' replied Edward dryly. 'Sure I'm not interrupting anything?'

'Nothing that won't keep,' Hugh replied, smiling at Eleanor and releasing her slowly.

Edward drawled, 'Hullo, Eleanor. Have you had a good day?'

Eleanor said hurriedly: 'Yes, thank you, we didn't expect you back . . .'

'Evidently not.'

'. . . or else Dodie would have waited up for you,' she finished firmly, and retreated to a chair outside the range of the table lamp.

'May I pour you a drink, Edward?' asked Hugh imperturbably.

'You may,' replied his host, and as the front door banged and voices were heard in the hall, he added mockingly: 'Dear me! This is unheard of—the Mansels at home so early on a Saturday evening! Whatever can be the reason?'

'It's certainly most unusual,' commented Hugh mildly, passing him a drink. '*We* had to put Dodie to bed. What's *your* excuse, Edward?'

Edward paused in the act of taking a drink, eyes narrowing as he looked at him consideringly. Their eyes held and then Hugh smiled, saying equably: 'This sounds like Vanessa.'

'Plus her escort,' observed Edward, taking a quick drink. 'Your tête-à-tête is rapidly disintegrating, old fellow.'

'Yes, it is, isn't it?'

The door opened and Vanessa swept in, looking radiant, followed by Philip Nolan. Eleanor wondered how things would go, but she was forgetting Vanessa's panache for such occasions, and whatever Edward's feelings, his inherent good manners, and good sense, came to the fore. As for Hugh, Eleanor saw with amusement that he was eyeing Vanessa with a keener regard than usual ... and Vanessa was giving a good performance. Her skill with the introductions, the pouring of drinks, arranging the seating and steering the conversation was worthy of a mature woman. Eleanor's attention was turned to Philip Nolan, whom she had not met before. He was a broad, well-built man with a rugged complexion, unruly fair hair, bold eyes and a ready smile. He dressed well and was articulate, and she could understand his easy, devil-may-care attitude appealing to Vanessa. Talk flowed between them and the time passed. Eventually Nolan made his apologies and left, and Edward, on Vanessa's return, said dryly:

'You've sent him home early, Vanessa. Not, I trust, with a flea in his ear?'

'Sorry to disappoint you, brother dear. He needs his beauty sleep. There's a vintage car rally on tomorrow and he's picking me up early,' and Vanessa smiled sweetly and said goodnight, Eleanor following her a few minutes later.

The next day, Dodie was disappointed to hear that she had missed Edward so finely. His gift had caused her much indecision the previous afternoon, and she had pondered long and deeply, twice changing her mind, finally choosing a beautifully illustrated natural history book. She was thrilled with it and wished Edward to sign it for her. On the way back from church she asked Eleanor if she thought Edward would be calling in before they left for the station.

'I doubt it,' Eleanor replied, and seeing her sister's disappointed face, added hesitantly: 'I suppose we could telephone and . . .'

'Oh, yes, let's do that, Nell,' broke in Dodie eagerly. 'Now! Please!'

Eleanor, although reluctant to bother him any more, did so.

'Edward? This is Eleanor. I'm sorry to disturb you, but . . .'

'You're not disturbing me. What's wrong?' His voice was not very encouraging.

'Nothing's wrong!' Eleanor said rather curtly, and then took a breath and began again. 'Dodie bought a book with your very generous gift and she wondered whether you were calling in here before she left so that you could sign it. I said I'd ask, but she knows how busy you are—so please don't bother if . . .'

'What time is her train?'

'One o'clock, but . . .'

'I'll pick you both up at twelve-thirty. Be ready and waiting, I won't have time to come in,' and barely allowing for Eleanor's gratified 'thank you' he cut off. Eleanor went to tell Dodie the good news, and found her in the study, reading.

'He's coming? Oh, good-oh! Will he bring the Jensen?' she demanded. 'Just wait until I tell the girls at school!'

True to orders, Eleanor and Dodie were assembled on the top step ready and waiting by twelve-thirty. Eleanor had been at fever pitch in case he arrived and they were not there. Seeing the Jensen nose its way into the Crescent,

Dodie flew down the steps, Eleanor following more sedately.

'Hullo, Edward, may I sit in front?' Dodie asked eagerly. 'Oh! Is this your dog? Isn't he a beauty!'

'Yes, to both your questions,' answered Edward, amusement in his voice, and he helped them in, plus all the parcels and packages. It wasn't necessary for Eleanor to contribute to the conversation on the way, the two in the front managed perfectly on their own, the previous day's happenings offered up minute by minute to Edward by the voluble Dodie.

'Hugh seems to have made a hit,' he observed, 'with both of you,' and Eleanor found blue eyes quizzing her from the mirror. She was proud of the cool smile with which she was able to answer him. They parked the Jensen and Dodie chatted excitedly all the way to the platform, suddenly remembering the book at the last minute.

'Edward! The book!' she exclaimed, mortified. 'Quick, Nell, a pen. Here, Edward, sign it, please.'

He did so, adding a few words. 'You have good taste, Dorothea,' he murmured when finished, and checked his watch. 'You'd better get settled in,' he told her, opening one of the compartment doors.

Dodie threw herself at Eleanor, nearly knocking her over. 'Goodbye, Nell darling. I do miss you, we all do ... when are you coming home?'

'When she's good and ready. Don't be greedy, Dorothea. You've had her for much longer than we have.' He looked at Eleanor. 'The train's rather crowded. Shall I install her while you walk along the platform?' and taking the satchel and case from Eleanor, he ushered Dodie on to the train.

Eleanor walked level with them and Dodie was deposited in a window seat and Edward placed the satchel and violin case on the rack above. He was talking and Dodie was nodding earnestly, and then to Eleanor's surprise, and surely Edward's too, Dodie reached up and gave him a kiss. He pulled her plaits teasingly and smiled. Lucky Dodie, thought Eleanor, to receive such a treat. Did she appreciate how lucky she was? But it seemed she did, for Dodie was beaming when she turned to look out of the window to find Eleanor. Edward joined her on the platform and amidst the hustle and bustle of the last seconds they stood together, having one of those ridiculous conversations with Dodie through the glass, when there was nothing more to be said, knowing their mouthing antics to be comic. And then the train began to move, slowly at first, and Dodie waved, pressing her face hard against the window as she was taken further and further away, until she finally disappeared from sight and the train was merely an anonymous row of carriages.

'I suppose she'll be all right,' said Eleanor, having a momentary qualm.

'The child managed to get herself safely here on Friday, so I wouldn't worry if I were you,' replied Edward briskly, as they walked back along the platform. 'I've had a word with the guard, he's going to keep his eye on her until York.' He shot her a keen look. 'That warm heart of yours will get you into trouble one of these days, my girl. Your family appear to take untold advantage of it.'

'There's nothing wrong with having a warm heart,' she responded crossly.

'Not for other people, certainly,' Edward said. 'Kate and Dodie would agree with you.'

'I'd sooner have mine than yours, any day!'

'Oh? And what do you know about my heart, Eleanor?' He saw the consternation on her face and gave a short laugh. 'Never mind, don't answer. I'll admit it's not so soft and vulnerable as yours.'

Why, oh why, despaired Eleanor, as she climbed into the Jensen, did they always end up arguing? She didn't want to. She tried hard not to. He had every right to bemoan her warm heart—for it had caused him nothing but trouble.

The journey back to the Crescent seemed very quick. As Edward pulled up at the kerb, he said briskly:

'I'll see you tomorrow morning at the shop. Usually I'll have left before you arrive and any messages will be on the pad, but for a while, until you get used to the routine, I'll hang on until you get there. Van can join you in the afternoons for a week at least, and I'll leave you a number to ring, should you need to contact me, and Ron Mann, the other part-timer, is a good man.' His eyes went up to the rear-view mirror and he added: 'Right, I think that's all, unless there's anything you want to ask me?'

Eleanor's eyes followed his and saw a car pull up behind them. Felicity Maddox stepped out, smiled and waved before locking up.

'No, thank you, Edward.' Luckily the seat belt came apart easily and she shot out of the Jensen, running up the front steps without a backward glance.

The following weeks were easier than Eleanor expected. Vanessa was able to spend some hours of every day with her, as her own place needed to be altered before she could move in. Ron Mann also put in extra hours during the early stages, until Eleanor felt more capable. She soon found her feet, made friends with her neighbours and life settled down pleasantly.

From the start, Edward set the pattern of their behaviour, which was totally impersonal and businesslike, which suited Eleanor. Half-way through the second week he took off suddenly for Yugoslavia, which made her spirits rise, for surely he would not have done that had he any qualms about her ability to cope. Eleanor had to admit that she desperately wanted to make a success of this venture, if only to prove that Edward's initial misgivings were unjustified.

She dropped a line to Maisie, telling her that she would explain all when she called to see her. When she finally did so, purposefully timing her arrival for near the end of the lunch period, Maisie was delighted.

'Oh, Nell! It is good to see you. Come and sit down. Are you eating? What will you have?'

'Hullo, Maisie,' and laughing at the quick-fire questions, Eleanor replied: 'Yes, I'll have lunch, please,' and followed her to a quiet corner table. 'What have you to tempt me today?'

Maisie pursed her lips. 'The steak and kidney's good,'

she offered, then added slyly: 'or you might fancy the Spanish omelette!'

Eleanor eyed her over the top of the menu. 'Very funny! I'll stick to the pie, thank you. Spanish omelette brings back too many memories.'

'I bet!' Maisie grinned. 'Righto, madam—steak and kidney it is,' and she whisked efficiently away. Later she brought across two coffees and joined Eleanor at the table.

'It's lovely to sit down. The trouble is, it's hell getting back up!' Maisie stirred her coffee and looked at her friend thoughtfully. 'Of course, I'm just dying of curiosity, about Spanish omelette, I mean, but if you don't want to tell me, I shall quite understand.'

Eleanor pulled a face and gave a shrug. 'There's not much to tell. He was angry I'd got the job without telling him.'

'When I saw him lead you off that night, I wondered whether to run for help,' Maisie said with a grin. 'He looked madly controlled on the outside, but a seething mass on the in!' and she rolled her vowels with dramatic relish.

Eleanor gave a burst of amusement. 'That's a fair description.'

'To tell the truth, when Spanish omelette dragged you off, I thought that was the last we'd see of you.'

'You were wrong then, weren't you? And Maisie, you can't keep calling him Spanish omelette. His name is Edward.'

'Edward.' Maisie lingered experimentally over the name. 'Yes, that suits him. Sort of proud and distinguished.'

Eleanor groaned. 'For someone you've only seen once, he seems to have made a deep impression on you!'

'Once seen, never forgotten. Anyway, he must think a lot of you, Nell, to ...'

'You're barking up the wrong tree, Maisie,' interrupted Eleanor calmly, and proceeded to put her friend into the picture as briefly as possible. When she had finished, Maisie said thoughtfully:

'It's a funny set-up—a bit feudal, really.' She eyed Eleanor narrowly. 'Sure he's not sweet on you?'

'Eleanor said firmly: 'Quite sure.'

'Pity. I've always wanted to go to a society wedding.'

'You'll have a long wait if you're relying on me,' replied Eleanor dryly. 'Edward's favourite lady-love is a gorgeous blonde, but there are others, equally stunning, to ring the changes. How's Joe?' she added, hoping to change the subject, and Maisie took the hint.

'He's been chosen for one of the angels in the Nativity play at nursery school,' she said with a grin. 'That little horror an angel! I'll have to go armed with a large hankie, I always make a fool of myself.'

'Take two and I'll come with you,' suggested Eleanor. 'Let me know the date. If you're not doing anything on Saturday, can we take Joe to the Zoo?' She finished her coffee and collected together her handbag and coat. 'I don't work Saturdays.'

Maisie's face brightened. 'That's a grand idea.'

'Good, that's a date.' Eleanor rose, eyeing the clock. 'I shall have to dash. Where shall we meet?' and the two girls made the necessary arrangements and after a quick word with Ken, Eleanor left.

During Edward's absence Eve paid a few flying visits to the shop, but for the rest was deeply involved with Vanessa's twenty-first birthday celebrations, and as the date neared, it seemed to be her sole topic of conversation. One evening, when Eleanor and Vanessa were alone at the Crescent, Eleanor remarked casually:

'This birthday of yours sounds as if it's going to be a grand affair.'

'Yes, it does, doesn't it?' agreed Vanessa lazily. 'Once Mother gets the bit between her teeth there's no holding her. Actually, there's something rather odd about Mother the last couple of days, have you noticed? A sort of suppressed excitement.'

'Excited about your dance, surely?'

'Maybe, but this is almost as if she has something up her sleeve and is going to surprise us all. Her expression is smug, to say the least.' Vanessa was sprawled out along the settee, idly thumbing through a pile of magazines. Eleanor, sitting at the writing desk, was penning her weekly letter home.

'Don't you want a big affair?' she asked.

'It's immaterial what I want, Mother would still carry on,' Vanessa said carelessly. 'I don't mind, actually, it gives everyone the chance to catch up on all the latest gossip. And I might as well go out officially into the big bad world with a splash.' She grinned. 'No, I don't mind, it's the thought of all those brush and comb sets I'm bound to receive that puts me off!'

'Oh dear!' exclaimed Eleanor tragically, 'that's the first idea crossed off my list!' and she neatly evaded a flying cushion from the direction of the settee.

Vanessa continued gloomily: 'I peeped at Mother's guest list the other day, and honestly, some of the people coming I barely know!'

'But your own particular friends are on the list, I hope?' asked Eleanor mischievously.

'Oh, yes, old thing, everyone I want to be there will be,' replied Vanessa with a drawl, turning a page with a flourish.

'Including Philip Nolan?'

Vanessa grinned. 'Including Phil.'

'Anyone else I know?'

'Hugh, of course, and you've met Felicity, haven't you? The Maddoxes will all be there—business associates, you see. I'll introduce you to some rather dishy cousins of mine, so you won't lack partners. There'll be Edward too, of course.' Vanessa tossed the magazine aside and stretched lazily. 'He should be back soon.'

Eleanor stopped writing and considered this.

Vanessa yawned. 'He's gone on the firm's business, but I hope he brings home some good contacts for my shop.' She sat up and clasped her arms round her knees. 'I want to build up a group of contributors exhibiting solely at my place—leather, pottery, paintings, all that sort of thing, plus foreign craftwork.' Her face was animated with enthusiasm.

'It sounds exciting. I'm sure it'll be successful, you're

such a determined person, Van.'

'Determination doesn't always bring out success,' said Vanessa slowly, 'but it's a darned good help. And I never give up without a fight.' She lay back, deep in thought, and whatever it was she was reflecting upon brought a brooding look upon her face and silence fell between them.

Without warning Edward walked into the shop on the following Thursday, entering the back way from the flat. He was dressed casually and looked tired. Eleanor had just made a sale and was showing a customer out when she looked up and saw him.

'Why, Edward!' She hurried forward, a smile of welcome on her face. 'Have you had a good trip?'

'Thank you, yes,' he replied, making his way into the tiny office which opened off the main room. He paused at the door, looking back over his shoulder. 'By the way, Eleanor, Ron Mann was singing your praises when I telephoned him this morning. He says you've settled in very well.'

Eleanor flushed with pleasure and followed him in, to stand hesitantly at the door.

'Edward, I haven't had the chance to talk to you before about my wages,' she began in a rush.

'Oh?' Edward sat down at the desk, his back to her, and began to open some envelopes. 'What about them?' His tone didn't inspire any more confidence than the little she could see of his face. She took a breath.

'Well, I thought you were going to keep them to pay off the debt?' She nibbled her thumb and waited. 'That was what we arranged,' she persisted after a moment. 'And you haven't.'

He glanced up at her briefly, voice impersonal. 'I decided you ought to receive something in your wage packet each week, Eleanor, if only for the look of the thing, so far as the family is concerned.'

'Oh, I see.' It was a valid point. 'But surely, this is too much...'

'Please allow me to decide that.' The swivel chair swung round sharply and he gave her his full attention. 'You aren't receiving something for nothing, if that's what's offending you. I've allowed you a minimum sum, the difference between that and what you should be receiving will offset the debt.'

'But it still seems to me...'

'And as you have no idea of salaries in this part of the country, you must allow me to be the judge of what I consider to be your worth.'

'But I'm living free at your parents' house,' Eleanor protested, colour high.

'My dear girl,' he drawled in amusement, 'can you see my mother's face if you offered her board?' He swung back and picked up a pen. 'Leave it alone, Eleanor,' he continued, voice dismissive. 'I'm sure, like any other woman, you can find something to spend your money on. I'm quite satisfied with the way things are.' He began to write, pausing when she didn't move. 'Are you?'

'Yes. Yes, indeed,' began Eleanor awkwardly, 'it's just that...'

'You want to pay the debt off quickly and return home?'

'No, I'm very happy here and would probably have looked for a job anyway.'

'Then stop being stiff-necked about it. I quite realise that you don't wish to receive charity from me, but at least accept gracefully that this is a working arrangement, benefiting us both.'

'You didn't want me here,' she murmured.

'No. I don't suppose you wanted to work for me either. We're both making the best of it.' He stopped writing. 'Eleanor, where's that mangy tortoise-shell cat come from?'

'I... er... I don't think he belongs to anyone.'

'I see. But now he does?'

'He's no trouble and an awfully good mouser,' she said persuasively.

'Hum... what about Sykes?'

'He tolerates him. If you ignore the cat then Sykes will.' She couldn't see his face, only his hand, the pen moving swiftly across the page, filling it with his large, bold writing.

'Keep the animal away from the display shelves,' he said at last.

'Yes, Edward,' she said quickly, and hastened away in case he changed his mind.

Vanessa insisted on dragging her round the shops to find a dress for the birthday dance. Eleanor protested that she was sure her pleated one would do.

'No, it won't,' replied Vanessa decisively. 'Mother is paying particular attention to what we're both wearing, and we mustn't let the old dear down. Anyway, she's seen you in that dress, and apart from anything else, I'm dying to get my hands on you and put you into something really stunning and then turn you over to my hairdresser.'

'Help!' yelped Eleanor, and Vanessa laughed, sobering suddenly.

'I say, Nell, I know money is an awfully non-u thing to discuss, but if you need a sub, I'll...'

'Bless you, Van, I'm in funds at the moment, with working,' said Eleanor quickly, more than grateful for Edward's foresight. As they began their mammoth task, traipsing in and out of shop after shop, she said worriedly:

'I can't think what Edward must have thought when you phoned and calmly told him I needed the day off.'

Vanessa shrugged, pulling a dress from the rack and thrusting it into Eleanor's arms. 'Try this one. Oh, Edward understood, and Ron was available. Anyway, he doesn't own you—if you want the day off, you ask for it.'

'Thus speaks the sister of my employer,' murmured Eleanor dryly, from the folds of the dress. Vanessa turned a surprised face, eyebrows delicately arched.

'Do you think of him as your employer?'

'Of course I do, chump, because he is! I can't take advantage...'

'Nell, darling, you are quaint. You do happen to be helping us out.'

'Maybe, but I'm getting paid for it, and not for gadding about looking for clothes! You have to have things on a businesslike basis. Promise you'll not do it again without asking me first?'

'Oh, all right,' agreed Vanessa, laughing at Eleanor's earnestness, adding teasingly: 'You're not scared of Edward, are you, Nell?'

'Scared to death,' replied Eleanor. 'Now, what about this?'

Vanessa watched her parade up and down, a frown on her face. 'No,' she said at last. 'Take it off. Black doesn't suit you. And don't look like that—we're finding you the right dress even if it takes all day!'

'It probably will,' sighed Eleanor, with deep foreboding.

'You'll not recognise yourself,' her determined friend promised.

Vanessa's promise was recalled on the evening of her birthday, two days later. Eleanor stood poised before the long mirror in her bedroom, assessing the stranger looking back at her. Of course, it wasn't quite a stranger, she could recognise herself—the hazel eyes, serious brow and sensitive mouth were all familiar features, but there were changes. The nut-brown hair was shaped into a soft flick-away style, framing her face in a most complimentary way, and she tilted her head questioningly. Yes, she liked the hair, she decided, but the dress—she wasn't so sure about the dress.

Eleanor ran her fingers over the silky material, feeling its cool smoothness on her skin. It was lovely, there was no doubt about that. She moved tentatively, the folds moulding flatteringly to her young slim body, clinging where it touched—rather disconcertingly so, the softly draped material complementing her femininity. Not, she thought wryly, a dress to go unnoticed. Red . . . a colour she rarely wore. Admittedly not a bright shade of red, more a warm, deep ruby, but . . . red, nevertheless.

No good being faint-hearted in a creation like this, Eleanor told herself sternly, and gave herself a liberal spray of her favourite perfume. When the knock came at the door she was just applying lipstick the exact shade of ruby. The figure reflected in the mirror was unexpected.

'Hullo, Edward. I didn't know you'd arrived. Is it time to go? I'm sorry, I am ready.' She was absurdly flustered and turned, picking up her evening bag to search for a non-existent article.

'Good evening, Eleanor,' said Edward calmly, 'there's no hurry. Van has sent me with this.'

'Thank you.' She expected him to leave the bracelet on the dressing-table, instead of which he held it out.

'Shall I clip it on for you? The clasp is rather awkward, I believe.'

Eleanor turned slowly, holding out her arm, the folds of the sleeve falling back to reveal smooth, pale skin. Edward clasped the wide silver bracelet round her wrist and snapped it shut. His hand, quite brown, contrasted the whiteness of her arm and his thumb lay lightly against the vein, showing delicately purple through the skin.

Eleanor caught her breath, her eyes held by the sight of his hand, feeling the blood coursing its way beneath his fingers. For one brief moment she recalled how once before Edward had held her so, had imparted a kiss on that same pulse, racing just as fast and furious as it was now. It brought that evening painfully back, and she wondered if he remembered it too and her eyes lifted to his face, but there was a remoteness there that chilled her and put a stop to such foolishness. Pulling her arm away as carelessly as she was able, Eleanor gave her attention to the bracelet, saying:

'Thank you, Edward. Van has impeccable taste, hasn't she?' She turned her back to him and studied herself thoughtfully in the mirror. 'She knew exactly what was needed to finish me off.' Her eyes went to Edward's reflection, tall, dark and rather forbidding, and something prompted her to add provocatively: 'Van promised to transform me for this evening—what do you think, Edward? Has she succeeded?'

His eyes flicked over her. 'No one who knows you well will be in the least fooled, Eleanor,' he remarked, walking to the door.

'That will teach me to fish for compliments—and I don't even know if I got one,' she said dolefully, and Edward paused, his eyebrows giving a comical quirk.

'My dear girl, you don't need to fish—and it was definitely a compliment.' He glanced at his watch. 'We'll be leaving in about ten minutes. Save a dance for me, won't you? I have a few young cousins who have an eye for a pretty girl and I won't get a look-in unless I book one now,' and then he was gone.

Eleanor mechanically collected together her things and just before leaving, surveyed the flushed cheeks and bright eyes of the girl in the mirror. Smiling idiotically at herself, she floated dreamily from the room.

CHAPTER SIX

'The heart has its reasons, which reason does not know.'

Pascal

THE ballroom looked splendid, couples dancing beneath glittering chandeliers, a mass of weaving colour. Vanessa broke away from a group of guests and drew Eleanor to one side.

'Nell, have you seen Hugh?'

Eleanor shook her head. 'Isn't he here?'

'No, not yet,' Vanessa said in exasperation. 'He's probably forgotten the day!'

Eleanor laughed. 'Don't be silly, he couldn't possibly have, the way you've been reminding everyone for the past few weeks.'

'You don't know Hugh,' exclaimed Vanessa darkly. 'I've got to speak to him before it's time for the toasts. Mother's asked him to make a speech and I want to find out if he has any ghastly anecdotes up his sleeve! If he has, I'll bribe him somehow to miss them out.' She took Eleanor's arm. 'Come on, I'll introduce you to one of my cousins, as promised.'

Eleanor did not lack for partners, nor admiring glances, and she was just regaining her breath from a more than hectic Gay Gordons when she saw Hugh.

'So you've finally arrived! Van was beginning to think you'd forgotten to come.' She laughed at the pained expression on his face and added: 'You've seen her?'

'I have, and been duly chastised,' Hugh confided. 'I made my apologies, quite legitimate ones to do with business, but I doubt they've been accepted.' Hugh's eyes wandered over the dancing couples and he turned with a smile. 'Do you care to dance?' he asked, holding out his hand invitingly. Eleanor accepted happily and as they were about to join the throng, Vanessa sailed by, giving them a wave, before being whirled away in the arms of Philip Nolan.

'How beautiful she looks,' said Eleanor warmly.

'Indeed she does,' agreed Hugh, 'but she has competition.'

'Why, thank you, Mr Latimer,' exclaimed Eleanor delightedly.

'My pleasure, Miss Ferrers.'

To her surprise Hugh was a good dancer and she thoroughly enjoyed herself. As they walked slowly off the floor a cool voice drawled from behind them:

'Beware of these quiet types, Eleanor, they very often turn out to be wolves in sheep's clothing.' It was Edward, and Hugh turned twinkling eyes to her, remarking smoothly:

'But wolves very rarely turn out to be sheep! Excuse me, I see Eve over there and I haven't begged a dance from her yet,' and he smiled blandly at them both and walked unhurriedly away.

A ridiculous constraint fell over Eleanor and for the life of her she couldn't think of a single thing to say, and then it was not necessary for her to say anything, for the music started up again and Edward said:

'A waltz, I think,' and drawing her into his arms, he danced her away. Unlike Hugh, she was not at all surprised to find that Edward was a good dancer. Out of the corner of her eye she saw a flash of peacock blue and knew that Felicity had her eye on them. Though why, I don't know, thought Eleanor crossly, she's had him for most of the evening so far, surely she doesn't begrudge me one measly waltz! When the music stopped Edward said gravely:

'I now understand why you're so popular. Thank you for such an enjoyable dance, Eleanor.'

'Oh, we do have a few social graces in Yorkshire, you know,' she answered airily, to cover the stab of delight his words gave her, and murmuring her own thanks, she excused herself and slipped swiftly into the crowd.

As the evening progressed Eleanor had so many partners that her feet began to protest and she escaped upstairs to the gallery, thankful to be on her own for a few minutes to catch her breath. She looked over the rail watching the sea of dancers below and was able to pick out Vanessa easily by the silver lurex gown she was wearing. Vanessa was dancing with her father, and James Mansel, himself looking eminently outstanding with his white hair and lordly bearing, was clearly proud of his radiant daughter.

Eleanor stayed in the gallery for some time, a longing for a cool drink finally making her move. As she made her way to the stairs she squeezed by a group of fellow guests blocking her way and came face to face with Felicity Maddox.

Eleanor hoped that a dutiful smile would suffice, when something in the other's face stopped her doing even that. The pallor of Felicity's skin was accentuated by the brightness of her eyes, which were hard and sparkling with anger. Felicity made to speak, but a group of laughing guests crowded up the stairs behind her and, lips tightly compressed, she pushed by Eleanor without doing so.

Eleanor gazed after her in consternation. Whatever was the matter? she wondered, feeling acutely uncomfortable, and she continued on down the stairs, her thoughts buzzing in all directions, and then she forgot all about Felicity Maddox as hands grasped hers and she was pulled into a weaving line of people doing the Conga. Suddenly the line broke and the hilarious dance disintegrated. Laughing and gasping for breath, she stood at the side content for the line to continue without her, and then Vanessa appeared, eyes bright and face glowing, and there was something in her expression that made Eleanor say quickly:

'Hullo, Van, is anything wrong?' and Vanessa shook her curls vigorously.

'Nell, you sly old thing!' she scolded happily, giving Eleanor a kiss and an enthusiastic hug. 'Come along, we've all been looking for you. Mother's dying to see you, and is as pleased as Punch, of course, but Pop's just as bad—they thought it would never happen!' and she laughed.

Eleanor found herself being propelled along the side of the ballroom, trying to make some sense out of Vanessa's excited chatter.

'Van, wait a minute! What are you . . .?'

'Ah, come on, no more games,' grinned Vanessa knowingly. 'All is revealed! Do come and tell Edward that he's being extremely nonsensical.'

Wishing that all could be revealed to her, Eleanor gave up and allowed herself to be drawn towards her host and hostess, meeting their beaming faces with an uncertain smile. Eve enveloped her and kissed her, saying in an almost reverential voice:

'My dear, dear Eleanor, you can't think what this means to me, to us—we're so happy . . . I could cry!'

'You are?' ventured Eleanor, frantically trying to find a glimmer of reason for all the joy and, as suddenly, having a blinding, devastating suspicion that didn't bear thinking about.

'Now do persuade Edward that tonight would be a beautiful time for your announcement,' Eve was saying persuasively. 'Yes, my dear, you may jump with surprise, but we know everything now, and Vanessa is as thrilled as we are, so you don't have to worry about stealing the limelight and upsetting her.'

'Where is Edward?' asked her husband.

'Looking for Eleanor,' put in Vanessa, and that Eleanor could well imagine, and wanted to sink through the floor.

'My son is very stubborn,' carried on Eve, oblivious to interruption, 'as you'll no doubt find out, but he'll give in to please you, my dear, and . . .' She broke off quickly and looked over Eleanor's shoulder confidently. 'Won't you, Edward?'

Eleanor made to turn, but before she could do so a pair of arms came round her and held her firmly, Edward's body cradling hers, his chin resting gently against her hair.

'Won't I what, Mother?' he drawled, well aware of Eleanor's nervous start as his arms enfolded her.

Vanessa said mischievously: 'You two really fooled me! All this businesslike efficiency at the shop and Eleanor actually saying she was scared of you!' she accused. 'She doesn't look scared, does she, Mother?' and thus appealed to, Eve said fondly:

'Of course she doesn't.'

Eleanor choked back an hysterical laugh. Little did they know!

'I think that perhaps Eleanor and I should have a talk,' suggested Edward, with deceptive meekness, and his father nodded in agreement.

'Yes, my boy, you do that. No one wants to influence you.' He turned to his wife, who was barely containing herself. 'Now, Eve, if the youngsters don't want to announce their engagement tonight, we must let them have their way.' He looked quizzically at Edward. 'I must say, it seems a good opportunity, but it's up to you. Off you go.'

'Come along, darling,' said Edward, his voice resignedly amused, his hand warm and comforting round her shoulders. Like a zombie, Eleanor was led across the floor and out through a side door, aware of a few curious glances following them. Once in the corridor she stopped and would have spoken, but Edward made for a small sitting room set aside for Vanessa's presents, and his hand was no longer warm or comforting as he thrust her before him. With ominous calm he closed the door, saying with savage civility:

'I must congratulate you! When is our happy day to be?'

Eleanor winced at the look on his face and stammered: 'What's happened? Why do they think . . .?'

Edward said scathingly: 'I was hoping you'd be able to tell me that!'

'Well, I can't,' she retorted, anger coming to her aid now that the horrified surprise was wearing off. A pulse throbbed in her throat and she made a strong effort to control her voice. 'I don't know what's going on.'

'I find that extremely hard to believe,' came the biting reply. 'The whole set-up seems too well organised not to have been contrived!'

'Maybe, but I haven't ...' Eleanor began furiously, and was silenced as Edward swung her roughly to him.

'My God, if I thought for one moment that you'd ...' He stopped and expelled an angry breath. 'We seem to have played this scene once before ... and that makes it twice too many!'

'I quite agree with you,' flashed Eleanor, white with temper, 'and I should be obliged if you would kindly keep your hands to yourself!'

Edward released her abruptly. 'I can't promise you that—my first instinct is to shake the living daylight out of you—but I'll try.'

'Thank you,' she said coldly, rubbing her arm where he had gripped her. 'What are we going to do?'

'What do you suggest? You'd better make it short and sweet or they'll think we've eloped!' The sarcasm was unmistakable.

'You could have denied it!' exclaimed Eleanor explosively. 'You should have—why didn't you?'

'My dear girl, there are certain situations that even *I* cannot control, and this is one of them. Do you seriously believe I would have allowed it otherwise?' He gave a short laugh and ran a hand through his hair. 'Deny it? When my own mother informed me so archly that she had had the news from such a reliable source?' He smiled unpleasantly, biting at the words. 'From her own dear Constance?'

Eleanor stood as though turned to stone, colour flooding her cheeks.

'My mother?' she squeaked incredulously.

'Your mother,' Edward repeated coldly, eyes narrowing as he studied her reaction. 'I could hardly call my prospective mother-in-law a liar, now could I? It wouldn't augur well for future relationships.' He leaned against the table and busied himself lighting a cigarette, his eyes never leaving her face. 'You do see my predicament?' he observed at last. 'You appear speechless. Am I to assume that you want me to believe you're as much in the dark as I am?'

'I don't care what you believe,' Eleanor ground out, finding her tongue, 'but it happens to be the truth.' She flung round at him. 'How many times do I have to tell you that I bitterly resent my name being coupled with you or your money, because that must be a serious consideration, surely? Neither could induce me to marry ...'

'I'm very pleased to hear it,' he replied harshly, 'because I make a most disagreeable ...'

'And I pity the poor girl who does!'

'... adversary when coerced into a situation not of my own making!'

The silence in the room was broken only by the systematic ticking of the grandfather clock standing in the corner. Blue eyes held hazel in a commanding glare and Eleanor was the first to tear hers away.

'Have you any ideas?' she asked stiffly.

'For getting us easily and cleanly out of this mess?' He raised a sceptical brow and when Eleanor nodded, he said without hesitation: 'No, my dear Eleanor, I have not. The only thing we can do at this moment is to go back in there and agree to an announcement.'

'You can't mean that?' Eleanor's mouth set obstinately.

'I do.'

'In front of all those people?' Her voice rose incredulously and then flattened. 'If that's the best suggestion you can offer ...'

'I'm quite willing to hear yours, but I should remind you that I've had somewhat longer to think about it than you have, and there's something else you should know.' Edward crushed his half-finished cigarette with some force. 'When my mother dropped her bombshell, we were at the time in a group consisting of numerous relatives and friends, all showing signs of being an appreciative audience. Even if nothing officially is said tonight, it will be common knowledge in about half an hour.' His lip curled. 'I'm supposed to be quite a catch, I would remind you.'

'I really don't know why,' said Eleanor witheringly, and was rewarded by a thin smile.

'Neither, my dear girl, do I. Many would agree that the boot is on the other foot. You are, by far, the better catch.'

'I can do without your peculiar sense of humour, thank you, and I wish you'd stop calling me your dear girl. I'm not and never will be,' she snapped, adding sarcastically: 'And if you've managed to elude the marriage net so far, how come you've been caught now?'

'*That* I mean to find out,' Edward replied formidably 'Why the devil I didn't strangle that damned Margot Slade, I'll never know, and as for your idiot sister . . .'

'She's not an idiot—and you thought it would die down!'

'I made a mistake, didn't I?' he responded grimly. 'Someone fanned the flames.'

'If you insinuate once more . . .' Eleanor began, and choked back the words, turning away to pace the floor. She threw out a hand in a helpless gesture. 'If only your mother had waited! Asked us when we reached home, at least! She seems to be lapping it all up.'

'My sweet innocent,' drawled Edward. 'Wait? When she's been trying to marry me off for the past five years? Lapping it up—this is double cream to my dear mama.' His eyes narrowed. 'By the look of you it's obvious you have no idea of what I'm talking about.'

'None whatsoever.'

'How lovely if my Edward should fall in love with your Eleanor!' he mimicked. Eleanor stared at him in horrified amazement.

'You're making it up! They surely didn't believe . . . It doesn't sound like my mother at all,' she exclaimed impatiently.

'It sounds all too true of mine,' Edward answered dourly.

'This is intolerable! We shall have to tell them it's not true.'

Edward sketched an exaggerated bow. 'Off you go,' he urged. 'See all the eager, expectant faces out there. I'll watch on the sidelines to see fair play.'

'Oh, stop being facetious,' flared Eleanor, rounding on him. 'You know I can't do that!' and she rubbed her forehead distractedly.

'Of course you can't, and now that we're back to square one, you'll just have to take my arm and we'll go in and smile like the revoltingly happy couple we're supposed to be.' He gave her a searching look, reflecting dryly: 'If that's the best face you can provide, then we're doomed to failure right away. You'll convince them I beat you already.'

'It's not funny,' said Eleanor, gritting her teeth. 'There must be a way.'

'There isn't. Not here and now.'

'It's wrong. What we're doing is wrong.'

'Of course it's wrong, in more ways than one, but at the moment there's no other way out of this mess, unless you want to make both our families a laughing stock?' When she didn't answer, Edward continued factually: 'We'll carry on the farce for a few weeks and then you can tell the world that I'm despicable, arrogant, conceited and any other adjectives that will, no doubt, spring readily to your lips—and everyone will be only too happy to believe you.' He lifted a dark brow mockingly. 'You can jilt me as dramatically as you like, no one will blame you. Are you ready for the fray?' and not giving her time to answer, he opened the door and swept her through. As they walked the corridor, he added casually: 'Naturally you'll have to be prepared to play up to them.'

'What do you mean?' asked Eleanor breathlessly, trying to keep up with his stride as well as his reasoning.

Edward sighed heavily and stopped, saying patiently: 'We *are* supposed to be in love, Eleanor.' His mouth gave a cynical twist and his voice left no doubt as to his feelings. 'For this to have happened to the elusive Edward Mansel it must have come with some force. Don't forget I've withstood the marriage-mart for a hell of a time, and as value on the unobtainable sends up the price, they'll believe you to be in the same state. So . . . this is no watery emotion we have between us.'

Eleanor wrenched away her arm and said dangerously: 'I see.'

'But don't worry,' he assured her, smiling with great charm. 'I'm renowned for my self-control. Just a few adoring glances from you will suffice for tonight.'

'Oh, will it?' she responded with a furious whisper, for they had reached the doors and music and voices could be heard the other side. 'I think you're insufferable! I wish I'd never set eyes on you! You're a . . . a . . .'

'Tut, tut, mind the language, parson's daughter!' His discerning eyes flicked abrasively over her. 'Yes, anger certainly does the trick, you were looking quite frightened before, now they'll be able to believe all the romantic twaddle we're about to dish out to them.' He pulled her deliberately to him and kissed her, long and lingeringly. When his head lifted at last he said softly: 'Such an eminently kissable mouth should look as though it has been thoroughly kissed—it's expected.' He put out a hand to the door and then paused, glancing down at her. 'Just one thing more . . .'

'What?' managed Eleanor, shaken to the core, the palm of her hand itching to wipe the lazy smile from off his face.

'For this to work at all, it must be solely between the two of us. No little confidences—to anyone. Not to Van . . . not to Hugh . . . not to your sisters. Not to anyone.'

'I have no wish for us to appear any sillier than we already do,' she responded icily.

'Good. Then in we go,' said Edward, adding a sardonic aside: 'and mind you blush happily, my love!' as he pushed open the door.

'Are you tired?' Edward's voice broke the silence between them.

Eleanor, laying her aching head back against the seat,

replied 'a little' in an uninterested voice, hoping to quell further conversation, and to underline her feelings, she turned to gaze out of the side window. The Jensen sped swiftly along the almost deserted streets, the smooth note of the engine changing slightly as Edward slowed for a corner. The night was particularly black, and cold, with low hanging clouds. Although it was warm in the Jensen, Eleanor felt frozen, in mind and body. Her face, as well as her head, ached—ached with the effort of smiling so much. Smiling! When that was the last thing she wanted to do.

Edward began to hum tunelessly beneath his breath and she moved her head to look at him, wishing she could know what he was thinking. Whatever it was, it didn't appear to cause him much concern. He was driving with his customary ease, the collar of his coat upturned, hands firm on the steering wheel, gaze impassive on the road ahead.

She felt a quick stab of resentment and closed her eyes, taking the image of his profile with her. No doubt, in time, the last two hours would fade away, diminish, so that it could be looked back upon as part of a crazy dream, a foolish memory. No doubt, in time.

'Things seemed to go well,' observed Edward.

'Yes.'

Eleanor purposefully remained with her eyes closed to discourage talk. Most of her troubled thoughts were of her own making. As Edward said, it had gone well—too well, showing her how it would have been had the engagement been authentic. Thinking how people would react in no way related to living through it. Thinking could not compare to feeling, and for her, what they were doing made a mockery of everything, and she hated herself. But once they had begun there was no going back.

Edward, as might be expected, had given a superb performance—beautifully controlled and in character, wearing the slightly whimsical air of a man renowned for his cynical views on marriage, finally succumbing. It was here in her thinking that Eleanor admitted the enormity of their deception in relation to him. No wonder, initially, he had been so angry, but no one would have known his true feelings as they circulated among friends and relatives, receiving their congratulations. Even Eleanor's outraged feelings had been lulled and smoothed. There was a point during the evening when Edward pulled her close in his arms for a slow, dreamy waltz. Her head fell naturally upon his shoulder, the lapel of his jacket smooth to her cheek. Their steps became smaller and smaller and his hand stroked the back of her neck gently, soothingly. When the music stopped she lifted her head and smiled dreamily. It was the cynical gleam in Edward's eyes that brought her back to her surroundings, that and the awareness of how close they were standing together, how thin her dress was, the very intimacy of contact bringing a disturbing vulnerability, and Edward looking down at her with a curious expression on his face.

'No need to overdo it,' he murmured.

Eleanor peeled herself from him. 'I was pretending you were someone else,' she said coldly, between smiling lips, and was rewarded by his sardonic smile.

Remembering this episode she wondered bleakly, was it so easy, then, to learn to say hateful things? and blinked away a stupid tear that threatened to spill over, giving herself a mental shake. Okay, so you're out of your depth, she told herself sternly, then you'll just have to learn to swim.

She gathered together her resources and said in a controlled voice:

'You needn't have brought me home, Edward, I could have gone with your parents,' but even as she said it, she knew she could not have borne their delight. At least with Edward she didn't have to pretend.

'Have you no soul, no imagination? That wouldn't have done at all,' Edward answered coolly. 'We shall be expected to arrive home much later than the others, having stopped on the way to talk—as lovers are apt to do, among other things,' and suiting action to words, he pulled into a quiet side-road and slowed to a halt. When the engine note died and the lights were dowsed, he turned a mocking face to her. 'We mustn't disappoint them.'

Eleanor shrugged. 'What do we talk about?' she asked

indifferently, pulling her coat more securely round her, not liking his nearness, nor the meaning of his words.

Edward swivelled in his seat so that he could look comfortably at her, one arm on the steering wheel, the other on the back of his seat, leaning his body lazily against the interior of the door. His teeth gleamed in the semi-darkness.

'You're being deliberately obtuse, Eleanor,' he replied equably. 'Surely you can guess at the form? For instance, we can say how surprised Hugh was, did you notice? or we can reflect on how disappointed my young and handsome cousins were that you had been plucked right beneath their noses. We can laughingly amuse ourselves with the thought that my dear mama already sees herself a proud grandmother, cooing over a baby or two. There's endless things we can talk about. And we end up by saying, rather smugly I fear, that apart from the outsmarted cousins, everyone seemed very pleased.'

'Not everyone,' said Eleanor flatly, and then wished she'd held her tongue. Edward raised a brow.

'Oh? Who wasn't?'

She moved restlessly beneath his probing look and replied shortly: 'Your girl-friend, Felicity.'

There was silence for a few seconds and then he said evenly: 'Why do you say that?'

She shrugged again. 'I just had that impression.' Some impression! she thought grimly, remembering the fury in the green eyes as Felicity took the chance to whisper: 'Don't think you'll be able to hold him with your stupid, old-fashioned innocence, because you won't—he'll soon tire of you!' Eleanor had felt like saying that she fully agreed.

'There's no need for you to worry about Felicity.'

'I have no intention of doing so,' she said, 'I'll leave that to you, but don't forget our bargain of silence,' and she deliberately turned her shoulder to him and gazed steadily out of the window.

After a moment Edward asked casually: 'What are you thinking?'

With an effort she moved her head, the smell and feel of

the leather seat close to her cheek. 'I was thinking how well you took your part,' she answered, 'and how painstaking you are to follow it through.'

If Edward noticed the edge of bitterness in this last remark he did not comment on it, and that was as well, for Eleanor could not have justified the bitterness. He said musingly:

'As a boy I came into contact with a very good drama teacher at school, who roped me into a play and gave me my first taste of acting, which interested me right through university. I remember this teacher telling us that to be a successful actor you had to think further than the words and action written down, that the mind and body needed to be submerged completely into that of the person portrayed, until you knew exactly how he would react in any situation. My ambitions in that direction faded, but his advice didn't.'

'How cold-blooded and efficient you are, Edward. Don't you ever allow yourself the luxury of an unpremeditated act?'

'Not often,' he answered, 'and whenever I do, I mostly live to regret it—hence the mess we're in now.' He watched the tinge of red flush her cheeks and added consideringly: 'You didn't give such a bad performance yourself, Eleanor, allowing for the fact that you'd had no rehearsals. It was a most praiseworthy effort ... sweet young girl, basking in the glory of getting her man—the tremulous smile, the maidenly blush, the downward, shy curve of eyelash—all very commendable.'

He was too near the truth for comfort and it frightened her. Not the cynical observations, but the way, once her initial anger had dissipated, she had slipped so easily into her part, the extraordinary blissful sensation of being part of Edward—a loving Edward. Such feelings were lunatic and incomprehensible.

She swallowed hard. 'May we go now, please?' She felt rather than saw him glance at his watch.

'I think we may.' Reaching for the keys, he paused. 'Ah! Here's the snow, I thought it would come.'

Eleanor opened her eyes and watched the windscreen becoming more and more spotted with thick white flakes until it was gradually covered over with a translucent layer. She sat up, suddenly stirred.

'Do you think we'll have a white Christmas? How lovely if we do—Dodie will be so thrilled!' She turned to him. 'It's ages since we've had snow at Christmas, isn't it? There's a hill at the back of the Rectory that's just right for sledging.' She peered into the darkness. 'Do you think it's settling?'

'Looks like it,' commented Edward absently, 'and according to the forecasts, the North has already been hit, so Dorothea will be able to sledge.' He was staring at her and making no move to start the engine. 'Would you like to go home for Christmas, Eleanor?'

'Go home?' she repeated stupidly, after a stunned silence.

'Yes. You miss them, don't you? If you want to go, I'll take you.'

Home! Suddenly, home was the one place she wanted desperately to be. All the familiar faces came instantly into her mind's eye, becoming immediately more dear and precious, and a longing for their warmth and love swept over her, leaving her physically shaken. There was a huge ache in the back of her throat and she could barely answer.

'It's very kind of you to suggest it, but ... no, thank you.'

'Why not?'

'It ... it would be better if I didn't,' she managed, and turned her head away, blinking rapidly. She almost jumped out of her seat as his hands touched her, forcing her round to face him.

'You want to go,' he said brusquely, searching her face, and then giving an exasperated sigh, added: 'If it's my presence that stops you, then go alone.'

'That would make it worse.'

'Really? I rather imagined that you disliked my company.'

She pulled away from him and said angrily: 'Oh, *you're*

being obtuse now, Edward! We're supposed to be in love, remember? My parents would think it most odd if I went home alone, and if we went together . . .'

'Yes?'

'It wouldn't be long before they knew something was wrong.'

Edward switched on the engine and it sprang to life. Without speaking he flicked the wiper switch and as the headlights burst through the darkness, snowflakes could be seen, hurtling to the ground. With deliberation he engaged gear and edged the Jensen away, gradually gaining speed. After a while he said:

'You really aren't cut out for this sort of charade, are you? My dear girl, people are getting in and out of engagements all the time these days.'

'But not you. As you said earlier, this is no watery emotion—those were your words. Doesn't that make nonsense of what you've just said?'

'Perhaps, but mistakes have been known to happen, and even hard-bitten bachelors and innocent parsons' daughters make them. For goodness' sake, stop eating your heart out for other people! Your parents and mine will soon get over it—yours certainly, you'll soon provide them with the genuine article.' He gave her a quick glance. 'Well, if you won't go, you won't. I suppose it would be asking too much at this early stage. Later you'll no doubt be more used to the idea and able to be blasé about it.'

'I thought we were going to break it off as soon as we could?' exclaimed Eleanor in alarm.

He looked pointedly at the dash clock. 'We've been engaged exactly one hundred and thirty-three minutes, Eleanor. I think we shall have to allow a little more time to elapse before we do that.' He took his left hand from the wheel and placed it over her own, staying them from turning the evening bag over and over in her lap. 'I quite realise that the whole thing is abhorrent to you, but you're not the only one who suffers. You'll just have to be patient.' When he felt her hands relax he took his own away.

'How can you take it all so calmly, Edward?' she asked.

'I know initially you were angry, but now you seem so matter-of-fact.'

'That's the difference between us, my dear. You're a romantic and I'm a realist. I *was* angry, I don't like being fooled, but what's done is done and we might just as well resign ourselves to seeing the thing through, with the minimum amount of fuss. You'll come out of it better if you can think that way too.'

Nothing more was spoken between them until they reached the house.

'You'll have to ring your parents tomorrow,' Edward said thoughtfully, 'and it won't be an easy thing for you to do, I'm afraid.' He shrugged. 'Perhaps you'll be able to piece together the whys and wherefores—not that it matters now, but it would be interesting to know.' He heaved open the door and ran round the car, snow settling starkly on his dark overcoat and hair. He opened the passenger door and helped her out and through the snow into the house, half carrying her up the steps to save her evening shoes from becoming wet. Everywhere was silent and in darkness.

'Goodnight, Eleanor.' Edward contemplated her gravely, brushing some flakes from her hair, and lifting her face to his, so that she had to look at him. 'Try and sleep. Things won't seem half so bad in the morning.' He raised her hand to his lips, kissing the inside of her wrist gently, and then turned on his heel and was gone.

Eleanor went slowly up the stairs, undressed and made ready for bed, purposefully keeping her mind a blank, but the minute she collapsed between the sheets her thoughts ran riot over the events of the evening. Only when the sky began to gradually lighten, did she fall into an exhausted sleep.

Eleanor left the telephone call to the Rectory until after lunch. She steeled herself for the happy congratulations and gave a creditable account of herself, asking some pertinent questions in return, and by the time Edward returned later in the day, she had worked out some idea of what had happened. She was giving Henry, the tortoise-shell cat, some milk, when he came in with Sykes at his heels.

'Hullo, Edward,' she said quickly, hardly looking at him. 'Henry's so much better, don't you think? His fur is improving daily and he's much fatter,' and she concentrated on pouring the top off the milk.

'I'm not surprised,' remarked Edward dryly, 'the amount of food you give him. I bet he hasn't thought of a mouse for days.' He took in her pale face and smudged eyes, but didn't comment.

'He's always hungry,' murmured Eleanor, stroking the cat, who was rumbling with a self-satisfied purr. 'And everyone thrives on a bit of love,' she added firmly. She followed Edward into the office and began a stumbling explanation of her telephone call home, which he broke into.

'Come up to the flat, we'll be more private. Ron can take over in here.' Once upstairs, he threw off his jacket and loosened his tie, saying: 'Do you mind of I get out of these first? Make a pot of tea, there's a good girl, and by then I'll have showered and changed.' He walked swiftly through to the main bedroom, leaving the door slightly ajar, and while Eleanor foraged in the unfamiliar kitchen for the tea things, she could hear him moving about, hear the noises of a drawer opening and shutting, the splashing of the shower—all homely, ordinary sounds, giving her a glimpse of Edward in his own environment which was oddly comforting. As she waited for the kettle to boil the telephone rang. The sounds from the bathroom made it obvious that Edward could not hear it, and Eleanor answered it after some indecision. She was just about to give the number when a female voice said tersely:

'Edward, I must speak with you.'

It was Felicity, there was no mistaking the voice. Eleanor was aware of a sharp stab of shock and then said quietly:

'I'm sorry, Edward is in the shower at the moment, can I take a message, or have him ring you back?' Afterwards she realised how provocative the words were, but there was nothing she could do about it, it was, after all, the truth.

There was a distinct intake of breath and then the line went dead.

Eleanor slowly replaced the receiver and went back into the kitchen. As she carried the tray into the room, Edward came through, hair wet, skin glowing. He draped his jacket round the back of a chair and began to fix his watch-strap.

'Edward. There was a phone call while you were taking a shower.'

'Oh, yes?'

'I . . . think it was Felicity, but she put the phone down . . . when she knew . . . when I answered it.'

His actions froze for an instant and a shutter came down over his face, and then the moment passed and he was saying easily:

'I intended ringing her today. I'll do it later.' He sank into an armchair and Sykes followed and sat heavily on his feet. 'Now, how did your call home go?' He lifted a brow. 'Was it as bad as you expected?'

'Not really,' said Eleanor, pouring out the tea.

'You don't sound too sure. Never mind, you're over the worst hurdle. Thank you.' He accepted his cup of tea. 'What did you find out?'

Eleanor took her own cup over to the window, her back to him, and sat on the chair there, looking pensively out. She made herself talk slowly, but still stumbled over the words which had seemed relatively easy back there in the kitchen as she had rehearsed them.

'I found out enough to know that it wasn't any one person or thing, rather a series of events, almost an inevitability about the whole thing. Of course, the beginning was Kate, nothing can alter that, and the fact that the Slades know your family—we should have done something, there and then, with Margot, we really should have, Edward.'

'We've already agreed on that,' he said briefly, 'and recriminations are useless.'

She took a deep breath and continued more steadily: 'Do you remember telling me that I could decide whether or not to tell Kate that it was you who had provided the eighty pounds? Well, I thought and thought, and in the end decided I would tell her. I was so thankful and deeply grateful to you, Edward,' she felt her colour rise and carried on quickly: 'I felt that she should know who it was had helped her out of the mess. I think she'd have guessed in the end anyway. I told her you didn't want any thanks, that I had thanked you on her behalf.' She shot him a look over her shoulder and saw that he was lying back, eyes closed, his face telling her nothing of his thoughts. She kept her voice as expressionless as she could. 'I should have explained in more detail, I'm afraid. I didn't say that I was working for you to pay it back. Rightly or wrongly I thought that Kate ought to do something in that direction—oh, not for the money, but for her own good, and I knew she would be more likely to do that if she thought that she was indebted to you. So I just told her there was no hurry and no need to worry. I see now that it was a mistake. I'd forgotten how old-fashioned we Ferrers are. You see, in her relief that everything was going to be all right, Kate confessed to the parents.'

'Good heavens! Why on earth couldn't she have done so in the first place?' demanded Edward.

Eleanor shrugged. 'The reasons she didn't still applied. All she had to do was confess, not ask for money.'

'Go on,' he drawled. 'Why was it a mistake?'

'It will be difficult for you to understand, I think. You'll have to put yourself into a hard-up parson's family to do so.' She frowned, seeking the right words. 'To us, Edward, eighty pounds is a great deal of money, and a great deal of money to *give* anyone. The fact that you did so, to me, seemed an enormous gesture, and a significant one.' She gave him another swift glance. 'Your generosity could only be attributed to one thing.' She swallowed. 'That you . . . loved me and . . .'

'Considered myself to be part of the family already,' he murmured lazily, a flicker of amusement showing as he saw her look of surprise. 'Go on,' he prompted again.

'There's not much more to tell. They waited for me to say something in my letters home and when I didn't my mother wrote slightly ambiguously to yours, which set your mother thinking . . .'

'I'll bet it did!'

'... and then she must have met up with Margot Slade. Your mother rang back home and they more or less confirmed each other's theories. Anyway, what with one thing and another, your mother ...'

'Took over and planned to force the love-birds out into the open in her own indomitable way—the success of which we know only too well!' Edward rose and took up his briefcase lying on the table. 'We're no better off for knowing, but it tidies things up. We can write finis across the whys and wherefores. And as you say, it all apears remarkably predictable.' While he was talking in that slightly mocking way he had, Edward reached inside the briefcase and brought out a small box. 'There's one thing more to complete the picture. Luckily Van helped with your finger size, I hope it fits.' He held out his hand for her own. Eleanor looked first at the box and then at his face and said in an appalled voice:

'I don't ... I hadn't thought there'd be a ring!'

The seconds stretched out between them.

Edward said: 'If there's an engagement, there's a ring, Eleanor. You know what a stickler I am for efficiency and authenticity, and you've gone this far, you can't balk at a little thing like a ring!' He held it to the light. 'I thought you'd like an antique setting, and rubies seemed appropriate. It didn't cost the earth, I hasten to add, in case you should feel guilty for my bank balance—although I quite realise that money, in the ordinary sense, wouldn't count with you.'

'What do you mean?' asked Eleanor, lifting startled eyes to his face.

He gave his familiar twisted smile. 'I haven't known you all these weeks without learning something of the way you feel. You love beautiful things, but people count with you.' He slipped the ring on her finger before she could protest. 'Good. It fits.' He studied her hand for a moment. 'Do you like it?'

'It's very beautiful,' she said quietly, seeing her hand in Edward's and the deep red stone on her finger in a peculiarly detached way. 'Why were rubies appropriate?' she asked suddenly.

'Mmm...?' He dropped her hand and walked away, saying carelessly: 'Oh, there's a proverb, more than one, about rubies ... but your red dress probably instigated the choice.' He turned. 'I can change it if you ...'

'No! I like it, truly, and anyway ... it doesn't really matter, does it? I mean, I won't be wearing it for very long, will I? It's not as if ... it means anything.'

'Exactly,' he said laconically. Eleanor bit her lip and plunged on.

'Edward, there's something else you must know. My parents' first thought, when Katie told them who had provided the money, was to scrape some from somewhere and send it to you. Kate persuaded them to wait until they heard from me, they were reluctant, but agreed. I ... explained about my job and they feel rather better about it all, but I have to pass on their thanks to you.' She took a swift look at his face. 'I know you don't want their gratitude, but I'm afraid you'll have to put up with it. My father is telephoning this evening. W—will you speak with him, Edward?'

'Oh, yes, I'll do what's expected.' He looked at his watch. 'We'll drive over to the Crescent and I'll wait while you change into your slinky red number, and then we'll go and eat.' He gazed at her critically. 'I have the feeling you haven't done much of that today, and some exquisite French cooking at a small restaurant I know seems in order. We'll try and rope Hugh and Vanessa into the scheme, we can pretend we're celebrating the ring. How does that sound?'

It sounded, thought Eleanor, following him out of the flat, as if once Edward took something on, he saw it through to the bitter end. It also sounded as if he didn't want to be alone in her company any more than she did in his.

On the edge of sleep, that night, she sat up in bed and switched on the light. It was ridiculous doing it now, she thought, flicking the pages until she found what she was looking for; tomorrow would have done.

In the once more darkened room, Eleanor closed her eyes, trying again for sleep, but the proverb seemed to be imprinted on her lids.

'Who can find a virtuous woman? for her price is above rubies.'

CHAPTER SEVEN

> 'Oh how bitter a thing it is to look into happiness through another man's eyes.'
>
> *William Shakespeare*

CHRISTMAS was highlighted for Eleanor by a long telephone call home on Christmas morning, but she found herself thrown into a whirl of social events that kept her busy and which, to her surprise, she enjoyed, and the holiday passed quickly. The snow obligingly stayed to make Christmas a white one, but was soon washed away by February rains.

As the weeks passed, Eleanor hoped that she would become used to their pseudo-engagement, but she did not; the strangeness of wearing the ruby ring on her finger was enough to be a constant reminder of the game she was playing.

During business hours it was easy, but when they were with other people and had to pretend it was always a shock when Edward made a loving remark or gesture. However, it was obvious that everyone else accepted the situation as being genuine and looked on with fond and indulgent benignity. Everyone, that is, except Felicity. Once or twice she was included in their arrangements and although she was all honey and sweetness on the outside, the green eyes held a special message for Eleanor which she could not fail to interpret. Miss Maddox was not going to allow a ruby ring to stand in the way of something she wanted.

Vanessa was now working full-time in her own shop, but as Mrs Fellows, the lady who had so conveniently broken her leg, returned, her help was not missed.

One evening in mid-February Edward informed Eleanor that he had organised private art tuition for her. As he chose to tell her this when they were in the company of his parents Eleanor could only murmur a suitable response. However, when Eve and James retired for the night, leaving the two of them alone in the study, Eleanor decided to tackle him further on the subject. They had all been to the theatre and Edward had opted for coffee before driving back to his flat. Eleanor loved the study, with its browns and golds, the mellow wood panelling on the walls making the room warm and masculine. She pulled the heavy curtains across the windows and busied herself with the coffee tray.

Edward lay all his length on the huge settee, having thrown off his evening suit jacket and bow tie, the top of his shirt being comfortably unbuttoned. His hands were behind his head and, eyes closed, he was listening to some Chopin.

'Shall I put another on for you?' Eleanor asked, when the record came to an end.

Edward put his cup on the hearth and relaxed back into his previous indolence. 'No, I don't think so, unless there's something you fancy?' but Eleanor shook her head and carefully replaced the record into its cover.

'By the way, thank you for my rose, Edward,' she said, glancing down at the single red rose on her dress, and feeling a compassion for the half-opened flower quickly unpinned it, slipping it carefully into a small posy bowl filled with early crocus.

'A rose for a Rose,' murmured Edward, and Eleanor, who had hitherto not cared for her second name particularly, thought she might change her mind.

The scene was intimate, peaceful and cosy, and she was loath to break the companionable atmosphere, but she felt compelled to do so, and rather reluctantly began:

'Edward, about these art lessons . . '

'I thought it wouldn't be long before we talked about "these art lessons",' he said lazily, lashes lifting to reveal cool blue eyes.

'You knew jolly well I couldn't say anything in front of

your mother and father,' protested Eleanor indignantly, settling herself on the hearthrug, the flimsy chiffon of her evening dress spreading itself round her like the delicate petals of a blue flower. 'I'm supposed to be working in the shop, not studying art!'

'You can do both, I suppose?'

'If I do that I'll have to take a cut in salary,' she declared firmly.

'Very well.'

She looked at him suspiciously. The reply was carelessly given.

'Now, why have you agreed without a battle?' she asked thoughtfully, and he smiled mockingly.

'I'm an astute business man, my dear.'

'Oh, yes?' she answered sceptically. 'I happen to know that you've paid Mrs Fellows' wages in full all the weeks she's been away with her broken leg. Hardly the action of an astute business man with his eye on his money, would you think?'

'Well, let's say that as we've managed to steer clear of battles for some time now, I want things to remain peaceful for as long as is reasonably possible.'

Eleanor wished she could read his face, but it was shadowed. Should she also bring up the subject of breaking off their engagement? The last time she had tentatively done so he had suggested it should be planned, like a military operation, and said he would let her know when the time was ripe. She hadn't much faith in his suggestion as he had been in a particularly sardonic mood at the time. It had not been mentioned since, and somehow, the evening had been such a happy one she didn't want to spoil it. She took the empty coffee cups back to the tray, still undecided.

'There's a present there on the desk for you,' Edward said casually.

She turned in surprise. 'For me?' and as Edward nodded, she frowned and said worriedly: 'You know we agreed . . .'

'*You* agreed,' he interrupted smoothly, eyes closed once more, hardly interested in her reaction. 'You wouldn't have me labelled Scrooge, would you, Eleanor? I have my reputation to consider, and besides, you shouldn't take away my pleasure by squabbling. Go on, open it,' he ordered carelessly, adding disconcertingly: 'and don't let the fact that it's from me spoil *your* pleasure.'

Eleanor stood quite still, gravely contemplating him. One arm was behind his head, the other hung limply down, resting on the thick, long piled carpet. The rise and fall of his chest was steady and his face was in deep repose. Giving an undecided sigh, she picked up the parcel, which was large and heavy, and brought it back to the hearth, where she knelt to open it. Everyone likes surprises and Eleanor was no exception, and even though she knew she ought not to be receiving presents from Edward, it was exciting pulling off the string and opening up the brown paper. When that had all been dealt with she sat back on her heels, her face lighting up, hands clasped in delight.

'Oh, Edward! Heavens, how marvellous! I'll never be able to live up to it!' and she explored eagerly the boxes of oil paints, brushes, assorted canvases and finally, the collapsible easel.

'Will it do?' he asked lazily.

Eleanor laughed. 'Will it do, indeed!' She turned helplessly to him. 'Edward! Did you buy up the shop?'

The dark lashes lifted. 'No. Just asked for the necessary basics for an up-and-coming young artist.'

'You really believe I can get somewhere, don't you?' she said slowly, a strange and wonderful glow sweeping over her. 'And knowing you, it won't be just any teacher you're sending me to—it will be someone good.'

'Mark Ives,' agreed Edward, smiling faintly at her perception. 'I've already given him some of your work to look at and he's extremely interested in you.'

Her cheeks flushed with pleasure. 'You have? Oh, how good you are, Edward! For someone who doesn't like to be thanked, you make it very difficult for me.'

'I can't bear waste,' he said laconically.

'Then I can't waste my thanks,' Eleanor declared, her natural warmth moving her to lean over and impulsively place soft, tremulous lips to his. Light and brief as the kiss was, contact was shattering. Drawing breathlessly away, her hands supporting her weight on his chest, she gazed wide-eyed into his face, feeling the rapid thumping of his heart, equalling her own, beneath her palms. For a long moment their eyes held and then, with a sharp intake of breath, Edward pulled her to him, crushing her body to his, lips hard and demanding.

With one accord they slid slowly to the floor, bodies compliant and yielding to the obstacles in their path, instinctively supple. They reached their destination, settling on the shaggy-piled hearthrug, and Eleanor's hair fanned out like a halo, the firelight throwing a warm glow on Edward's dark head as he bent over her.

As his kisses became tender, soft, demanding sweet promises, exploring new territories, Eleanor reached the point of no return, now knowing that she loved him. She gave him her lips responsively, innocently and generously declaring her love, thrilling to the strong weight of his body, quivering to his touch.

Afterwards, in the still, small hours of the night, as she lay and tortuously relived those bitter-sweet moments, the memory both thrilled and frightened her, for she had been swept along on a tidal wave where there was no room for sense and reason, and the knowledge overwhelmed her. Had Edward asked, she would have given herself completely to him—and he must have known, could not have failed to know.

What would have happened she couldn't guess ... probably what did happen, without any outside help, for Edward was no callow youth, physically swayed by his emotions against reason. His sense of occasion would have been offended, and his intuitive perception and capability for self-preservation would have brought him to his senses sooner or later.

The telephone finally made them both aware of their surroundings and they lay still for a moment, listening to its shrill ringing. Edward raised himself on to one elbow and looked down into her face, his own suddenly withdrawn and remote, and she closed her eyes, turning away, unwilling for him to read there what her heart desperately longed to tell him. He sat up and reached for the telephone, and through half-closed lids Eleanor watched him hungrily, visually devouring every inch, every facet of him as though she would never be able to look upon him again. She saw him react to whoever was on the other end of the line, answering in murmured monosyllables, once giving a low laugh, his free hand smoothing back the fall of hair from his forehead, then tucking in his shirt that had somehow become adrift, rising to his feet as he did so.

Somehow! She gave an inward hollow laugh, remembering how her hands had revelled in caressing the bare smoothness of his back beneath the crisp cotton of his evening shirt, feeling the lean strength of his body beneath her palms. Remembering this, and how his own had drawn tumultuous feelings from the very depths of her being as they caressed and held her close, swept her with excruciating pain, and she sat up and leaned her head on the arm of the settee, gazing with unseeing eyes into the fire.

She heard the click of the telephone as it was replaced and felt the reverberation of his tread as he returned, sensed the tall, brooding figure looking down at her in the pause that followed.

'The devil with playing a part,' he said at last, 'is that after a while you begin to believe in it.' He reached down and took her hands, gently lifting her to her feet. 'I am, after all, only human, and you are a very attractive leading lady.' As if she were a child, he carefully covered her shoulders, calmly smoothing the neckline of her dress back into place where it had been disarranged, replacing a strand of hair clinging to her cheek and generally putting her together again as new. Eleanor allowed him to do so, knowing she would never be the same again, that all his efforts for normality were useless. As his fingers impersonally touched her skin, icy cold now where so recently she had been afire with his kisses, she wondered whether she had dreamed it all, whether this was the same man who, a few minutes earlier, had been demanding the compliance which she had been so willing to give.

He lifted her chin, forcing her to look into his eyes, observing the effect of his words, and added wryly:

'I should have realised that that warm and generous heart of yours would be the undoing of us both. Gratitude is a dangerous game to play, my dear, and leaves a bitter taste in the mouth.'

She raised her eyes, looking at him properly for the first time, and contemplated him gravely.

'Then we won't play that game, Edward,' she replied, marvelling at her composure, 'for it would be a shame to spoil our newly-found peace, wouldn't it?' She smiled faintly. 'Don't worry, Edward, I do know the rules of the game, you know.'

'Do you, Eleanor?' Edward said heavily, holding her look and frowning slightly. She nodded and picked up his tie which he had cast aside earlier in the evening.

'May I?' she asked, holding it up. 'I'm quite good at it, you'll find.' She reached up and gave a laugh. 'You'll have to sit, Edward, you're too tall for me.' He sat on the arm of the settee and allowed her to skilfully tie his bow tie, first of all doing up the two top buttons.

'I think you have a set of rules all of your own, Eleanor,' he murmured, as her fingers touched his neck and her hair swung against his face.

'Oh, I don't think so,' she replied, stepping back to admire her handiwork. 'I'm not at all unique, and you know there are lots of your girl-friends who would be able to do your tie just as well.'

'And you don't consider yourself one of my girl-friends,' stated Edward evenly.

'No,' Eleanor said thoughtfully, and gave another small smile. 'I can't classify myself as one. A girl-friend implies freedom of choice. Everything we've done together you've been coerced into.' She flicked him a quick look and his face was inscrutable, his eyes dark and hooded. 'I do know how awful it's been for you, Edward, having to put up with me. It must be a bore, and a strain on your other friendships. Can we put an end to our engagement now, do you think?'

At her words Edward paused in his task of shrugging on his jacket and looked at her steadily.

'We must discuss it some time,' he agreed, his voice sounding suddenly tired, 'but not tonight.'

'Very well.' She looked round for her shoes, which had somehow become lost. Somehow. No, she wouldn't think of that, not here, not when she was doing so well, keeping her pride intact.

'That was Felicity on the phone,' said Edward, handing her the shoes.

'Oh, yes?' she responded, with just the right amount of interest, thinking how ironic that it should have been Felicity who had brought them both back to their senses. Almost prophetic, although she didn't believe in such things.

'She was confirming the house-party at her place next weekend. Van and Hugh have also been invited.'

'That will be fun.' The shoes, strappy evening sandals and very fiddling, were finally on, and she turned to him with a smile. 'Goodnight, Edward. Thank you for my present. I shall have to work hard and show you that I deserve your faith in me.'

'Goodnight, Eleanor. I'll see to the fire and the lights.'

With a swirl of blue chiffon she swiftly left the room.

The following morning was filled with resolutions. Forget Edward. Forget Mark Ives and the chance to study. Go home.

The day suited her mood, being dismally wet and turbulent. When she reached the shop, Eleanor found that Edward had gone to Paris, but he had left the address of Mark Ives on the pad, together with other instructions pertaining to her job. She wasn't very busy and was glad when Mrs Mansel came in, later on in the morning, bringing with her some new stock which she had recently purchased at a sale.

Eve looked at her closely. 'My dear girl, you look tired to death! You shouldn't let my thoughtless son keep you up so late in future!' She smiled and patted her cheek fondly.

'It's time you two were married and in your own house, instead of having to pack the old fogies off to bed so that you can have some peace together.'

Eleanor smiled wanly and murmured that she was all right. Eve pursed her lips.

'I've put a great restraint upon myself and not asked questions—but have you set a date yet?'

Eleanor swallowed painfully and felt her cheeks redden. 'No. We thought we'd let Kate get hers over with first.'

'Well, don't keep Edward waiting too long, my dear. He's not the most patient of men. I'm surprised he hasn't rushed you to the altar before now.' She looked sharply at her. 'In fact, I've never believed I'd get Edward into a church for a full wedding. You aren't tiptoeing off to the Registrar's Office and doing it on the sly, are you?'

Eleanor forced a laugh and shook her head. Eve always made her feel terrible, the guilt lying heavily where she was concerned. So obviously delighted with their engagement, she was in for a bitter disappointment when it was broken off, and that must be soon. But she could not do anything until she had discussed it with Edward, and he was not available. One part of her bemoaned the delay, while the other, the weak feminine part, was glad, ridiculously glad that she had a legitimate excuse to stay on a little longer—how humiliating love could be!

Eve clucked like a mother hen all morning over her washed-out appearance and persuaded Eleanor to go home and rest that afternoon, convinced the girl was about to sicken for something. Eleanor thought ruefully that she had already sickened and fallen, and would have liked to assure her kindly hostess that hearts did not stop beating no matter how bruised they were.

She knew she wouldn't sleep, even though she was consumed with weariness, for her mind was over-active, a jumble of questions and answers. She decided to do something constructive and washed her hair, finishing it off by sitting near the fire, drying it, Sykes at her feet.

The bull-terrier hated Edward's absences and to her surprise attached himself to her and condescended to be comforted. Eleanor knew very well that as soon as his master returned he would switch his allegiance immediately, but she was ridiculously touched and welcomed his heavy weight on her legs. Her hair was nearly dry when the door bell rang and Hickman's steady step along the hall could be heard. Eleanor listened to the voices and was ready with a warm smile as the door opened.

'Hullo, Hugh, do come in. I'm so pleased to see you, I was getting lonely and in the doldrums.' She glanced over his shoulder at Hickman, who was waiting in the background. 'May we have tea, please, Hickman, with some of those lovely pastries that Mrs Hickman excels herself with?'

'I thought I could depend upon you, Eleanor,' said Hugh comfortably, as Hickman disappeared. He closed the door, took off his coat and joined her at the fire, rubbing his hands and holding them out to the flames appreciatively. Seating himself in a nearby chair, he took off his glasses, which were rain-splattered, and wiped them on his handkerchief.

'What a miserable day,' he observed. 'Why are you lonely? Where is everyone?'

'I'm not supposed to be here myself,' confessed Eleanor, 'but Mrs Mansel has sent me home, with orders to rest. I feel a fraud, really, as I'm all right, only a little tired. Edward is away, he's had to go to France.'

'And you miss him,' stated Hugh quietly.

Eleanor felt herself colour. 'Sykes too, poor old thing,' she replied, scratching the dog's ear.

'I thought Vanessa might be here. I rang her shop, but Ron Mann said she was out, gone to a sale some hours ago.'

'Yes, that's right, I remember now. Ron was going over to relieve her,' said Eleanor. 'She was going to fly to this sale and . . .'

'Fly?' Hugh put on his glasses, and replaced his handkerchief, frowning slightly.

'So you see, you're a welcome visitor. I haven't seen you since . . .'

'Are you *sure* that Vanessa's flying?' Hugh demanded, not listening, his question making her aware that he was no longer sitting relaxed in his chair.

'Why, yes, I think so,' she began, and seeing the look on his face continued uncertainly: 'I understood her to say that there was something special she wanted at this particular sale.' She frowned, trying to remember. 'Somewhere in Oxfordshire, I can't think of the exact place.' Her anxiety was growing. 'What is it, Hugh?'

He crossed to the window, peering out, his usually impassive face stern. 'It's not flying weather, not for small craft.' He turned abruptly. 'When did she go?'

'Early this morning, I think. The weather wasn't too bad then.' Eleanor hesitated, but he'd have to know sooner or later. 'Philip Nolan picked her up and they went straight to the aerodrome.'

A pulse flickered in Hugh's temple as he stood silent for a moment. Taking another look out of the window, he walked to the telephone and began to dial.

'Perhaps they decided against going,' suggested Eleanor, although not very hopefully, knowing Vanessa.

'Perhaps,' Hugh replied briefly.

'Or if the weather worsened, they might have decided not to fly back.'

Hugh didn't reply and after a few seconds of intent listening, replaced the telephone. 'The weather forecast is more rain, visibility poor with high winds, no change in outlook.' He began to re-dial. Eleanor heard Hickman outside and went to the door to take the tray from him, smiling her thanks. She placed it on a low table and began to pour out. She could hear Hugh's voice, short and clipped, asking for information about Vanessa's flight.

'What do they say?' she asked uneasily, trying not to listen to the rain beating on the windows.

'It was touch and go whether they went, the weather was fair at that time, but it seems that with Vanessa's usual impetuous manner she prevailed upon Nolan to take a chance on conditions staying the same.' His voice showed exasperated anger. 'Why on earth Nolan didn't refuse ...'

'He must have thought it safe,' said Eleanor gently. 'And we don't know what's happened the other end.'

'If the luck holds out once it should never be pushed further. Wretched girl! To risk her life for such a paltry reason! I knew something like this would happen some day. It was just a question of time.'

'What sort of pilot is Philip?' asked Eleanor, handing him a cup. 'A good one?'

'One hopes so,' said Hugh grimly, absently taking a drink. 'He'll need to be on a day like this.' He walked to the window and looked out again into the abnormally dark afternoon. 'I'm sure the wind's rising.' The telephone rang and Hugh clattered down his cup and crossed quickly to answer it.

Eleanor began to feel very worried now. If calm, dependable Hugh was panicking, then things must be serious. His face was brooding as he returned to her side.

'That was the aerodrome again. They've made inquiries and it seems they took off for the return journey. If everything went according to plan, they should have been back an hour ago.'

Eleanor shivered. 'What can we do?' she asked miserably.

'Nothing. Just wait.' Now that Hugh knew the worst he seemed calmer and completely in control, although his face was drawn and set. They drank the tea, but food was unthinkable, and twenty minutes of desultory conversation seemed interminable, and when the telephone rang, making them both jump, they sprang to their feet and Hugh snatched it up. He listened, a frown on his face, answering in monosyllables. Eleanor stood by his side, a hand on his arm, fearing the worst. When the call was finished, he took her hand.

'They're all right. They had to make a forced landing and Nolan's broken a couple of ribs and they're keeping him in a nearby hospital. God knows how she made them, but Vanessa was allowed to return to London on the understanding that she had medical attention. She must have begged a lift in. That was the Social Worker from Guy's asking for someone to fetch her. She has cuts and bruises and a suspected broken wrist.'

Eleanor fell into his arms and burst into tears of relief, laughing even as she did so.

'Hugh, how awful it's been! Poor Van. You'll go to her?'

'Yes.' He handed her his handkerchief and she wiped her eyes, saying ruefully: 'How predictably feminine I am!' She tucked the linen back into his top pocket. Hugh glanced at his watch before putting on his coat, saying reassuringly:

'It will take me at least an hour.'

'Give her my love.'

He smiled briefly and felt in his pockets for his car keys. 'A similar thing happened to me not so long ago, although we didn't crash. It's nerve-racking. She'll probably have delayed shock, so have her bed warmed and she can go straight up if necessary. I'll be as quick as I can.'

At the window, Eleanor watched the Porsche out of sight and then settled down to wait. As the room darkened she switched on a small lamp, preferring the room to be subdued, suiting her mood. Her vigilance was at last rewarded as Hugh's car drew up outside again. She saw him get out and open the passenger door, and then Vanessa emerged, her arm in a sling. Eleanor ran to the front door before they had time to ring.

'Van darling, how thankful I am you're all right!' she exclaimed.

Vanessa gave her a tremulous smile and walked on ahead into the lounge. Eleanor, aghast at the whiteness of her face, looked at Hugh, who was hovering in the doorway. 'She looks dreadful,' she whispered in dismay.

'The wrist is broken, and they want her back at the hospital tomorrow for the permanent plaster. I'll call for her.' Hugh was most un-Hugh-like, his own face was colourless and his manner stiff and forced. 'Get her to bed, Eleanor, will you?' He hesitated, said a short 'goodnight' and left abruptly. Eleanor closed the door, wondering at the oddity of his manner, and hurried into the room after

Vanessa, who was standing gazing into the fire, her body drooping wearily.

'Hugh was most peculiar,' Eleanor began, and then seeing Vanessa's face, said gently: 'What is it, darling? Are you in pain?'

Vanessa turned despairing eyes to her and gave a bitter laugh.

'Oh, I'm in pain, but not quite the sort you mean!' Her face crumpled and she fought for control. 'Do you remember me once saying that I wanted to make Hugh angry, just once, to see what it was like? Well, now I know.'

'Do sit down, Van, I'm sure you should,' urged Eleanor, and Vanessa sank to the carpet, brushing her good hand wearily across her eyes. 'Does your head ache?' Eleanor asked, kneeling by her side.

Vanessa gave a mixture of a sob and a laugh. 'It does, but not as much as my heart! Poor old heart! Oh, Nell, you should have heard him! So cold and polite—not Hugh at all!'

'He was worried, Van, we both were. We didn't know what had happened to you for ages.'

'I tried to tease him out of it,' continued Vanessa dully, 'I usually can, and he lost his temper and said the most awful things—and then I lost mine.' Sobs shook her.

'You care what Hugh thinks of you, don't you?' Eleanor said softly.

Vanessa wiped her tears, little girl fashion, on the sleeve of her jumper, and said crossly:

'Oh, yes, that's the ridiculous part of it—the laugh of the year! You've guessed, of course, and I don't mind you knowing.' She shot Eleanor a guilty look and said hurriedly: 'I was pleased about you and Edward for your own sakes, but there was part of me that was thankful you were no longer free. I thought Hugh might fall for you, you see, and I wouldn't have blamed him, you'd suit him much better than I would.'

'I don't love Hugh, you idiot,' retorted Eleanor firmly, 'and he doesn't love me. I like him enormously—although the way he's upset you now, I'm not so sure.'

'Don't blame him, Nell. He was right in everything he said.' Vanessa thrust a hand through her hair. 'He was so blisteringly angry, I didn't dream he could be.'

'He'd no business to go on at you when you've been through all this. I'm surprised at him,' said Eleanor wonderingly, 'especially as he was telling me earlier that something similar had happened to himself. He should have known . . .'

'It was then that I first knew how I felt about him,' broke in Vanessa. 'He was with Edward and they were missing for two hours in fog. I was worried about Edward, of course, but suddenly I realised how desperate I was for Hugh, and I'd known him all my life!' She turned to Eleanor, who was again shocked at the sight of her face. An ugly bruise was beginning to show up on her forehead and she was deathly pale. Eleanor wanted to suggest that Vanessa went to bed, but knew that now she had begun to talk, she had to finish.

'What did you do then?' Eleanor prompted gently.

'Oh, I tried to tell myself I'd imagined it all—it rather knocked me for six. I began to go out with anyone, as an antidote, but it didn't work—in fact, it only made things worse. And I knew how hopeless it all was. Hugh sees me as a little girl, he knows me too well. Then you arrived and I was beastly to you. I was so wrapped up in myself that I couldn't be bothered, and then you got on so well with him, I could hardly bear it, I was so jealous. He treated you as an adult, he only indulged me. What made it harder was that I began to like you.' She sighed. 'There's a refreshing honesty about you, Nell, I couldn't help liking you, the same, I suppose, as Edward couldn't help loving you.' She smiled wearily. 'You do see how complicated my life was? Anyway, it was then that I decided to change my tactics. I concentrated on old Phil, the same age group as Hugh, to see if that would make him realise that I was no longer a child. There was no chance of hurting Phil, his heart's already engaged elsewhere, only she's in America at the moment. He fitted the bill beautifully.'

'And did it make Hugh realise, do you think?'

Vanessa hesitated. 'I don't know. Sometimes when we were out together I thought so, but it was probably wishful thinking. He certainly made it quite clear today that he considers me a spoilt child who wants her bottom spanking and sending straight to bed.' She rose and walked restlessly round the room. 'There's something else that will make you laugh. This sale we went to today—it was for one particular lot.' She rummaged awkwardly in her handbag and brought out a packet, handing it to Eleanor who opened it carefully. 'It's a snuffbox, a special one, as you can see,' Vanessa continued apathetically. 'I was going to give it to him when . . . if ever . . . well, you can see what I mean,' and she gave a short, bitter laugh.

Eleanor did see what the gift represented, taking in the delicate heart design entwined all over the box. 'It's beautiful, Van,' she said gently.

Vanessa shrugged. 'So that's that!' Tears were streaming relentlessly down her cheeks. 'Oh, blow! Take no notice of me, Nell, only I'm so fed up.'

Eleanor went to her. 'Of course you are, love. Why don't you let me help you to bed? You'll feel much better. Has the hospital given you anything?'

Vanessa nodded and brought out a small box of pills.

'Good,' carried on Eleanor, 'they'll be to help you sleep, I expect.' She paused as something caught her eye out of the window. 'Why, surely that's Hugh's car? Has he forgotten something, do you think?'

'What?' Vanessa turned a startled face and peered out. 'Yes, it is! Nell, he's coming in! I don't want to see him—I can't see him! What shall I do?' she gripped Eleanor in a panic, but it was too late for escape. The bell was rung and Hickman was answering it. Vanessa, halfway across the room in flight, dropped with a stifled sob to her knees by the fire, her back to the door. Eleanor stood helplessly by the window, not knowing what to do for the best.

Hugh came in, closed the door behind him and walked slowly over to Vanessa, looking down at her.

'Van? My dear, I'm so sorry. I shouldn't have gone on at

you like that, it was inexcusable of me. Will you forgive me?'

Vanessa, cradling her injured arm, head bent low in order that he should not see her tear-stained face, whispered:

'It doesn't matter.'

'It does. Your forgiveness matters a great deal. I was halfway home before I came to my senses. I turned right round and came back, as you can see, wholly repentant, my only excuse being that anger is a normal follow-up to relief.'

'There's nothing to forgive,' Vanessa said in a rush, voice a little stronger. 'Everything you said was true. Honestly, Hugh, it's all right.'

'You're very generous, my dear.' He hesitated. 'And to cap it all, I seem to remember you saying that you'd gone to that damned sale on my behalf.'

'No,' denied Vanessa, adding more calmly: 'No, you were mistaken.'

'Even when I'm angry,' he said thoughtfully, 'I have a remarkably good memory.'

Vanessa swallowed hard. 'I might originally have bought it for you, but I've changed my mind.'

'I see. I get my just deserts. May I, at least, see it?'

'No!' replied Vanessa fiercely, tears beginning to stream again, and she stumbled to her feet, making a belated escape. Hugh caught sight of her face and gave a muttered exclamation, catching hold of her as she went to pass.

'Don't cry, Vanessa my dear, I can't bear it. You make me feel so guilty,' and he gave her his handkerchief which she grabbed gratefully, her shoulders beginning to heave. 'Please don't,' he repeated gently.

'It's not that,' sobbed Vanessa crossly, furious for breaking down and determined to put him straight. 'You ... you mustn't feel guilty. I deserved everything you said and if Edward had been here he would have acted j—just the s—same. You know you've always been like a s—second b—brother to me,' and she ended on a sobbing hiccough.

'The hell with that!' exclaimed Hugh vehemently, abruptly releasing her and moving away. 'I'll tell you now, Vanessa, that it's a long time since I've felt brotherly to you!' and then he saw the snuffbox on the table where Eleanor had placed it.

As the words and the manner in which they were spoken penetrated, Vanessa turned to him, trying to control herself, and followed his gaze. She stood rooted to the spot, holding her breath, while a dull red crept swiftly across her face.

Hugh tilted his head and looked at her gravely, before returning his attention to examination of the box. After a moment he picked it up and carefully studied it, his voice reflective.

'Late eighteenth century, I'd say at a guess . . . good condition, rose quartz set in gold mount . . . most probably a betrothal gift.' He placed it carefully back on to the table and moved across to her, holding her gaze, until he was very close. 'May I have my present now . . . Vanessa my love?'

Vanessa nodded, suddenly enchantingly shy.

'Good,' said Hugh softly, 'because I have every intention of taking it,' and tenderly holding her face between his hands, he kissed her.

Eleanor felt as though she had been holding her breath for ever and said despairingly:

'You won't forget that I'm still here, will you?'

Hugh and Vanessa turned, both looking slightly dazed. Hugh said mildly:

'So you are, but we hardly gave you a chance to disappear, did we?'

'I daren't, I might have spoilt everything! What a pair of idiots you've been,' she teased, giving them both a warm embrace.

'We have, haven't we?' agreed Hugh, carefully wiping Vanessa's cheeks.

'Darling Nell,' said Vanessa tremulously, 'I can't believe this is happening!'

'It is,' Hugh told her firmly, looking anxiously at her wan face. 'I think you ought to go to bed, you look worn out. May I leave her in your care, Eleanor?'

'I shan't sleep,' declared Vanessa, giving an involuntary yawn. They laughed.

'I'll go and organise a hot drink,' suggested Eleanor, adding demurely: 'and you can have suitable privacy for saying goodbye.'

'Thank you,' replied Hugh gravely, 'we appreciate your tact.'

When Eleanor returned Hugh had gone and Vanessa was sitting with a dreamy expression on her face. She accepted the cup with a grateful smile and said thoughtfully:

'Isn't life amazing? It doesn't seem possible that one can be desperately miserable one minute and in the next be as blissfully happy!' She yawned and gave a laugh. 'I suppose I am awake?'

'Well, you're not dreaming, or if you are, then I am too,' Eleanor told her affectionately. 'Come on—to bed, Hugh's orders.'

'Goodness, I'm feeling hopelessly shaky!' And Vanessa clung to her friend as they climbed the stairs. Finally tucked up in bed, she said sleepily: 'Thanks, Nell, I couldn't have managed on my own.' She turned a comic face. 'Oh lord! What on earth will Mother say? Both her offspring to be married! She'll be speechless!' She yawned again. 'Night, Nell. I'm awfully happy.'

Eleanor switched off the light. 'Goodnight, Van. I'm so glad things have turned out well for you.' She closed the door quietly and made her way thoughtfully down the stairs. As she entered the lounge, Sykes lifted his head and his tail quivered in a greeting. Eleanor sank down beside him and the dog moved fractionally and laid his head on her lap.

'You'll be glad when your master's back, won't you, boy?' She stroked him gently and he closed his eyes, snoring intermittently. 'So shall I,' she murmured. For Vanessa was wrong about one thing. Eve Mansel would be planning only one wedding. The other had to be broken off ... and the sooner the better.

Henry, the tortoise-shell cat, was missing. After a whole day of non-appearance, Eleanor was convinced that something had happened. It was so unlike him to stay away for long without returning to be fed, and she wandered round the Mews, whistling and calling, but to no avail. When he didn't turn up the next day either she began to be really concerned. Eleanor had become very fond of the tortoise-shell—too fond. She would miss him when she left, but it was no good trying to change her nature ... she needed someone to lavish love and affection upon and Henry fitted the bill. He, in his turn, visibly blossomed, no longer qualifying for the term 'mangy'. Whether Henry returned her feelings or whether regular meals were the attraction was a debatable point. And now he was missing.

Nor was Henry her only concern. It was Friday. Edward had been away for four days and it was unknown whether he would arrive back in time to take Eleanor down to Felicity's house-party that weekend. Vanessa and Hugh were insisting that if this happened, then she was to go down with them. This dashed Eleanor's hopes that she would be able to miss the visit altogether, for the last thing she wanted to do was to spend two whole days in the company of Felicity Maddox, especially as she had decided that it was to be this weekend that Edward took his ring back. When he did so, she wanted to put a great number of miles between herself and Miss Maddox.

These thoughts were running through her head as she made her way back to the Mews late that evening. She had been visiting Maisie and returning home by tube, suddenly decided to make a detour and go to the shop. It was an impulsive decision and a daft one, she admitted. Henry wasn't a mollycoddled cat who couldn't take care of himself, but an erstwhile alley-cat, who knew all the tricks of the trade—one of which was to inveigle himself into the warm heart of a softie like herself.

There was no sign of Henry waiting in his usual place in the porchway, and to satisfy a niggling doubt that he might have been accidentally locked inside somewhere, she found her key and let herself in. Even as her hand went out to the light she remembered that the mains were off for the night.

'Drat it!' she muttered, fumbling for the burglar alarm switch, having no desire to be mistaken for an intruder. She opened the back door to the shop, ignoring the stairs leading up to Edward's flat, and stepped into the kitchen. By the light of the window she half-heartedly opened first a broom and then a store cupboard, calling the cat's name softly. It didn't surprise her to have no answering furry form wind itself round her ankles, she had been continually passing in and out of the kitchen area over the last couple of days and would certainly have heard Henry's cries to be let out. The only place she had had no cause to go to was the cellar, which opened off the back of the showroom, under the stairs. Feeling her way cautiously across the shop floor, she found the cellar door and opened it, calling out 'Henry!' quite sharply into the dark void below. Ears straining for the slightest sound, she sighed. It was no good; she would have to go down and look properly. She fumbled back to the kitchen, loath to go up to the flat to switch on the lights at the mains, and found a box of matches. She returned to the cellar and struck one carefully, finding the top step by its tiny flickering flame.

'Honestly,' she said crossly to herself, as she felt her way down the stone steps, 'I could be fast asleep in bed by now instead of . . .' Her foot encountered something unexpected, a draught of fresh air wafted out the flame, her balance went and she fell.

She lay winded, an excruciating pain in her head, which she had struck on the iron rail on her way down, and in her wrist, which took the first impact against the cellar floor. She could not be certain how long it was before she was aware that the lights had gone on in the shop and that Edward was saying urgently:

'What the devil's going on?' She heard his footsteps clattering down the stone steps as she blinked at the sudden light, heard his startled: 'Eleanor!' followed by a series of colourful oaths under his breath as he saw her sit up. 'What the hell do you think you're doing, prowling around in the dark like this, woman! No wonder you fell! What a damned fool thing to do! Are you hurt?' he demanded as he helped her to her feet.

'Please don't shout, Edward ... my head aches ...'

'I should think it does—there's a bump on your forehead as big as an egg,' he replied grimly, and scooped her up into his arms.

'I'm sure I can walk,' protested Eleanor feebly, but for all that, content to rest her head on his shoulder, nausea coming over her in waves. She felt somewhat better lying flat on Edward's sofa, vaguely aware that he was telephoning, and then a cold, wet flannel was placed on her forehead and she was told to lie still. She was quite happy to do so.

Edward disappeared downstairs to secure the premises and on his return she opened her eyes and said disarmingly:

'I didn't think you would be back until tomorrow.'

'It's a good job I managed to hustle things. You could still be down there now,' Edward retorted, switching on the gas fire.

'Oh, no,' she protested. 'I only slipped a few of the steps. What did I trip over?'

'A roll of carpet,' he replied, frowning down at her.

'The match blew out,' she offered meekly.

'When I opened the outside door, probably. You really are a little idiot, Eleanor. Ah, this sounds like the doctor!'

'I'm sure I don't need a doctor,' she began, but gave up.

When the doctor left, her wrist was bound and in a sling, and she had been given a thorough examination. Edward returned from showing him out, saying crisply:

'He thinks the wrist is only a sprain, he wants it and your head x-rayed tomorrow morning. Any signs of sickness and he's to be sent for.' He mixed himself a drink and downed it in one swift gulp.

'He told me he didn't think I was concussed,' murmured Eleanor, adding: 'You look tired, Edward. Have you had a wearying trip?'

'Stop trying to change the subject,' Edward replied

firmly, sitting down opposite. 'What were you doing down the cellar?'

She gave him a sideways look through her lashes. 'Didn't the doctor say I was too ill to be questioned?' she asked hopefully, and Edward's lips twitched.

'No, he did not, my girl. Come on, out with it.'

She sighed and eased her bruises. 'You'll be cross.'

'I'm quite sure I shall be, but don't let that deter you.'

'I should love a cup of tea.'

'You shall have one when you've said your piece.'

'You really are a bully, Edward, aren't you? Oh, all right! I came because of Henry.'

His face went blank for a few seconds.

'Henry? Don't you mean Joe?'

It was her turn to be puzzled. 'Joe? No, of course not. I mean Henry. The cat.'

'The cat?' He rose abruptly and moved to replenish his drink. 'Oh! Henry!' He rubbed the back of his neck irritably. 'I knew that damned cat would cause trouble.' There was a pause, and then: 'What about Henry?' he prompted, back still turned.

'He's missing, he's been gone for two days. I was worried and wondered if he could have been accidentally locked . . .'

'. . . in the cellar. Yes, that sounds like you, Eleanor.' He crossed back, shaking his head in wonder. 'Why, in heaven's name, didn't you turn on the lights?'

'Well, it meant coming up here and I thought I could manage with a match, and I would too if Ron hadn't put that carpet on the stairs. It wasn't there the last time I looked.'

'Nevertheless it's there now,' said Edward repressively. He gave a heavy sigh. 'Oh, well, it could have been worse, I suppose. You were lucky you didn't break your neck, my girl.'

'I know,' admitted Eleanor humbly.

'You're a menace.'

'I know.'

Edward gave an exasperated bark of laughter. 'Don't you dare go all subservient, Eleanor, or you'll tempt me to give you a shaking! I will now go and fetch you that cup of tea. If you can manage to stagger to the bathroom, a wash wouldn't come amiss.'

They timed their arrival back into the room in unison. Edward scrutinised her critically.

'You're going to have a lovely bruise. How do you feel, walking?'

'A bit stiff, but not too bad. Er ... Edward?'

He looked up from pouring out the tea and eyed her warily: 'Yes?'

'You know I said I came to look for Henry ... well, he isn't Henry any more ... I've just found him in the airing cupboard with six kittens,' and she bit her lip to stop herself from laughing at the comical expression on his face.

Edward covered his face with a hand, and after a moment's thought, looked up.

'So Henry has kittens. How very remarkable! No wonder he gained weight. And just how long do you think he'll occupy my airing cupboard?'

'I'm not sure,' said Eleanor apologetically. 'We shall have to move him eventually, of course, but at the moment he's comfortable. It's warm in there, you see, and he's tucked himself away so cleverly at the bottom corner that ...'

'Let him stay,' Edward declared with a philosophical wave of the hand. 'God knows what Sykes will do, and have you considered the delightful prospect of taking a shower with seven pairs of eyes looking on? Slightly unnerving, don't you think?'

Eleanor gave a splutter of laughter. 'Oh, Edward, you are funny!' and he smiled, a real one, the alluring and elusive dimple very much in evidence, and she found herself smiling idiotically back. For a few moments happiness spread over her, giving her a sense of well-being, and then she remembered what she had to say.

He lifted a brow above shrewd eyes. 'What is it?' he asked, and seeing her look of surprise, said impatiently: 'Your face is an open book ... here, drink this tea while it's hot and tell me what you have to say.'

Eleanor gulped the tea gratefully and Edward settled himself, eyes on her face. Discarding the empty cup, she began hesitantly:

'Edward, may we end our engagement, please?' She took a deep breath. 'I know we decided to wait until after Kate's wedding, but that's only three weeks away and I find I can't go through the pretence any longer. I think you'll be relieved too.' She shot him a quick glance and hurried on 'I'm very . . . gratefu . . .' her voice shook over the word, 'I appreciate everything you've done, and know how you must have hated it, how much it must have inconvenienced you. If we finish now it will let you off having to come home with me. The . . . eighty pounds is paid off now, isn't it?'

There was silence and she chanced another swift look, dropping her eyes as she met Edward's hooded contemplation. When he spoke, his voice was matter-of-fact.

'As you wish. There's one suggestion I would make. I can understand your reluctance to take me along to the wedding, but don't make the break between us official until after it. Your parents will have enough on their minds without worrying over you, and they will if they think things aren't right with you.'

Eleanor turned a troubled face to him. 'But that means I'll still have to go on pretending.'

'Easier to do on your own.' He eyed the engagement ring that she was twisting back and forth. 'You can keep that, as a memento.'

She stared at him. 'I can't do that.'

'Keep it, give it away, throw it in the back of a drawer—I have no use for it.'

Eleanor had no intention of doing any of these things, but her head was aching so badly now that she didn't argue. Instead, she said doubtfully: 'How shall I explain your absence?'

He shrugged. 'An unexpected business trip, no doubt I can arrange something to satisfy this end too.' He looked at her closely. 'It's late. I think it would be as well for you to stay tonight. Our friend the doctor advised as little disturbance as possible and there's a spare bed here. There's some night things and a new toothbrush in the bathroom linen cupboard—and the clothes *are* Van's, should you think otherwise.'

Eleanor flushed vividly and said: 'I didn't suppose them to be anyone else's, and if they were, it's none of my business. Thank you, I would prefer to stay, I don't fancy travelling back to the Crescent.' She swung her legs to the floor and rose gingerly, giving Edward a reassuring smile as he watched her frowningly. She hesitated before leaving him and said reluctantly: 'Shall I have to go to Felicity's tomorrow?'

'We'll see how you are, shall we?' Edward replied evenly. 'I don't particularly wish to upset the arrangements, but if you're not fit then of course we'll not go. Felicity's father has some interesting paintings and the house and surrounding countryside are pleasant. You need not do much.'

It was obvious he wouldn't go without her. 'I expect I'll be all right,' she answered, making an effort to sound enthusiastic. At least Vanessa and Hugh would be there for support. Suddenly remembering, she turned at the door, a smile on her face. 'Of course, you don't know, do you? It happened while you were away,' and answering his look, explained about his sister's broken wrist and her engagement to Hugh. 'So you see,' she finished off, 'Hugh will finally become an official member of your family. Are you surprised?'

To her annoyance Eleanor found herself blushing, although she was able to hold his steady appraisal. There had never been anything but friendship between herself and Hugh—and if Edward thought differently, that was his affair!

'Not about Hugh,' he said at last. 'Van, yes, I didn't know she had that much sense.'

'That's a typically male reply and you don't really mean it,' she replied with a show of spirit.

'Perhaps not. Goodnight, Eleanor. If you need me, don't hesitate to call.'

'Goodnight, Edward.'

Before leaving the bathroom, Eleanor opened the airing cupboard wider and Henry lifted his head sleepily. She stroked him, listening to his contented purring.

How uncomplicated your life is, she told him, a twinge of amusement striking her as she realised that Henry was going to pay for his duplicity by always being a he, so far as she was concerned.

She lay for some time, just thinking, and before sleep overtook her, she realised that her sprained wrist could be turned to some useful purpose. She would have a legitimate excuse for not riding a horse this weekend, and thus deny Felicity the opportunity for some amusement.

CHAPTER EIGHT

'For her price is above rubies.'

Proverbs

'My God!' said Vanessa, 'has he been beating you already?'

'Very funny,' replied Edward, getting out of the car. 'You ought to say snap,' he added, looking from Vanessa's sling to Eleanor's.

'Mine isn't broken, thank goodness,' explained Eleanor, 'it's just a bad sprain.'

'I understand I have to congratulate you, Hugh. Do you know what you're taking on?' Edward asked dryly.

'I think so,' his friend assured him with a smile.

Edward ruffled Vanessa's hair. 'You've been a sly one, brat, but I applaud your good sense. Come here and be kissed.' Vanessa laughed and accepted a hearty kiss, while Hugh turned kindly eyes towards Eleanor.

'My dear girl, what have you been doing with yourself?' he asked with concern.

'Falling down cellar steps,' Edward informed him

crisply, heaving the cases out of the boot. 'Take this one, there's a good fellow,' and as they walked towards the house Edward outlined the previous night's happenings.

'Luckily it's not your painting hand,' commented Vanessa, linking up their good arms. Edward, a few yards ahead, turned his head.

'You've been to Ives, Eleanor? How did you get on?'

'I'm sorry, I forgot to tell you. Yes, I've been, and he hasn't said much, but I find him fascinating, very clever.'

Edward nodded with satisfaction and Eleanor lapsed into silence, listening with only half her attention as Vanessa rambled on about her visit to Hugh's grandmother in Devon that week. Why I bothered to go to Mark Ives, Eleanor thought despondently, I'll never know! What's the point, if I'm going home soon anyway? But it had been exciting and tremendously rewarding to have the talented painter's judgment and criticism of her work, and she only hoped he would not be too annoyed when she left. He was interested in her wild flower collection and had kept the folder, saying that he had contacts who might be able to use them.

'Don't, however, raise your hopes too high,' he warned her, 'as publishers are inundated with work. What's this?' and he indicated another folder.

'Some charcoal sketches that I've done since I've been in London.' Eleanor told him. 'I only brought them because Edward said to bring everything I've done—they're not very good, rather instant impressions, although I'm quite pleased with the one of Tower Bridge.'

Mark Ives nodded and pursed his lips as he leafed through the drawings.

'This one has a good line—shall we work on it further?'

It was a drawing she had done of Sykes. She had managed to capture the 'waiting look' conveyed in the eye and the body, even though the position was one of repose.

Sykes was, at this minute, greeting one of Felicity's dogs further up the drive, and it was obvious by the wagging of tails, that they were buddies, and Eleanor came back from her interview with Mark Ives to hear Vanessa saying:

'This weekend will probably be a bore, but we'll have to make the best of it. I wanted to get out of coming, but Hugh says that Edward asked him particularly to make the effort. Here's Felicity,' and their hostess appeared at the open door, calling out gaily:

'Thought you were never going to arrive, Edward darling! I was so worried something might have held you up.' She smiled, threading an arm possessively through his and then, almost as an afterthought, noticed Eleanor. She raised beautifully arched eyebrows. 'My goodness, we have two wounded heroines—first Van and now you! Not serious, I hope?'

Eleanor smiled and shook her head, knowing there was no real interest in her health.

'What a shame! Now you won't be able to ride with us,' mourned Felicity, and Eleanor repeated her smile, this time with a little shrug, knowing full well that Felicity was highly delighted at the prospect of having Edward to herself.

'I've pinched the bed near the window,' said Vanessa, 'we're sharing a room—first right at the top of the stairs.'

'I'll take your case up for you,' said Edward, and Felicity pointed a finger with provocative warning.

'Be right down! I'll tempt you with a drink and then you must come and see the gelding, he's a beauty.'

'Both suggestions meet with my approval,' drawled Edward, and Eleanor, following him closely up the stairs, knew she ought not to have come. He placed the suitcase at the foot of the bed and regarded her intently.

'How are you feeling?'

'Not too badly. Do you think Felicity would mind if I rested for a while?'

'I'm sure she wouldn't. I've told you to do exactly what you feel up to. I'll warn Van not to come bursting in, in case you manage to sleep.' He paused at the door. 'Sure there's nothing I can bring you?' and Eleanor shook her head.

'Have a good ride.' She sat on the edge of the bed, her back to him, easing off her shoes. She looked up and saw his reflection in the dressing table mirror as he stood by the door.

'I won't be riding, it's too late, the light will have gone. I'll go out tomorrow, probably. Can you manage the sling?'

'Oh, yes, I don't really need it all the time. I can easily slip it off.' She hesitated and said quietly, 'Felicity will be wondering where you are.'

'I'll see you later,' and after one more searching look, Edward left her.

Rather to her surprise Eleanor did sleep, and felt more refreshed when she finally went down to join the others. The house party consisted of a dozen people, and Eleanor was glad that Vanessa and Hugh were there, as she did not know any of the others. The thought struck her that that was probably why Edward had wanted his sister and friend to be here, to keep her amused while he went off and played with Felicity.

Even as the thought came, she squashed it, dismayed by the rush of bitterness that came with it, and she turned to her next door neighbour, and started a conversation. As he was something to do with television programmes, the documentary kind, he was interesting to talk to and soon it was time to get ready for the meal that was booked for them at a nearby Country Club, and they all went to their rooms.

Vanessa and Eleanor managed to cope by helping each other, the process reducing them to giggles. Vanessa zipped up Eleanor and whistled approvingly.

'I take it all back. Black does suit you. You look stunning, Nell, you really do.'

Eleanor studied herself critically in the mirror. The dress was very plain, high-necked, long-sleeved, fitting closely to the figure until mid-thigh when it flared to the ground.

'You don't think it's too . . .?' she began doubtfully.

'No, I don't.'

'I bought it in a rush when I knew we were coming here. I mean, Felicity takes some living up to, doesn't she?'

'Why try?' responded Vanessa calmly. 'She's no threat to you, Nell,' and when Eleanor did not reply, added: 'I know you must still be feeling rather shocked, falling down cellar steps isn't funny, and I know being here can't be easy, but don't start imagining things. That ruby ring is on *your* finger. Edward loves you. You love Edward. Keep remembering that.'

Eleanor managed a smile and nodded, touched by her concern. 'I suppose I am getting some reaction from yesterday. I still feel quite exhausted, and yet I haven't done anything to warrant it.' She slipped on her evening sandals and struggled, one-handed, with the tiny buckle. 'I'm never very good in a roomful of strangers, anyway,' she murmured. 'Thank goodness you and Hugh are here too.'

'Oh, I don't know,' said Vanessa airily. 'You were coping very well a few minutes ago.'

Eleanor finished her task and sat up, pleased with herself. 'Mmm? Oh, he was most interesting—something to do with television programmes. I found him quite amusing.'

'I noticed. So did Edward,' asserted Vanessa, grinning at her through the mirror.

'Don't be silly,' Eleanor said feebly.

'Believe me, Nell darling, I'm not being,' replied Vanessa decidedly, and giving them both one last look-over, she led the way downstairs.

During the evening Edward took Eleanor's hand and moved to the dance floor, and as his arms enfolded her, she sighed inwardly and relaxed, giving herself to the line of his body and the rhythm of the music. His arms felt strong and comforting and she welcomed the rush of emotion that swept over her. This would probably be the last time she would feel his arms round her and she would make the most of it.

'You've gone very quiet, Eleanor,' Edward murmured, his lips close to her hair.

She raised her eyes to his. 'I ... don't feel like talking.'

He lifted a dark brow. 'Then we'll just dance,' he said lightly, and pressed her head to his shoulder.

In the darkness of her room, Eleanor listened to Vanessa's steady breathing in the bed next to hers and relived that dance, telling herself she was a fool, but even fools could be given some small crumb of comfort. When it became quite definite that she was not going to be able to sleep, she decided that she would have to take the sleeping tablet that the doctor had given her—Sunday would be unbearable if she did not achieve at least a few hours of rest.

Slipping on her dressing-gown and tiptoeing so as not to wake Vanessa, she gently opened the door and padded along the dimly lit landing to the bathroom.

On her return, a murmur of voices came floating up the well of the stairs and she hesitated, caught in a welter of indecision as to whether to try for her room in the hope of not being seen, or declare her presence and have to go through tedious explanations. Then the moment to move was lost and she chose concealment, drawing into the recess of the curtained window, the decision being made for her by the sight of Edward, his arm round Felicity's shoulder, head bent low to catch her soft words.

Obviously the last to retire, they were ascending the stairs, their elongated shadows diminishing as the wall lights were dowsed, one by one. It was without surprise that Eleanor saw Edward follow his hostess into her bedroom, heard Felicity's low laugh and saw the door close behind them.

For some seconds she remained where she was hidden, staring quite calmly at the glass in her hand, then she moved quietly to her own room, found the sleeping pill and downed it in one swallow.

The bells were ringing for the morning service as Eleanor joined the line of churchgoers up the path towards the church. It was very similar in structure to her father's church—old, beautiful and friendly. She felt a welcoming peace steal over her as she sang the well-known hymns and found herself thinking of her parents and their steadfast love for each other and their children. Eleanor reflected that most children took their parents for granted until they left home and missed them; only then was it possible to be objective about them. She certainly found herself being so, and could almost hear her father saying, in his kindly patient way, that it was time to cut her losses.

She had to admit that she was waiting for the impossible. Deep down she had been hoping that Edward would grow to love her, as she had done with him, the more they were thrown into contact with each other. He had given her no encouragement to fall in love with him, the reverse in fact, making his cynical views on love very plain, and she had only herself to blame for stupidly allowing herself to be ensnared by cool, amused eyes, lips that quirked, a shocking sense of humour and a sharp, analytical brain. As she handed in her hymn book and shook hands shyly with the vicar on her way out, she could even feel able to mock herself for falling for a man so opposite to her young girl's romantic ideal! Guy had been that, of course, and had been as real as a puff of smoke.

She walked slowly down the path towards the gates, her steps faltering slightly as she saw a figure leaning indolently against the stone wall surrounding the churchyard. He was still in riding clothes.

At the sight of him Eleanor's heart began to beat rapidly and she felt colour come to her cheeks. It really wasn't fair, she thought despairingly, all her new-found resolutions dying a death, the coming to terms with the situation wafting away like ashes in the wind. And how dare he look so absurdly familiar and dependable, with that half-smile on his face as if butter wouldn't melt, having just spent the night with another woman! How dared she feel so stupidly weak at the sight and sound of him!

'Good morning, Eleanor.' He took her arm. 'I thought I'd find you here.'

'Good morning, Edward. I *am* honoured! Does Felicity know you're here?' She felt, rather than saw, him glance at her sharply. Yes, she thought grimly, the little country mouse can bare her teeth too!

'You were not awake when I set off this morning,' he replied mildly, 'and I wouldn't allow Van to disturb you. Did you have a good night's sleep?'

'How kind of you to be so concerned. Yes, *I* did, eventually, thank you. Did *you*?' The unexpected sarcasm brought him to a halt and they stood in the middle of the lane. Head tilted slightly and eyebrows raised, Edward took in her heightened colour and sparkling eyes with watchful interest.

'Something's upset you ... what's the matter, Eleanor?'

'I don't like being made a fool of, Edward, any more than you do.'

'Oh?' His voice was suddenly guarded. 'And how have you been made to look a fool?'

'Surely we need not pretend any longer!' she retorted icily. 'Think a bit harder and you'll come up with a good reason.'

'I was never keen on riddles, even as a child.'

'I can't imagine you as a child, Edward, though I suppose you must have been one!' She gave an angry sigh. 'Oh, come on, stop being obtuse. I thought we agreed that no one was to be told that our engagement wasn't for real? That's what you said.'

'And that's what I meant.'

'Really?' Her tone was scathing. 'Do you mean that Felicity allows you to spend the night with her knowing you're in love with me?' She shrugged disdainfully. 'It's not beyond belief, I suppose. Were you able to persuade her that pride is an unnecessary accoutrement to one's pleasures? I presume she didn't need much persuading.' Stop, oh, stop, a voice inside her was crying, but she couldn't, humiliation and hurt wouldn't let her.

Edward was standing quite still, a disconcerting look on his face.

'May I ask how you know?' His voice was dangerously soft.

Her resolve wavered and then quickened. 'I ... I saw you go into her room.'

'I see. How providential for you, Eleanor. Is it too much to hope that your presence was accidental, or were you practising the part of the outraged wife and doing a spot of spying?'

'I couldn't sleep and needed a drink,' said Eleanor between her teeth, white where before she had been fiery red.

Damn his eyes, she thought furiously, and added contemptuously: 'I'd have made my presence known had I thought you'd be pleased to see me, but I considered I'd be rather de trop!'

'Most de trop, my dear.'

She began to walk on, thrusting her good hand deep into her pocket. The conversation wasn't going quite the way she had expected. There was no embarrassment in his eyes, no apology on his lips, but why should there be? she thought bitterly. He had never set himself up as a puritan . . . but oh, she had trusted him not to wound her feelings, her pride, especially with Felicity!

Once again Edward stopped her, this time with both hands on her shoulders, swinging her round and making her look at him. His expression was sardonic.

'I can hardly deny it, can I, and wouldn't anyway, you've already prejudged me. So, I spent the night in Felicity's bed, either with her knowledge that we are not truly engaged—in which case I broke my word to you, or without that knowledge, which doesn't do much for my character. But then you never had much of an opinion of that, did you, Eleanor? Remember my devil's portrait?' He thrust her hand to his hair, holding it close to the thick waves. 'Can you feel the horns, Eleanor?' he asked mockingly, adding: 'I wonder which explanation it is that's made you so angry?'

'Does it matter?' she flashed, wrenching her hand free.

'Oh, yes, I think it does. On the one hand you could be disappointed that I've at last lived up to your original opinion—gratitude may have blinded you into seeing a halo instead of horns, just lately!' He paused and added insultingly: 'Or it could be that you wished it was your bed I was climbing into . . .'

Eleanor's hand came round and struck him across the face. The noise sounded like an explosion in her ears. They stood like statues, normal country noises going on around them, Eleanor's face stricken, Edward's shuttered, devoid of expression. And then the tableau was broken as Edward took her hand, still wavering between them, tucking it beneath his arm and forcing her to walk on.

'We will, I think, continue slowly, the way lovers do,' he said, in a conversational tone, head bent close to hers. 'Van and Hugh have just turned the corner and are coming this way. I don't believe they saw our Victorian melodrama, and I quite realise that you would much rather be flouncing off in high dudgeon.' He pointed into the hedgerow. 'My goodness, isn't that *Slapatim Vulgaris*? Oh, no, it's just a dead piece of wood. Ah, good, you've stopped shaking and I'm hopeful that you won't faint at my feet...?' He raised his brows in question.

If it was possible to admire and dislike someone at the same moment then this was what Eleanor was doing. She swallowed hard and nodded, lifting her eyes to his face. The angry weal had faded slightly and no one looking at Edward's debonair figure and whimsical expression would imagine that only two minutes ago he had been white-hot with anger.

'Good. I do believe that if I took my arm away you would be able to stand on your own two feet, but I won't do that, of course, as lovers prefer bodily contact. I think we can turn round now and be sociable ... hullo, you two!' he said, raising his voice.

'There you are, Edward,' called Vanessa as they came nearer. 'Felicity's been looking everywhere for you. She thought you were going riding with them all and seemed quite put out when you disappeared without a trace,' and she winked at Eleanor.

'I changed my mind,' Edward said carelessly, ignoring Eleanor's start of surprise.

'If I were Eleanor I'd be very watchful of our dear hostess ... she's a bad loser,' teased Vanessa, her eyes dancing.

'Ah, but Eleanor trusts me implicitly, don't you, darling?' appealed Edward, blue eyes smiling down into hazel ones, planting a kiss on the end of her nose. 'And if I were Hugh, I'd give you a good hiding every day.'

'I do,' said Hugh comfortably.

'Good man,' and Edward ignored the tip of the tongue that his sister daintily showed him. 'By the way, you don't mind if we buzz off this afternoon after lunch, do you? Eleanor still isn't one hundred per cent fit, and we've had enough of people for one weekend.'

Hugh smiled. 'We understand your feelings and will be generous and allow you to escape first.'

Vanessa groaned. 'Oh, lord! I suppose it would look bad if we all scarpered together.'

'I hope you'll soon feel better, Eleanor,' said Hugh, and looked at the girls. 'You know, you were very lucky, both of you.'

'And still are, darling,' soothed Vanessa, hugging his arm, 'because we have you two. Come on, I'm famished!'

Edward allowed them to go on slightly ahead. 'Everything is panning out nicely,' he remarked with approval. 'Pack your case...'

'Edward, I...'

'... and we'll leave after lunch. Yes, *after* lunch, I think. I seem to remember roast beef and Yorkshire pudding being quoted as our fare, and it would be a pity to miss that.'

'Edward!' Eleanor stopped, forcing him to do the same. She shook her head despairingly. 'Edward, you're hopeless!'

'Yes, I rather think I am.'

She gave a choking laugh. '*Slapatim Vulgaris*! Honestly!'

'A pity I was mistaken. I fancied finding a rare plant... might have made a name for myself.'

'Edward, I'm sorry I slapped your face.'

'Are you, Eleanor? I think I deserved it.'

'And, Edward, about...'

'We'll not discuss anything more, Eleanor, not here.' He held the door open for her to pass through. 'It's not the right place.'

'But you're away next week, and I'm leaving on Friday for home,' she told him, suddenly aware of the fact herself, desolation sweeping over her.

'So you are,' he said lightly. 'Oh, well, a time will come,' and she nodded, unable to speak, and went into the house.

Saying goodbye to her host and hostess was difficult, more difficult than Eleanor had supposed. They had both been so kind to her, and spoke as though she were coming back, and she hoped that they would forgive her for deceiving them. Vanessa and Hugh drove her to the station.

'Bad luck Edward had to be called away,' said Hugh, and Eleanor replied brightly:

'I expect I'll have to become used to it.'

'There's something on the back seat that should interest you,' Vanessa said smugly. 'Something from Edward.'

Eleanor turned a startled face and looked back at the seat. Sitting squarely at Vanessa's side was a large basket with a lid. She felt a curious restriction to her throat.

'Henry?' she managed.

Vanessa grinned. 'Plus a few. Edward thought you'd miss them—you're making him quite human in his old age, Nell!'

'Stop showing disrespect to your brother,' demanded Hugh, eyeing his lady-love through the rear view mirror.

'Yes, sir,' teased Vanessa, planting a light kiss on the back of his neck.

'And stop distracting the driver,' he ordered, in mock anguish.

They helped her on to the train and Eleanor's feelings were mixed as they disappeared from her view. Would she ever see them again? she wondered sadly, but closed her mind to the future.

Her father was at York to meet her and she made a fool of herself by promptly bursting into tears, hiding her face in the rough tweed of his jacket.

'Now I know it's my Nell,' he joked, handing her his handkerchief. 'For a minute you had me fooled there, this smart young lady in the new suit—it is new, isn't it? But the floodgates have reassured me.'

Laughing through her tears, Eleanor said chokily: 'What a fool I am! Hullo, Daddy, it's lovely to see you, lovely to be home.'

'So I see. Good gracious! What's this? A cat basket? You have come back with more than you went, haven't you?'

Eleanor smiled happily and helped with the luggage. How good it was to see his kindly, loving face ... just the same, even down to the old grey pullover he habitually wore.

Hilary Ferrers led the way to the rather battered estate car and they loaded it up.

'In you get, Nell. They're all waiting for you at home.'

'How is everyone?' she asked, settling herself into the front seat, realising she was sitting on the dog's rug which was covered with hairs. 'You didn't bring Lass,' she added, removing the rug to the back.

Hilary peered left and right and swung out of the station yard. 'No. You know how excited she gets and she takes up so much room. You left the Mansels well?'

'Yes, they sent their regards.' She hesitated. 'I don't think Edward will make the wedding.'

'Oh?' Hilary gave her a shrewd look. 'Pity. Never mind, you'll be able to show him off some other time. When are you going back?'

'I ... don't know, haven't decided yet. I might stay on for a week or two.'

'Good. Do your mother a favour and put some roses in your cheeks while you're here—you're looking as if you could do with a spot of healthy country air.'

'I'm all right, truly,' said Eleanor quickly, and launched into an account of some of the happenings over the past few weeks.

Home fitted her like a comfortable glove and after a few days it was as if she had never been away—at least, when she was with the family. When she was alone too many memories crowded in on her, too many questions remained unanswerable. Another difficulty was the inevitable village interest in her ring and her 'young man' which proved a great strain on her resources.

Constance Ferrers began to despair of ever being ready in time as, one by one, unavoidable crises occurred.

'I honestly would not have believed that the child could have grown an inch in three weeks,' she pronounced, gazing in dismay at her youngest daughter.

'She couldn't have been wearing the right shoes when we measured her,' said Kate crossly, giving the bridesmaid's dress a downward tug.

'I did then,' exclaimed Dodie indignantly. 'I've grown, I tell you.'

'I can let it down, Mother,' soothed Eleanor, 'there's enough material.'

'Bless you, Nell,' replied Constance, and thankfully left her to it.

Dodie struggled out of the dress, demanding: 'Why isn't Edward coming?'

'He's away on business,' said Eleanor calmly, snipping the stitches.

'Funny you disliking him so much, when you first met,' commented Kate, anxiously looking in the mirror at what looked suspiciously like a spot on her chin.

Hilarious, thought Eleanor bleakly, giving an obligatory smile. Kate muttered something despairingly about looking a fright tomorrow, and rushed out of the room. When the door closed behind her, Dodie said darkly:

'I wish Edward was coming—I was looking foward to seeing him. I like him much better than Guy. Guy's a stuffed shirt. He and Kate make a good pair ... neither of them have a sense of humour.'

'You shouldn't say things like that,' reprimanded Eleanor automatically.

'It's true,' Dodie insisted, stroking Henry who had jumped up on to her lap. 'Edward's fun. You don't think he's laughing, because his face is serious, but then you see his lips twitch and his eyes give him away. Do you know what I mean?'

Eleanor paused, scissors held poised. 'Yes, I know what you mean.'

'You'll jolly well have to invite me down to your place when you're married, Nell.' Her face brightened. 'I say, if I get in at St Thomas's I could stay with you both—that *would* be convenient, wouldn't it?'

Eleanor stifled a sigh. Oh, what a tangled web we weave, she thought worriedly. 'You've decided against music, then?' she asked.

'Yes,' stated Dodie. 'I had a long chat with Edward when I knew I'd passed the exam and ...'

'With Edward?' Eleanor looked at her in surprise. 'When?'

'Oh, ages ago,' Dodie said airily. 'You don't mind my asking his advice, do you?'

'No, of course not, only he didn't say anything to me about it.' Eleanor pulled a face. 'Poor Father's phone bill!'

Dodie picked up a kitten that had been trying to climb her trousers. 'Anyway, I've decided to go for medicine,' she declared, 'so you see how useful it will be, you living in London.'

As Eleanor threaded the cotton through the eye of the needle she told herself that there was plenty of time to worry about Dodie and medical school when the time came. After all, she might very well be living in London by then ... on her own. Surely London could hold both Edward and herself without too much difficulty?

Kate's wedding day proved to be a sunny one, April showers belonging only to the song. As Eleanor listened to her father taking the ceremony it seemed a million years ago that she had fancied herself in love with Guy. Looking at him now, standing next to Kate, she was deeply thankful that she could pray for their happiness sincerely and with no reservations.

Coming out of the vestry Dodie whispered gleefully:

'All the village seems to have turned up—and someone else too!' and Eleanor followed her sister's gaze and felt the blood rush to her cheeks and just as quickly disappear.

Edward! Her heart turned over at the sight of him. What on earth was Edward doing here? Walking down the aisle she kept her eyes rigidly in front, but as they drew level she was compelled to shoot him a quick look. She could sense heads turning with curiosity, could imagine the news, that Eleanor's fiancé was here, after all, passing swiftly along the pews.

While photographs were being taken her eyes were constantly drawn to where he was standing, a little away from the crowd, looking—oh, well, she thought helplessly, looking just Edward! Why had he come? As she saw him being introduced to more and more people the whole situation began to take on a nightmare quality. How dared he make the whole thing more complicated, she thought angrily, anger being the only emotion she could allow herself. She found the opportunity of dodging round the back of the onlookers and seeing her approach, Edward came forward and kissed her lightly.

'Hullo, Eleanor darling,' he said. 'I made it after all,' and seeing the startled look in her eyes, murmured: 'We have an audience, my love.'

Making herself smile, Eleanor said under her breath: 'What are you doing here, Edward?' How dreadfully tired he looks, she thought worriedly.

'I've come to see a wedding,' he replied whimsically.

'You've ruined everything,' she retorted. 'You obviously know nothing whatsoever about village life or else you'd have realised that they've sized you up and married us off the first minute they set eyes on you!'

'Perhaps we'd better not disappoint the village,' he murmured, 'and don't forget to smile, there's a good girl.'

'They may be swayed by your broad shoulders and Savile Row suit, but I'm not!' Eleanor said with some asperity.

'I know,' he replied dolefully.

Eleanor bit her lip. 'Edward Mansel, I just do not understand you!' and then she had to return to the wedding group, taking with her a mental picture of him staring at her, blue eyes suddenly wary.

It was useless trying to talk to him during the reception, even if she could have found him in the same place for more than two minutes. Miss Hawkins, the village librarian, was sipping her sweet sherry, face rather pink, next to Eleanor, who was listening with only half her attention to what the elderly lady was saying, until she said:

'Such a lovely young man, my dear Eleanor, so well-mannered. I thought so when I first met him and today he even remembered my name!' and Miss Hawkins beamed benevolently.

Eleanor's attention swung completely to her companion.

'What do you mean, Miss Hawkins?' she asked, puzzled. 'Have you met Edward before?'

'Why, yes,' Miss Hawkins assured her, taking another sip from her glass. 'I was visiting the dear vicar at the time...'

'But when?' pursued Eleanor, her head beginning to whirl.

'I remember the library van had just called,' began Miss Hawkins thoughtfully, and then gave a hiccup which she hastily turned into a cough.

Oh, goodness, thought Eleanor in dismay, she's getting tipsy on the sherry! and led Miss Hawkins hurriedly to the food. She then searched for her mother and said urgently:

'Mother, I've been having a word with Miss Hawkins and...'

'Is she all right, Eleanor?' asked Constance worriedly. 'You know how quickly sherry goes to her head.'

'Yes, she's eating now,' answered Eleanor impatiently. 'Mother, what's this about Edward coming over to see you? When was it?'

'You've found out, have you?' Constance smiled and said with satisfaction: 'Your father and I thought he showed a deep concern for our feelings by coming. He knew what it must be like for us, you being away, and he felt we ought to have the chance to see for ourselves the man who was taking our daughter from us. He stayed nearly a whole day, had a long talk with your father, but wouldn't stay the night. We both like your Edward, Nell darling,' she finished warmly.

'But when did he...?'

'It must be about five weeks ago. He wanted it to be a surprise.' Constance peered round the hall, unaware of the impact of her words. 'Have you seen Dodie anywhere? She's disappeared. I do hope the wretched child keeps out of mischief. You know what she's like.'

'I'll keep my eyes open for her,' promised Eleanor, while her brain was hammering—five weeks ago! and nothing made sense any more.

'Ah, there you are, Nell, I've been looking for you, my dear,' Hilary said, taking her arm and leading her to a reasonably quiet corner.

'And I'm looking for Edward,' she answered, in growing frustration. 'Do you know where he is, Daddy? I must talk to him and I can't seem to manage it.'

Hilary looked at her consideringly and said: 'He's waiting for you at home,' and he absently brushed confetti from her hair.

'He is?' she replied, surprised.

'You'll find him in the study.'

'Oh ... right then, I'll go.' She gave his cheek a quick kiss and he held her to him for a moment.

'Be happy, my dear Nell,' her father said, and gave her a push out of the door. Eleanor threw him a startled look over her shoulder and paused in flight, but Hilary smiled and shook his head, motioning her to go, and closed the door firmly behind her. Puzzled, she ran through the church grounds and across the Rectory gardens, lifting the skirt of her dress high with one hand, the other still holding her bridesmaid's posy. The Rectory was very quiet as she let herself in and the study door was wide open, and as her steps sounded in the hall, Edward turned away from the window and she stood in the doorway, suddenly shy. The window through which he had been gazing looked out on the path by which she had come, and she wished she had walked calmly and sedately, embarrassed that he should have seen her running so urgently. Now that they were alone, her opening lines flew right out of her head and she was glad of the excuse to catch her breath.

Edward smiled slightly and crossed to close the door behind her and she said breathlessly: 'F—Father said you wanted to see me,' and twisted the posy nervously between her hands.

'I thought we should talk, Eleanor. I'm sorry to take you away from the festivities, but I must leave in a couple of hours. It was good of you to come.'

'Why, not at all,' she replied, decidedly correct. She searched his face desperately for some clue. The last time she had seen Edward in London he had barely looked at her, his goodbye had been casual and offhand. There was nothing casual or offhand about him now. There was a suppressed air of tension belied by the indolence of movement and his eyes had not left her face since she first entered the room. His regard was unnerving and she added quickly: 'Edward, why have you come?' He stopped a yard from her and folded his arms across his chest.

He gave the question his consideration. 'Oh, one or two reasons,' he drawled, and reached out and took one of her hands. Contact, as always, was electric between them, and the blood rushed to her cheeks. Raising her eyes to his, she said with desperate calm:

'Edward, that's not fair.'

'No, I know it isn't, but life isn't fair, is it? and I need to hold your boxing hand, I feel safer,' he reproved gently, amusement in his eyes.

Eleanor was quite happy to gaze into his eyes, to feel the warmth flowing from his hand to hers, but sanity returned and she said feebly:

'W—what reasons?'

'Oh, to thank you for my picture of Sykes.'

She raised her brows. 'You could have sent a thank-you letter.'

'I'm a terrible letter writer!' he responded heavily. 'I thought Henry might be missing me,' he said, after thought.

'You're outrageous!'

'Yes, I know. I hoped you might be missing me.'

There was a long silence while Eleanor's hand trembled in his grasp. She swallowed, and whispered unsteadily: 'You know I've been missing you, Edward.'

He let out a deep breath. 'I rather hoped you were. Dear, sweet, generous Eleanor.' He raised her hand and held it to his cheek. 'I didn't know. My egotism has been slightly undermined over the past few weeks and so I only hoped. I will now give you back your hand, I don't want to take an unfair advantage of you—besides which, I find it difficult to think clearly,' and he let it go, thrusting his own in his pockets, contemplating his shoes. 'Now that the time for talking has come I want to explain about Felicity.'

'There's no need, truly,' said Eleanor.

'Oh, but there is,' asserted Edward emphatically, 'if only because I've rehearsed the damned words all the way over here.' He took a breath. 'I was invited into Felicity's bedroom that fatal night to give my expert opinion upon a French clock, which the lady in question had recently purchased. I left within ten minutes.'

The explanation was given in such a fatalistically calm manner as if no one in their right mind could possibly believe it. No one in love is in their right mind, thought Eleanor, an absurd bubble of extraordinary happiness stirring inside her, and she observed gravely:

'It makes a change from etchings.'

'Yes, it does, doesn't it? The clock was a particularly fine example of Buhl—I was quite envious.'

'She couldn't persuade you to stay longer?'

'No.' His eyes held hers and she felt the colour come again to her cheeks.

'I'm desperately sorry, Edward, for ... hitting you. I'm deeply ashamed.'

'Don't be,' he said quickly. 'For once in my life it mattered what another person thought—my past reared its ugly head and laughed in my face.' He paused and tilted his head. 'And talking of ugly heads ... I bumped into our friend Mark Ives, who thought I should have one of your masterpieces. He sent it round the other day and I found it was a most interesting one of myself.'

'Oh,' said Eleanor, foolishly unable to meet his eyes.

'It showed me that you can see me without horns now and again—which boosted my morale. There was no halo, of course, but it was nicely flattering.'

'It was nothing of the kind,' protested Eleanor indignantly, rising beautifully to the bait. 'And it's a long time since I thought of you with horns.'

'How have you thought of me, Eleanor?'

'Y—you know perfectly well,' she said feebly, going ridiculously weak at the knees at the look on his face.

'Your father rang me last night and said I was to come and put the light back in your eyes. Will you give me the chance to woo you, Eleanor? Will you let me touch you . . . and kiss you . . . knowing I mean it, knowing I love you?' His voice was making love to her and he took her hands. 'I tell you now, Eleanor, that the Mansel arrogance has no intention of letting you walk out of my life. I've put this ring on your finger and that's where it's going to stay! Dear God, these two weeks without you have been endless. Will you marry me, my darling? Take pity on a poor tired bachelor who doesn't know what's hit him?'

She raised her eyes, face beautifully aglow, and said demurely:

'So long as it's clearly understood that I'm only doing it for your money . . .' and then she was swept into his arms and most thoroughly and satisfyingly kissed.

'Sweet heaven,' he murmured, after a long moment, and kissed her again, reluctantly lifting his head when a banging on the window made them both swing round. Dodie's face was pressed hard against the pane and with an exasperated groan, Edward strode over and opened the window.

Dodie leaned through. 'I've got it, Edward,' she said triumphantly, holding up a shoe box with remarkably grubby hands. Her face was bright with excitement and she beamed with pleasure when Edward said: 'Good girl,' taking the box from her and digging into his pockets for some coins.

'I don't think I ought to take any money,' she declared doubtfully.

'Why not?' Edward put the money into her palm. 'That's what we agreed.'

Dodie grinned. 'Okay, but I think you're crazy to . . .'

'Dodie!' exclaimed Eleanor in horror, coming out of her bemused state and taking a good look at her sister for the first time. She rushed over to the window. 'Your dress! Wherever have you been? You're covered in mud, Dodie, and just look at your shoes!'

'Don't fuss so, Nell,' grumbled the object of her dismay, brushing the dress ineffectively. 'Oh, golly, I am in a bit of a mess, aren't I? Do you think they'll notice?'

'Of course they'll notice, you nitwit,' wailed Eleanor despairingly. 'Don't you dare go back in there—Kate'll have hysterics!'

'Oh, well . . . it's awfully boring at these do's—the food's the best part. Just think! I've got to go through it all again for you two,' and Dodie gave them a dark look.

The thought was too new and disturbing and Eleanor said faintly: 'Do go and change, Dodie, and keep out of sight of the school rooms!'

'Righto. I didn't tell her, Edward, about your visit, I mean,' and giving a quick once-over round the terrain, Dodie dodged out of sight. Edward closed the window, amusement on his face.

Curbing her curiosity over the box, Eleanor watched Edward place it carefully in the middle of the table and said shyly:

'Why did you come—five weeks ago, I mean?'

He raised a dark brow and pursed his lips. 'It was an impulse.'

A laugh burst from her. 'I don't believe you do anything on an impulse, Edward!'

His lips went down wryly and then he asked quietly: 'Eleanor, who is Joe?'

She could hardly comprehend the question. 'Joe?' she echoed uncertainly, and then it dawned on her. 'Oh! Joe!' The warmth crept into her cheeks. 'He's Maisie's little boy. He's four . . .' and her voice trailed.

'You little devil!' and his eyes gleamed as he pulled her to him. 'You're right. I've come to the conclusion I never do anything on impulse,' and he gently kissed her eyes, her nose, and sweetly lingeringly, her lips. 'I've thought deeply and seriously about doing that for a long time,' he murmured softly, sweeping her off her feet and carrying her to the old armchair, sitting her possessively on his lap and settling them both comfortably.

'Of course, I came to the wedding to compromise you,'

he said complacently. 'I was my most charming to all the old biddies and openly made love to you with my eyes.' He laughed. 'If you could have seen your face when you saw me!'

'Oh, I quite realise how hopelessly transparent I was,' grumbled Eleanor lovingly. 'You knew perfectly well I loved everything about you.'

'Even the eyebrows?'

'Even those,' she agreed with a smirk, 'but they only come second to this dimple,' and she stabbed his cheek with the tip of her finger. 'When you first genuinely smiled at me I was done for.'

'Rubbish. You disliked me intensely,' Edward said fondly. 'You told me so often enough.'

She took his hand in both of hers, holding it to her cheek. It was the same hand she had known for a long time, but now it could be explored, viewed with new eyes . . . it could be caressed, kissed, and fingers could be entwined.

'I know you think me an innocent,' she murmured into his chest, 'but I knew from the start that there was some spark between us, and it seemed easier to be anti and ward off trouble.'

He threw back his head and gave a bark of laughter. 'Ward off trouble? My dear girl, you've been nothing but trouble to me from the minute I set eyes on you,' and he shook his head in mock despair. 'You brought out the worst in me, I'm afraid, purely for self-preservation . . . I interpreted the gleam in my dear mama's eyes the minute she knew you were coming . . . I was anti before I'd even seen you! And then you turned up with that ridiculous accent and my interest was roused, and gradually you wormed your way into my life so that you came between me and everything I did! I wasn't the same! All my confidence that no woman could make me dependent upon her—and certainly not a slip of a thing who shouldered everyone's troubles!—it all went . . . with alarming rapidity. I didn't go down without a fight, though.'

'You were horrible to me,' she murmured reproachfully.

'I'll make up for it,' Edward promised, moving slightly

to accommodate her more comfortably. 'By the way, your father knew about us.' Eleanor twisted a startled face up at him. 'How the engagement happened,' he added. 'I told him when I first came.'

'You told him . . .?' Words failed her and she could only gape incredulously.

'Everything,' he said, a tinge of amusement creeping into his voice as he shrugged slightly, 'well, nearly everything, but what I didn't say, he guessed, hence his telephone call last night.'

Eleanor expelled a long breath. 'Good heavens! All this time he's known!' She put hands to hot cheeks. 'And Mother?'

Edward shook his head. 'No, there was no need to tell your mother, we decided it would only worry her. Of course, I didn't tell him I loved you, I was still fighting my losing battle, but he's very astute, your father, and he knows how adorable is his Eleanor Rose.' He kissed her upturned lips gently. 'Such an eminently kissable mouth!' His arms tightened and his voice was rough. 'Dear God, Eleanor, when I saw you crumpled in a heap at the bottom of those damned cellar steps, for a moment everything stopped, I was finished, and then, when you moved, the relief that swept through me was unbelievable, the final link in the chain that bound you to me. Fool that I was, instead of telling you, there and then, what you meant to me, I dragged you off to Felicity's to try—well, heaven knows with what intent! I suppose I still wasn't completely sure that you loved me.' He gave a snort of derisive laughter. 'Instead of propounding my love I received a thwack across the face that nearly knocked me off my feet!'

'Poor love,' comforted Eleanor, caressing the offended cheek tenderly. 'I was so angry because you were right about the jealousy . . . in fact, that's probably what you intended me to feel that weekend, so that your declaration would be received with open arms!'

'I deny it,' drawled Edward, turning his cheek to her hair and savouring the perfume that wafted his way. 'My real intent was to see this stupid charade through to the bitter end and start again. Your gratitude was a dreadful barrier, my dear, and . . .'

Eleanor groaned. 'Gratitude! Edward, you seem obsessed with that word! You were kind to me and my family, and yes, gratitude has played its part, but it would never make me do anything against my wishes.'

This rather revealing statement brought the colour to her cheeks as she remembered their passionate lovemaking that night in the study.

Edward, obviously following the same line of thought, said softly:

'Perhaps it's as well I didn't know that. You're so beautiful, Nell my darling, so warm and compassionate, loyal and true, you went to my head the night I gave you that damned present like a rocket exploding into the sky, and your response only fanned the flames!' He smiled wryly. 'I ran away to Paris to sort myself out!' He gazed down at her face, at the sweet curve of cheek, lashes fanned across creamy skin, wispy tendrils curling along slender neck, the once tidy coronet of hair becoming appealingly astray. 'How long are you going to make me wait, Nell?'

Eleanor's lashes trembled, a small frown creased her forehead.

'There's such a great deal to organise with weddings, Edward.' She held the pause for as long as she dared. 'Would . . . a w—week be too long, do you think?' and as she met his eyes, exclaimed: 'Edward! I was only j—joking! It's not possible in a week!'

'A week you said . . . and a week . . . it will be!' he ground out between ruthless kisses, and with a groan, he thrust her from him. 'You're dynamite, young woman, and should only be handled in small doses!' He heaved them both out of the chair. 'I think we'd better make sedately for the bosom of your family.'

Eleanor dimpled and said teasingly: 'Oh, well, if you can't stand the pace!' and evading his grasp, dodged round the table, helpless with laughter, until he caught her and pulled her roughly to him. They clung together, the laughter dying as their eyes held, hearts thumping in unison, and their lips slowly met.

'Three weeks,' said Edward thickly.

'Three weeks,' echoed Eleanor faintly, breathing softly: 'Edward, I do love you so.'

He stood, holding her close. 'I can't think why, but I'm very glad to hear it.'

'And we w—will be happy, won't we?' She buried her head in his jacket. 'I'm a bit scared, Edward. You're sure . . .?'

'Quite, quite sure, and stop being an idiot,' he told her lovingly. 'It's not going to be easy, nothing worth while ever is, but we're going to work very hard at our life together.' He grinned. 'You know how efficient I am,' he teased gently.

After a while Eleanor said dreamily: 'I hate to be mundane, darling, but my left foot has the cramp and your box is moving.'

'Good lord, so it is!' Edward released her reluctantly and they looked at it. 'I'd forgotten the darned thing,' adding with a grin, 'I had other things on my mind.'

'Well, now you've remembered, are you going to show me what's in it? I know you think I'm a paragon among women, but I'm consumed with curiosity!' Eleanor wailed.

'Patience!' ordered Edward, leaning against the table, and pulling her comfortably back into his arms. 'Once upon a time,' he began, 'there was a beautiful princess, whose name was Nell . . .'

'Beautiful?' queried Eleanor sceptically.

'Beautiful,' Edward repeated firmly, 'don't interrupt. Princess Nell was kind, warmhearted and as beautiful in spirit as she was in looks. One day she became involved with a huge, slimy toad who conned her into kissing him. Lo and behold, the toad turned into a tall, dark—fairly handsome—prince, who kissed her hand, like this,' and Edward gently put his lips to her palm.

'Very nice,' said Eleanor, with full approval.

'Of course, they fell in love,' went on Edward, 'as all

good princes and princesses do, and lived happily ever after.'

Eleanor stood contentedly in his arms. She was glad of the cramp in her leg—it was a reassuring, everyday sort of thing, showing her that she wasn't dreaming, that the arms holding her so possessively were real.

'May I look inside now?' she asked, and gently raised the lid. Sitting squat in the middle of the box, resting his large fat body on a bed of leaves and grass, sat a splendid toad. 'Oh, my goodness,' she gasped, 'what a beauty!'

The 'beauty' gave a huge leap for freedom and the next few minutes were chaotic, reducing Eleanor into paroxysms of helpless laughter, tears streaming down her face. Edward's reaction was a mixture of oaths and commands, and when they finally recaptured Mr Toad, he was put back into the box and the lid was replaced firmly.

Breathing heavily, Edward eyed her narrowly. 'A fat lot of good you were, woman,' and he burst out laughing, brushing down his clothing ruefully. 'His name is Edward, by the way.'

'Of course it is,' agreed Eleanor, adding thoughtfully, 'I don't think it would be any good if I kissed him. You see, I'm not a real princess and I'm already spoken for, we've had our transformation scene.'

'Poor old toad,' said Edward, looking down at her, his eyes warm with love. 'Doomed to being a toad for the rest of his life. Ah, well, he probably has a wife and family waiting for him. Dorothea will have to return him to his pond ... and this sounds like her coming now,' he continued, with resignation in his voice. 'I suppose we should be grateful she's left us alone this long,' and the door burst open and Dodie's sturdy figure came charging in, Lass bouncing at her side. She stopped short at the sight of them and wrinkled her nose. 'It's quite usual,' Edward asserted, rather apologetically, retaining his arms round Eleanor.

'I know that—Kate and Guy were doing it all the time,' Dodie acknowledged with philosophical acceptance.

'We promise we won't do it all the time,' he replied soothingly, and Eleanor choked back a laugh.

'Do come on, you two,' Dodie urged. 'It's time the newlyweds are off, and I do so want you to give me a ride in the Jensen, Edward. So that all my friends can see me.'

Edward gave an exaggerated sigh. 'Very well, brat. But first of all I want you to do something for me.'

'Hmm...?' Dodie's eyes had been drawn to the box. 'Have you still got him?' she asked with interest.

'Only just. We want you to put him back, please,' Edward told her, lips twitching as he saw the outraged expression appear on Dodie's face.

'Put him back?' she blurted out in disbelief. 'In the same place?'

'Yes,' said Eleanor, striving to keep her voice even, her shoulders beginning to shake.

'Do you two realise just what *tremendous* trouble you've got me into?' her sister demanded, voice rising indignantly. 'Father caught me all muddied up and . . .' Words failed her for a few seconds, and then, mustering her second wind, she managed: 'Hell's bells—you want me to put him *back*?'

'In the same place,' repeated Edward, with unimpaired amiability.

There was a pregnant silence and finally Dodie took up the box with deep mistrust and uttered: 'I'm *never* going to fall in love! It sends folk *daft*!' and giving the offending pair a withering look she stalked out of the room.

'She could well be right,' mused Edward, turning Eleanor to him, his eyes searching her face. 'All I know is, I'm reet daft about you, luv.'

'I won't fratch with that,' responded Eleanor, eyes shining. 'Eh, lad, happen you've picked up t'accent a rare treat! Aye, we'll be champion.'

'Champion,' Edward promised, sealing his agreement with a kiss.

A shout from the garden made them look guiltily through the windows at the girl and the dog waiting for them at the gate.

'I'm afraid we've gone down in Dodie's estimation,' Eleanor said with a grin.

'I'm afraid so, my love,' and Edward smiled his devastating smile. 'Never mind, we have a long time ahead of us to put things right,' and his brows raised in silent question.

'Happen we have,' agreed Eleanor happily, and together they walked out into the April sunshine.